GIGA TROUBLE

A cybercrime novel

MICHAEL A. PYLE

GIGA TROUBLE
by
Michael A. Pyle
Published by:
Armstrong Media Group, LLC
144 S. Oleander Avenue
Daytona Beach, FL 32118
www.michaelapyle.com
info@michaelapyle.com
mikepylewriter@gmail.com

Copyright 2025–Armstrong Media Group, LLC

All rights reserved. No part of this book may be reproduced, scanned, or distributed in any printed or electronic form without permission. Please do not participate in or encourage piracy of copyrighted materials in violation of the author's rights. Purchase only authorized editions.

This is a work of fiction. Names, characters, places, and incidents are either the product of the author's imagination or are used fictitiously, and any resemblance to actual persons, living or dead, businesses, companies, events, or locales is entirely coincidental.

ACKNOWLEDGMENTS

First and foremost, I must thank my long-time editor, Leonor Sierra Salas, whose dedication has been instrumental to my journey as a novelist. She revived my first work of fiction, *White Sugar, Brown Sugar*, cleaned it up, and reprinted it several times. She also submitted it to contests, resulting in an honor that meant the world to me.

For my second novel, *Cuban Roots*, she supplied invaluable resources—photos, articles, and historical materials about Cuba, especially her hometown of Santiago de Cuba—that helped me understand and authentically portray the setting. She then edited and published that book as well.

Now, with *Giga Trouble*, she has been my steadfast partner throughout the nearly five years I've spent writing it, editing every draft and managing all aspects of bringing it to publication. I simply could not have completed this novel without her unwavering involvement and expertise.

While I read numerous nonfiction books on cybercrime to educate myself, I could never have achieved the technical accuracy this novel required without two key people.

My brother, Frank Pyle, Jr., possesses extensive knowledge of computers, the internet, and cyber security. He read the complete manuscript at least twice, correcting faulty technical vocabulary and clarifying complex technical explanations. His expertise allowed me to describe these elements with confidence and precision.

My good friend, Vincent Guyaux, also contributed his considerable understanding of cyber security. Though I only met him quite late in the process, he reviewed specific portions of the manuscript and helped me resolve technical misstatements and ensure accuracy. Beyond the manuscript itself, Vincent assisted with website development, marketing strategies, and the creation of the cover for *Giga Trouble*.

These three dedicated and knowledgeable people have contributed immeasurably to perfecting and completing this book.

ABOUT THE AUTHOR

Michael A. Pyle, born in Daytona Beach, Florida in 1953, holds degrees in English, Linguistics, and Law from the University of Florida, where he also was an Associate Professor of English as a Second Language. After over 40 years practicing law—mostly with a firm he founded—Pyle recently retired to focus on his passion for fiction writing.

He began writing his first novel, *White Sugar, Brown Sugar*, at age nineteen but didn't publish it until 2012 at age fifty-nine. This historical novel explores racism, addiction, and recovery in mid-20th-century Florida. It was named a finalist for the American Legacy Book Awards in Inspirational Fiction (2024). The Wall Street Journal's "Readers' Choice: The Best Books of 2013" voted it #2. *White Sugar, Brown Sugar* was reprinted through Amazon in October 2025, so that is the latest version.

Pyle began *Cuban Roots* twenty years ago, drawing on accounts from people who left Cuba in the 1960s. When the U.S. first allowed family visits to Cuba in 2010, he began traveling there and continued for quite a few years, visiting museums and libraries across the island and exploring historical sites of wars, battles, and imprisonment. He met Cuban history graduate students, where he was presented different versions than he'd learned before. Pyle presented *Cuban Roots* twice at the Instituto de Historia de Cuba in Havana. *Cuban Roots* examines contrasting perspectives between Cubans who remained on the island and those who fled, shaped by age, timing of departure, and family political involvement. This research partly inspired the Cuban setting in *Giga Trouble*.

Giga Trouble follows characters from Pyle's first two novels. *White Sugar, Brown Sugar* features David "Jude" Armstrong and Roosevelt "Red" Harris, whose now-grown children—Jude's son Mark and daughter Kim, and Roosevelt's son Tad—are major characters in *Giga Trouble*, alongside their fathers. *Cuban Roots* centers on Luis Morales, whose grandchildren Michele and Miguel (children of Franklin Morales) also play major roles, along with their father.

The reader does not need to read the earlier books to follow *Giga Trouble*, but they provide rich backstory if you're interested in the families' histories.

Monday, March 16, 2020

Chapter 1

Michele's face and eyes stung from the piercing smack as she hit the water. Seconds passed while below the surface, hearing and feeling the grind of the colossal yacht churning through the mouth of the inlet toward the ocean. She stroked furiously to avoid being sucked into the massive yawning propellers. Her heart pounded as she switched to a sidestroke so she could scan the water and shore for refuge while also searching for prying eyes on the decks of the floating prison fading behind her. As the yacht forged into the darkening sea, she glimpsed the glittering blue letters, "Giga Blue", hinting at the mammoth vessel's size.

******

The scorching Miami sun glinted off Giga-BATS' sleek office building shortly before nine in the morning as Michele joined the stream of employees flowing from nearby parking lots and transit stops. She caught her reflection in the window, her fingers instinctively smoothing her dark hair and adjusting her blouse. She thrilled that her new Mediterranean diet seemed to enhance the tone of her skin and trim of her figure.

Her friends Tad and Kim were also reflected in the glass as they headed for the entrance. Dark ringlets bounced around Tad's shoulders as he strolled casually ahead, his smooth brown skin glowing under the morning sun. A geeky co-worker strode alongside him, ghostly pale in contrast, though matching Tad's loping gait. Their animated chatter seemed like a jumble of tech jargon that might as well have been alien speak.

Tad had become quite attractive as he'd closed in on his 40th year. Her gaze lingered on him as she admired his easy smile and how his shirt strained against his muscular arms. How in the world had they sporadically become more than friends the previous evening?

Michele fretted about Kim's waifish figure, gaunt face, sharply jutting cheekbones and dark circles beneath her sunken eyes. Was it just workplace stress, or something more?

Nearing the office entrance, Michele frowned at the sight of idling buses. She clicked her iPhone to open the digital entry card, which also showed her photo and name, Michele Morales. Around her, coworkers followed the same routine, some still fumbling with physical cards.

Supervisors, all middle-aged Anglo men dressed in coats and ties, and security personnel, younger men wearing dark-blue button-up shirts with the company name, "Giga-Blue All-True Solutions", surrounding the company's logo on the left breast, and the abbreviation, "Giga-BATS" on both sleeves, stood in front of the access card readers, pointing to the buses and instructing workers to board them instead of entering the building. When questioned about the destination, a supervisor barked, "Company meeting on the yacht," while security guards silently maintained their steadfast countenance.

Michele grappled with the unsettling possibility that Giga-BATS, her once-shining beacon of hope, was involved in something sinister. The thought of leaving her employ filled her with dismay. What had begun as exciting career moves within the company and its subsidiaries had gradually transformed into a nightmare, stifling her spirit. The exhilaration of being valued for her talents had faded, and her once-proud strides through the doors of the renowned international company had morphed into hesitant steps. As she shuffled forward with the crowd, echoes of past low-paying, unfulfilling jobs caused her again to question whether quitting was the answer.

The odor of burnt weed wafted from the guy in front of her as she inched forward with the herd. Ahead, Tad gesticulated wildly, seemingly oblivious to the tension around him. Kim's troubled expression mirrored Michele's own unease.

Michele's cousin, Pedrito, a security officer who wore a lighter blue shirt, emblazoned with "Security Officer," to show that he was above security guards, waved the group toward one of the buses. He looked the other way as Tad walked by, and Tad ignored him too, perhaps because of their apparent dislike for each other or because Pedrito was concerned about the meeting the night before. When Michele approached Pedrito, they also ignored each other.

Finding a window seat, Michele caught Tad's eye. He winked, the gesture so unexpected it momentarily derailed her. She turned to the window as her thoughts drifted back to Pedrito. She could see the shared heritage of their ancestors from northern Spain in their faces.

Although Pedrito had worked for the law firm founded by her grandfather, Morales & Morales, and had earned a law degree, he'd apparently never passed the Bar. She considered how his advice had led her, Kim, and Tad to join the company. Now, with Kim's accusations echoing in her ears and her own misgivings growing, Michele couldn't help but wonder if they'd all made a terrible mistake.

As the result of Kim's insistence over several weeks, Michele had arranged a meeting of the two of them, Tad and Pedrito the previous evening. In her multiple tense texts, Kim had written messages like, "I can't believe you got me into this. We are screwed. This isn't going to last. I think that asshole cousin of yours, Pedro or Pedrito, or whatever his name is, duped us. Some friend you are, and some stupid idiot your midget cousin is. Or maybe he's not so stupid. Maybe he got a bonus for dragging us in."

Michele had been losing her patience with Kim, thinking that the arrogant bully she'd married was probably pushing her to make such allegations. Michele had worried if she scheduled the meeting as Kim had requested, Pedrito might report them, or maybe he would get into trouble for talking with the workers about their thoughts of deserting the company. Kim had insisted that their employer was somehow monitoring all their communications. She'd even indicated that the company regularly gathered data from their phones and used the gifts of home security and smart home apps as a means of penetrating their privacy. Michele thought about whether Kim's rants had raised her concerns but decided that she'd been worried before Kim began pushing her nagging misgivings.

Pedrito had been defensive when Michele had called him the night before the meeting to tell him of her trepidations. He'd insulted her when he'd turned it back around on her, almost yelling into the phone, "What do you really have to complain of? You are paid well. You and your friends have been promoted several times. There's nothing even a little bit questionable about the company. Kim is just being a stupid bitch. If you listen to Kim, you are just as stupid."

While munching on snacks during their pre-meeting before Pedrito's expected arrival at seven o'clock the previous night, Michele told Kim about Pedrito's attitude.

Kim said, "Of course he's defensive. If we leave, he might lose the bonus he probably got for getting us involved."

Michele decided not to counter Kim's words but was sure that was not the case.

Tad said, "Well, I was initially proud when the company moved me around, thinking they were promotions to honor my good work, but then I started wondering if they were testing me. In the cyber security department, I was developing procedures to protect the company from cyber-attacks. But the work involved intruding into sites of other businesses. When I questioned that, they said the best way to secure protection was to know the vulnerabilities of others. I didn't feel confident about the company's intentions after that. And then I was placed in their cryptocurrency exchange company, where I was asked to hack into similar entities, followed by their artificial intelligence department, where I learned that the company had created its own AI, which they said was being used for marketing, but they were cloning competitors' employees' looks, manners, voices and other personal traits. How could that be related to marketing and advertising?"

Michele said that because her degree was in finance, she'd been moved into the banking and investment side of Giga-BATS. She'd been questioned about how digital money was moved internally and externally. "I kept telling them that the technical aspects of holding and moving funds were not addressed in studying finance, but they kept quizzing me on similar topics. Finally, they instructed me to probe the digital footprints of competitors…ostensibly to enhance security of Giga-BATS' internet presence, yet I'd say it was more likely to gain leverage for Giga-BATS."

Kim said her latest position was in funding and promoting election of candidates and political parties favored by the company. "I guess it was because of my degree in political science. But I couldn't understand how political involvement was in any way connected to any of the businesses to which I'd been assigned."

Tad said, "So, we've all worked for various of their sub-companies. I don't know whether you've had to breach systems like I have. I think they're preparing something devious, because all the companies seem to gather personal and private data from customers. I'm particularly concerned about the world-wide financial system. I think their purpose is to grab it all."

Michele said, "Who is they?"

"Who knows? Whoever is behind Giga-BATS. That's the problem. Nobody has any idea who is behind anything."

Michele tried to take it in. She said, "So, if somebody has all of something that exists in a digital form, and nobody else acknowledges the authenticity of what they have, do those who have it really have anything?"

Tad looked at her. "Huh?"

She smiled. "O.k. Let's talk about digital currency. If Giga-BATS takes all the world's cryptocurrency, it will no longer be currency, will it? Nobody will acknowledge it, other than the one who has it. Right? So, nobody will be able to buy anything with it because it is worthless, right? In fact, same question if they stockpile all the paper money and coinage, and no other party has any. They then have nothing, right?"

Tad gawked at her, mouth agape, nodding. "You have a point."

The bus finally pulled to a stop next to the wooden dock that led to the company's yacht. Michele followed somber workmates plodding silently like a herd of sheep toward the vessel, moored just across the channel from Miami's cruise ship terminals. She'd heard executives of the company touting it as a giga yacht, indicating it was much larger than a mega yacht. How apropos that both the immense yacht, "Giga Blue" and the employer, "Giga-Blue All-True Solutions", incorporated the first word into the yacht's and the company's ostentatious names, hinting at the supersized egos of those behind the business.

Michele glanced up at the behemoth of a vessel, seeing supervisors, security personnel and men wearing white button-up shirts with black bow ties and vests carrying trays holding drinking glasses.

The gangway connected to the largest deck, the second one above the water, with the largest outdoor area. Each deck above was somewhat shorter. At the end of the ramp, supervisors instructed workers to join lines outside the interior areas.

Fewer employees exited the indoor areas on the higher decks than those who entered on the main deck. She wondered if they were being fed or interviewed or exactly what was going on. She tried unsuccessfully to discern the facial expressions and gait of those exiting.

Something is fishy here. I should leave. Turn around and go. Forget this job. Something is wrong, wrong, wrong.

Her face felt on fire from the scorching sun. The drenched fabric of her blouse stuck fast to her back and sides in the steaming heat. Rivulets of perspiration slithered from her underarms, unaffected by the useless anti-perspirant she'd applied. Yet, sweltering heat was completely normal in Miami, even in the springtime.

Michele considered the climbing number of cases of the new coronavirus in Miami, which the media was now starting to call COVID-19. She'd seen news reports that Governor DeSantis and Mayor Gimenez were contemplating the temporary closure of numerous businesses, including bars and restaurants. Michele's employer had not said a word about changing the work environment because of the virus, which, according to the World Health Organization, was the beginning of a global pandemic. She wondered if mingling among this large group was unwise.

Mounting the gangway, she evaluated the demeanor of the hosts and guests. Supervisors and servers at the end of the ramp were all smiles. Guards never smiled. She wasn't at all sure she could escape even if she tried. She looked down at the short, nearly empty outdoor deck of the yacht below the main deck, outfitted with fixed deep-sea fishing chairs, tackle and outrigger poles leaning toward the stern. That would be the best place to escape if necessary.

Mr. Brown, a supervisor she'd never liked, oversaw security guards as they scanned credentials, while others waved metal detectors. Sweating through his polo, he smiled and said, "Welcome, Miss Morales."

She didn't respond.

A server stood at the end of the line behind the security checkpoint offering drinks to each worker. Michele paused and asked, "What is it?"

"Iced tea or lemonade."

She accepted the lemonade and moved onto the deck, sniffing and considering whether it was safe. Finally, she took a light taste, not detecting alcohol or unusual bitterness. She determined to sip very slowly, monitoring whether it produced any effect.

Michele moved into the shade beneath the next upper deck and sat on a lounge chair, while trying to determine a pattern of movement of workers, supervisors and security.

Mr. Brown approached her with a sinister grin and sat on the chair next to hers. He glanced around and wiped his brow with his wrist, "Your area is finance and digital marketing, right?"

She glared at him, clenching her jaw at his false cordiality. "You know what I do."

"Uh, have you ever done URL spoofing?"

She scowled. "Mr. Brown, do you mean do I know how to create a hyperlink to trick somebody and lead them to a site or page they did not intend? Of course, I know how to do that. I believe everybody who works in the computer area can achieve such a result."

What the hell was this guy getting at? Were they pushing staff to cheat customers? With its maze of sub-companies, she could cycle through a new position every day. His probing raised her suspicion.

Mr. Brown dabbed his brow. "We are simply trying to perfect the ability to grasp possible customers who are searching for information and steer them to our own sites."

She eyed him again. Sweat slid down his forehead and around his eyes. "Mr. Brown, in these times, there are many ways to track and send direct marketing to people who are searching in general without tricking them. We all know that if you research on-line or if you have any smart speaker or virtual assistant and even speak about an interest in anything, you get ads almost immediately. You can align with any of the established businesses to accomplish that."

Mr. Brown laughed. "Of course, you know, Miss Morales, that we are a legitimate family of operations. We just want to lead customers of one of our affiliate businesses to our other businesses. What's wrong with that? In fact, if you say those marketing processes are offered by legit businesses, why cannot our company do the same?"

"I suppose nothing is wrong with that, Mr. Brown." She worried that she was too flip in saying she knew how to forward from one URL to another. "I'm just wondering why you don't use existing businesses instead of trying to create internal new programs. Anyway, I'm not sure I'm qualified to do exactly what you want."

She tried to maintain a positive countenance.

He squinted his eyes and frowned. "We want you to do more in protecting our banking outfits from internet intrusions."

She smiled and shook her head. "Mr. Brown, I told you I am not a computer or Internet specialist." She wondered whether the goal was similar to something Tad had surmised—that they wanted to act like they were protecting the company while gaining access to data of other institutions.

Mr. Brown grimaced, rose and strutted away, like a peacock fanning its feathers, scouting another victim. Michele looked around, noting that she hadn't been sent to a line yet. It probably wouldn't be long.

Michele continually shifted beneath narrow bands of shade cast onto the deck from the next deck up. A server slithered along the deck encouraging workers to imbibe. If a person's glass was partly empty, he'd say, "Drink up. I'm here with a fresh one." Now, the man stood above her, clearing his throat. She tried to focus on something else, but he wouldn't leave.

"Have a drink, Miss."

Michele recoiled. "No, thank you."

Yet, having reluctantly accepted the plastic cup he forced into her hand, she tentatively sniffed the liquid. After a minute or so, knowing that he continued watching, she raised it to her lips and tasted. Her lips tingled slightly, leaving the tang of a bitter medicinal flavor. It did not appear to be harmless this time. She carefully spilled a few drops onto the deck as close to the leg of the chair as she could. She glanced across the deck and was alarmed that she might have been seen.

Then she realized that a woman who Brown previously interrogated was being ushered inside, ahead of the line of workers patiently waiting. The line was getting shorter and only a few, like she herself, were not in line. She still couldn't fathom what was happening. She walked toward the rear of the main deck and looked up. All the workers on higher decks seemed to stagger. What could that mean? Perhaps those who were forced to imbibe had somehow failed the inquiries or refused to cooperate with demands. It was apparent that workers on the main deck were also being offered tainted drinks though none seemed affected, perhaps because they weren't drinking it, like she wasn't, or perhaps it was much weaker than what was served above.

She spotted Pedrito on the deck just above her, gripping the railing and swaying, his legs quavering unsteadily. She was shocked to see that the arm insignia and logo on the front of his shirt had been cut off, exposing his flesh. He forlornly stared into space like a shell-shocked soldier after an intense and bloody battle.

A young woman who worked in Michele's area stumbled and swayed across the deck above and grabbed the railing to the left of Pedrito, the corners of her mouth turned down, her eyes apparently focused on nothing. Alarmed, Michele asked, "Destiny, is everything all right?"

The desolate facial expression she received in return was horrifying. Suddenly, a supervisor appeared, lifted Destiny by her elbows and marched her away, saying, "Let's get you something to drink or eat."

Mr. Brown approached a young man on the main deck and led him to one of the lines. Michele glanced at her watch; it had been about twenty minutes since he'd chatted with the same person. Few workmates had not been assigned to lines or taken inside.

She would touch the cup to her lips when she thought a waiter or supervisor was watching. A server headed in her direction, so she held the glass up like she was taking a sip. When he turned, she sat for a second and poured a little more under a lounge chair.

She moved close to the side of the deck, just beneath where Pedrito sat. Looking up, she was blinded by the intense sunlight, so she ducked a bit under the shelter. She climbed onto a bench and whispered, "Pedrito, what's going on?"

He glanced down at her—dull eyes—desolate smile.

"Pedrito, are you Okay?"

His downcast eyes and silence devastated Michele as she worried that her setting up the meeting had caused his ruin.

Michele scoured the emptying upper decks yet saw no sign of Kim or Tad. Were they locked away somewhere? Although Kim had displayed an attitude for quite a while, she was still a dear friend. They must be inside somewhere. Could the yacht be preparing to head out to sea?

Depression descended on her. Whatever this was, it was her fault for not recognizing—for turning a blind eye despite Kim's insistence and her own worries.

The sun seared her skin. People shuffled about like zombies. She considered calling her father. But why? She'd struggled for a long time to display her maturity and earn her independence. She wouldn't want to display a lack of self-confidence to her father now. But she felt afraid. She needed him. He was her rock, always there for her. He wouldn't be negative to her—ever. But she so wanted to stand on her own two feet, not be asking Daddy for help. She needed to be strong.

She glanced at the screen of her phone several times, looked at the people on the decks of the yacht again, opened Siri and said, "Call Dad."

He picked up. "Hi, Michele. What's up?"

"Daddy. I think I'm in trouble. I'm afraid." She realized her voice was shaking.

A supervisor appeared from nowhere, ripped her phone away and disconnected the call. "Who were you calling?"

She didn't answer.

Clutching her phone, he silently walked away.

Now she couldn't even erase her texts, her contacts, her call log; incriminating data had to be all through it. If they could access it, they'd see all the communications with Pedrito, Kim and Tad, and they would know for sure. But maybe they already did know.

More nervous than before, she decided there was no time to waste. She needed to make decisions and act. She was about to climb down from her perch on the bench when Kim staggered to the edge of the deck near where Pedrito sat.

Michele whispered, "Kim." But the response was a dull, disinterested look toward nowhere.

"Kim," she said a little louder.

Seeing a supervisor eyeing her, Michele hopped off the bench. Fear gripped her. Was this luxury yacht going to sea, as a transport to a sinister destination, like a train hauling European Jews to a death camp? She glanced over the side and examined the dock. The ramp to the main deck on which she and the others had entered was empty. A couple of workmen unloaded provisions from a truck and rolled a flatbed stacked with supplies along a service gangway. Why were they loading provisions? Was the yacht going to depart? No deckhands were preparing to cast off.

A long line of fellow employees staggered out the door on the main deck. She'd seen some of them on upper decks. They must have been brought down via interior stairs. Supervisors helped those who seemed unable to steadily traverse the deck. Two supervisors directed Michele and others on the deck to move away from the line. As the departing employees approached the gangway, guards scanned their credentials, glanced at screens and checked them out.

Her desperation exploded into terror as the yacht's engines rumbled to life. *Oh, no. The yacht is leaving the dock. Those people who just left are the last to avoid a trip to–to where?*

She almost ran to the side facing shore. The line of workers who had left were now being pushed into the buses that had brought them. Deckhands tossed lines to other crewmembers and jumped aboard.

The yacht slowly left the dock and entered the channel. She feared more and more that this trip seemed like a train to Auschwitz. There would be no future. She had to escape. When? How?

The yacht cruised easterly along Government Cut, the main channel used by large vessels, toward the inlet and open sea, passing the now-vacant dockage of Carnival, Norwegian and Royal Caribbean cruise lines, on the right, and Palm and Star Islands, with residences of the rich and famous across MacArthur Causeway, on the left.

Small craft lolled atop gentle swells as their occupants fished or watched vessels edging toward the sea. Three young men on a speedboat stood in unison, turned and mooned the passengers on the yacht. They were probably accustomed to cruise ship passengers laughing and cheering but their antics drew no response from the subdued workers on Giga Blue.

Michele noted a lull in the security and interrogations. She thought it was not very smart to let their guard down here, but the ability to escape was at hand. If she didn't leave, nobody would ever know what had happened to her and her colleagues. It was her duty to get free and report.

GIGA TROUBLE

The only supervisor on the main deck walked inside. The ship continued eastward along the deep channel, passing the departure point for Fisher Island and heading toward South Miami beach. The light blue water turned to a richer, darker blue as the yacht neared the ocean, and the depth increased.

The mooners' boat was the last before the inlet. She rushed down the ladder to the deep-sea fishing deck, praying to avoid discovery. Clear.

Her heart thudding, she climbed onto the transom and glanced up at the steps. Still clear. Monitoring the current, she considered whether it was safest to dive straight out from the stern or to a side. Sucking in a shaky breath, she tensed, poised on the knife's edge between extreme danger and escape. *Now or never.*

Chapter 2

Fearing the worst as she scissor-kicked westward, Michele felt and heard the rumble of the yacht's engines. She saw nobody on the decks looking her way.

A shout pierced the air. "Fuck, that chick jumped. She's heading toward us."

She adjusted the angle of her sidestroke and realized she was heading straight toward the speedboat of the guys who'd mooned the yacht. Looking back at the yacht, her heart pitter-pattered as she glimpsed the head of a person on deck. But he didn't seem to be searching.

Another fisherman said, "Man, I been praying for years that some vixen would jump overboard for me."

Ignoring the crude remark, she maneuvered to the western side of the boat, so she'd be out of view of anybody scanning the water from the yacht.

Over the caw of two seagulls battling over a fish, one of the guys said, "Hey. You all right? What the hell? You like our naked asses that much?"

She would have laughed but was still too frightened. "Is anybody from the yacht looking this way?"

The three men turned, one using binoculars. They all shook their heads.

"Would you get me out of here before 'Jaws' gets me?"

Several strong hands reached down and hauled her over the transom.

One asked her what happened. She tossed soaking hair out of her face and eyes. "I didn't feel safe."

A man said, "Should we call the police…or the Coast Guard?"

She wasn't sure whom to contact. Her dad would know what to do. She needed to do something to stop the yacht from disappearing with all those souls on board. She said, "I'm not sure yet. Can you take me ashore to where I can get a taxi or something? They took my phone. You have one I can use?"

One handed her a phone. She tried and tried to remember her father's cell phone number. But since it was a favorite on her phone, she never had to dial it. The problems of the modern age. "Can I Google to get my dad's office number. I can't remember."

"Sure. What's your name?"

"Michele."

The man smiled reassuringly. "We're Hank, Jorge and Butch," he said, pointing at each.

Still petrified that the guards on the yacht could track her or her parents with data they probably already had, she dialed her dad.

*****

So tense he thought he could have a heart attack, Franklin Morales paced the floor. Michele's broken voice, saying the childlike "Daddy" she hadn't used in years, echoed in his mind, each imagined scenario more terrifying than the last. The declined calls when he tried to call her back only fueled his growing panic. Where in the world could she be? Why wasn't she at work on a workday, in the middle of the morning?

When the receptionist announced over the intercom that Michele was on the line, he lunged for the receiver like a drowning man grasping for a life preserver. His palms pouring with sweat, he said, "Michele, what is it? What's happened? Are you all right?" The words tumbled out, tripping over each other.

"Daddy, I'm safe now. We shouldn't talk by phone."

"Thank God you're safe, baby girl." Franklin hadn't referred to her as "baby girl" since she was young. He held his palpitating chest. "Are you in Miami?"

"Miami Beach."

He decided to use their private clue of a safe location, the name of the family boat. "Can you get to M&M?"

"I don't know how long it will take me, but yes. I don't have my phone, so just wait if I'm not there when you arrive."

"Whose phone are you calling on?"

"It belongs to somebody who's helping me…on a boat…but I won't have it after they leave me on shore."

A muffled voice in the background, "We'll help you get to your location, Michele."

"Okay, Dad. I'm sure you can see the number I'm calling from, so you can call back."

Franklin's stomach clenched. "Are you safe with these people, Michele?"

After glancing at the three men, she said, "I think I am. I certainly hope so…much safer than half an hour ago."

He hoped she was right but felt so unsettled. "I'm leaving now," he said, grabbing his keys. "Be careful, Michele." The receiver clattered as he dropped it and ran down the hall toward his son's office.

******

The world tilted and spun lazily around Kim as she fought against the drug-induced haze, struggling to steady the pitching and swirling. Bile built in her throat as she half-recalled being coerced to imbibe a chemical cocktail. Her stomach roiled.

Memories of her youth and happier times swirled through her mind like leaves caught in a whirlpool. Daytona Beach, swimming and sunning on the beach, hanging out at disappearing island, boating in the river and ocean, waterskiing in the Inland Waterway and the Tomoka River, traveling with family along country roads, enjoying picnic lunches, fishing, and sliding down rocky streams in inner tubes. And then, the childhood memories morphed into hoped future memories with her darling child.

She remembered her history with Tad, from when they were very young, when Tad and his family were not permitted to join Kim and her family at the yacht club because of the color of their skin. She reminisced about when she and Tad were about ten, on a trip to Miami with their dads, who were in business with Michele's dad, and walking into the home of Michele's family, which seemed to her and Tad to be a huge mansion.

Jolts and the sound of creaking aluminum and wood told her the yacht was cutting through rather large waves. They must be in the ocean, heading who-knew-where. The movement coupled with whatever was still in her system made her woozy. Her stomach rolled as the room flipped.

What was going on? Were they imprisoned? Why were they here? Where were they going? What danger would she and the other workers face? When would she see Denver and Nevaeh again? Would she ever? Tears welled up and streamed unchecked down her cheeks.

Dim light emanated from recessed bulbs where the walls met the ceiling. She glanced around the tiny, bare, white-walled room. Four cots crammed into the corners. No toilet or door to a bathroom. A door in the middle of one wall. Two other beds held girls, fully dressed but sleeping. It seemed the walls were moveable. She surmised that larger rooms had been altered, perhaps temporarily, into super small rooms.

She struggled to remember what had occurred. Slowly, she began to recall sitting in a tiny room across the table from a supervisor, who quizzed her about her knowledge of computers and told her she needed to perform work for her employer. She remembered standing up to the guy, refusing to cooperate. She was proud of herself for that. Denver would be proud of her too. Or would he? Lately her darling husband was such a jerk. Her parents would be proud. They'd always had her back and touted her courage and independence.

Had she been raped? She rubbed her hands over her clothing. All seemed intact. She didn't feel anything odd in her private parts.

She had a recollection of standing—swaying—next to Pedrito on the deck of the yacht earlier in the day as Michele talked to them from the deck below. Suddenly she wondered about Tad. Where could he be?

She sat up. *Oh God.* Dizzy. Weak. She fell back on the bed, trying to pull it together. She didn't know if she'd ever felt worse. Sick, debilitated, hungover. Awful. Did she feel like vomiting? Not really. Her stomach didn't hurt. She sat up again, slowly. She moved closer to the edge of the bed. Her feet touched the floor. Numb. She pushed on the bed with her hands and tried to stand. Wobbly legs. Dizziness hit her. She tried to just maintain her balance. *God, help me.*

She closed her eyes and prayed to her God. *Please, protect me God. Please, help me get out of this ... whatever this is. I want to hold Nevaeh. I want to hold Denver.*

She willed herself to stand without support. She moved a foot forward and felt herself leaning to the right. Her left foot came off the ground. *Please, let me stand. Let me walk.* She took a step, and then another, toward the door. Slowly, slowly, she inched around the cot in front of the door, grabbed the door handle and pushed down. She pushed and then pulled. Nothing. Nothing. *Damn it.* It was locked from the outside. There was no button to unlock it. Only an empty keyhole. She was locked in. *Oh no.* She choked, trying to hold in tears, fear invading her.

She remembered the asshole telling her she had probably lost her job for refusing to do what he demanded. But then why didn't they just fire her and send her away? Why was she here, locked in? Were they going to take her out and force her to perform the computer tasks they were asking about?

She moved slowly to a cot on which a thin, teenaged girl sprawled, face up, and gently swept the blonde hair off her face. Shadowed eyes fluttered, but the girl didn't awaken. Kim put a hand on her shoulder, leaned down and whispered, "Hey, are you all right?" The girl gave a slight "hum", but no more. Kim moved the girl's shoulder back and forth, but the girl groaned and shook back.

On the adjacent cot, a lean girl with a thin but strikingly beautiful ebony face dozed. Kim moved a stray ringlet of hair behind the girl's ear. The girl swatted Kim's hand and grunted, but then opened her eyes a bit, grimacing and covering her eyes with her hands. Then she spread fingers and peered between them. "What happened? Who are you? What did you put in that drink?"

Kim rubbed her shoulder. "I'm Kim. Just a worker, like you. I didn't give you anything. They drugged me too. We're locked in a room."

The girl sat up quickly, closed her eyes, put her hands on her head. "Oh, man." She lay back down and pulled her pillow over her face.

Slowly, she slid the pillow aside and opened her eyes again. "What you mean we're locked in?"

Kim nodded. "What's your name?"

"Honesti."

"Honesty? That's your name? Honestly?"

"Yeah. Ends in an i. What's happening? Is this boat moving, or is it just me feeling hungover?"

"It's moving. I think in the ocean."

Honesti's eyes bulged. "To where?"

Kim shook her head and shrugged.

Pointing across the room with her nose, Honesti said, "Who's that?"

"Don't know. She didn't wake."

Honesti stood and tried to open the door. "Where could they be takin' us? What can we do?"

Kim's voice squeaked as she answered, "I wish I knew."

******

A slight shudder resonated through the soles of Tad's shoes, followed by the faint yet unmistakable feeling of the hull of the yacht rising and falling. They must be in the ocean. But going where? What would

GIGA TROUBLE

become of him and his co-workers? Beads of perspiration pearled along his temples. He should sign the document that had been left in front of him by the asshole who'd interrogated and threatened him. He could play along and later quit this job, if he ever could leave the boat.

He looked at his watch, worrying about Michele. Was she being interrogated and harassed too? He hadn't seen her arrive on the yacht, but he had seen her on the bus. Then again, he'd been quickly sequestered without a later glimpse of the outdoors. He hoped to God that she was all right. He recalled their brief but electric encounter and kiss the night before.

He wondered what Pedrito could be up to. The bastard surely knew what was going to happen before their meeting.

Tad considered the weight of the decision he was about to make, inhaled slowly, steadied his nerves, and scrawled his name on the dotted line. Not long after, the man entered the room, saw the signature page and said, "Good decision. Let's go."

The man led him through the bowels of the ship and into a large room, in which a group of workers sat at computers facing a projection of the instructor's computer that showed the settings of a social media application. Tad's monitor displayed the instructor's computer on the left and an open browser window on the right. Tad considered probing but was unsure whether his actions could be monitored. Still, with access at hand, he felt compelled to discreetly investigate.

Tad scanned the room, but the eyes of most of his colleagues were fixed forward in placid indifference or dulled resignation. Tad bristled as the instructor demonstrated rudimentary skills like fashioning bogus social media pages, a task that any kid could grasp intuitively.

The man in front of the room continued his droning explanations as to different types of long-standing social media applications used by older generations to the new, hot, instant gratification apps used by youth. He realized that the attendees were being groomed to assist the company in somehow using private information that the company had acquired for inappropriate purposes. Tad stewed more and more as realizations came to him.

Then, the instructor said that the internet access on the yacht was provided by the company's own connections through its own satellites. Tad knew that the company's fledgling, but growing internet provider and e-mail host operated under a different name, and that it also offered VPN connections with the promise that a user's identity, IP address and location were protected. But he was also sure that all the data it acquired was being used for nefarious purposes and probably was even a Dark Web provider, so nothing was protected at all.

The instructor spoke in a horrible monotone, constantly exhibiting a knowing, geeky grin. "I'm going to be presenting certain programming procedures. If this is simple for you, let me know. If it's new to you, don't worry. You don't have to program. Only to understand the basics. The real geeks have made a whole procedure just for you. You answer questions and provide information, and it all happens." The instructor clicked on a few pages on the large screen and then asked, "Who here could create this kind of procedure?"

Tad certainly could, but he didn't want to. If the company went down, he wanted to be a lowly employee, not a creator of means to perform illegal procedures.

After a while, the speaker announced that there would be a break, staggered by row, and that workers had to sit silently until it was their turn.

They couldn't speak to each other, and one person at a time could enter a restroom.

As he stood in the restroom line, a security guard stopped in front of him. "Do you have a phone?"

He hesitated, having planned to text his father while in there.

The guard tapped Tad's pocket. "Give it to me," the man ordered.

As Tad pulled it out of his pocket, he said, "When will you give it back?"

The guard shook his head.

Tad was livid, but also fearful. He tried to figure how to escape. How far from shore could they be now? Could he jump overboard and swim to shore? The thought of being in the deep ocean water petrified him further. He remembered fears as he'd read President John F. Kennedy's book 'PT 109', as well as the horrifying movie, 'Open Water'. He shuddered.

He thought some fresh air would do him good. He would have taken a great run like every day if he'd been free today. Maybe he could walk or run on deck. He looked around the narrow hallways trying to figure which led to the outside. He started walking in what could be the right direction.

He turned a corner and found himself face-to-face with a uniformed security guard. "Excuse me, sir. The class is back there."

Tad stopped and looked around. "I was trying to figure out where there's a door to the outside."

"No, sir. Turn back."

Now he knew for sure that he and the others were virtually imprisoned. He had to return and continue learning, while trying to figure out how to communicate with the outside.

He made his way back toward the classroom but was stopped by another guard. "Mr. Harris," the man said, "Please come this way."

Hesitant and concerned, he followed the man down a hallway. The man opened a door and ushered Tad into a room at which some of those he worked with at Giga-BATS stood around a series of computers. Glancing through a large glass window, he saw the room he'd been working in, still occupied by workers who obviously had less computer savvy than those in the server room did.

Another man dressed like a supervisor said, "Whether or not you have admitted it, we know that you all have the technological background to lead the workers out there to perform important tasks. Many of you revealed it by searching during the instruction. Now, you will be performing searches as we direct, creating programs and procedures and instructing the others to take certain actions. You will each sit at a server and follow instructions. Please don your headphones."

Despair hit him as he realized he'd become a player, complicit in their schemes. All he could do was pray that somehow, someway, he would find a way out of this labyrinth of lies and corruption before it consumed him entirely.

And through it all, the fate of Michele haunted him. Was she safe, or trapped in her own nightmare somewhere on this godforsaken yacht?

Chapter 3

Michele smiled at her dad's use of the comforting endearment, "baby girl." She glanced at the peninsula beside the channel, and then back at her saviors.

Butch asked, "Where should we take you?"

She hesitated, "I need to get to shore to get a ride, near here or closer to Brickell."

"What's your destination?"

She paused again, warily glancing at the three but somewhat reassured by their compassionate smiles. "Grove Isle Marina."

Hank said, "We can take you to the marina by boat, cutting across from out here. It'll be much faster. Agreed, guys?" He glanced around.

The others smiled and nodded. "We got you, Michele," Jorge assured her, his smile warm and genuine.

Butch mashed the throttle down. The bow rose as the boat planed smoothly and surged forward. The slight chop pitter-pattered against the hull. Michele's gaze drifted to the horizon, where the yacht carrying her friends and loved ones had shrunk to a mere speck. Dread about their unknown fate settled in her stomach like a lead weight.

Her mind drifted to a bittersweet memory of moments with Tad after Pedrito had marched off and Kim had left the previous evening. Tad and Michele had sat on a dock gazing at the star-sparkled sky. "It's so beautiful," she'd said.

"Stellar," he said.

She smiled thinking it was an unusual but fitting term.

As they chatted, he touched her arm and leg from time to time, and she found herself resting fingers on his wrist and hand. Having been friends for so long, but never having been romantically or physically involved, her sudden attraction to him surprised her. She wondered whether it resulted from the stress arising from their mutual concerns or instead was a rebound from the unexpected recent end of her relationship with Marco. She'd expected to marry him but concluded that the relationship was shallow, and that he was insincere. Had that been an error too? Had she dumped him for no real reason?

Michele had found herself gazing into Tad's engaging brown eyes, and then to his slightly plump, brownish, pinkish lips. Why'd she never thought of those lips before? He leaned in a bit, and she did the same. Soon, their lips came together, softly, sensually. His lips tasted so sweet, felt so smooth and soothing. As he turned his head a bit to the side, his tongue caressed and darted between her lips, tapping her tongue. She returned the tap.

"Well," Michele said. "That was a pleasant but unexpected surprise."

Tad smiled. "I didn't expect that either. I loved it."

She checked herself. It was not the appropriate time for relationship considerations. Anybody would know it was a rebound reaction. She gazed into his eyes. "Tad, I don't know whether we should have kissed like that or not, and whether that will lead to something else or not, but we've got big, important matters on our minds right now, and I think we should put a pause on kissing or whatever for a bit."

"Damn, girl," Tad had responded, looking hurt. "That's the quickest relationship end ever."

She smiled. "You're funny, Tad. You call a kiss a relationship?"

He grinned. "Well, I wouldn't mind having a relationship with you."

"Tad, I don't think I would mind having one with you either. But not now. Not tonight. Really, we have serious things to worry about."

He smirked. "Have you ever been with a black guy before?"

She glared at him. "That's a rather presumptuous question, don't you think? Should I ask you if you've ever been with a Latina before? And what do you mean by 'been with'? A little kiss? Something physical? A long-term relationship? Let's go, Tad."

He smiled, glumly. "Sorry."

She returned his smile. "You're fine, Tad."

He grinned again. "Michele, is that the new use of that word, like in 'that's all right, no harm done,' or the old meaning like, 'damn you fine'?"

She stood, grabbed his elbow and helped him up. He moved in with arms open to hug her, but she swooped to the side, turned and walked away. "Tad, you don't listen."

The electricity of their kiss still tingled on her lips, in spite of her immense fear of the future.

******

Franklin stuck his head into his son's office. Miguel, with his headphones from the office phone over his head, glanced up, looked concerned, and hit the mute button on the office phone. "¿*Qué pasa, papá*?"

Franklin answered in English, "I don't exactly know. Michele is in some kind of trouble. I'm going to get her."

"What? Oh God. I hope she's all right. Keep me informed. I'm talking to the mayor's office about their plans to announce closures of businesses because of the coronavirus."

His mind spinning in a whirlwind of worst-case scenarios, Franklin drove along the two-lane streets of Coral Gables beneath a tunnel of arching trees that filtered the sun, worrying about Michele. What could possibly be happening? Was it a problem with a dating relationship? Had that bastard ex-boyfriend Marco edged his way back in or threatened her? What could have happened?

He called his wife. "Diana, something has happened with Michele. I mean, she's all right; she called me. But she said she's in some kind of trouble. I'm going to M&M to meet her and find out."

His wife gasped. "What in the world?" She choked up. "Call me immediately when you get to her."

Franklin's phone showed his office calling. He quickly said goodbye, ended the call and picked up the other.

"Hi, Franklin, it's Teresa. You know the Mathers estate? The jewelry and collectibles were retrieved from the home yesterday and were supposed to be brought here. The jewelry appraiser is in the reception area to do the appraisal, but the jewelry hasn't arrived. Do you know anything?"

He hesitated, his mind whirring. "Uh, we used that same security company we've been using, right? They told me yesterday they had the instructions from you via email I think."

She answered. "I sent a secure email with an attachment."

"Okay, Teresa, can you please call and find out where the stuff is?"

At a traffic light, he glanced at a Mercedes stopped next to him, driven by a pretty, dark-haired teen, her nostrils adorned with bone-like studs. He was chagrined when she looked back and caught him staring, offered a half smile and looked away. The blare of a horn jolted him back to reality.

He glanced up, saw the light was green and moved forward, reminded that he'd been on the phone with Teresa. "Franklin, are you there?"

"Uh, yeah. Sorry."

"Also, some of Mrs. Mathers' investment accounts were being liquidated and transferred to the new estate bank account, but I don't see them yet in the account by viewing the on-line record. Do you know about that?"

He had trouble changing course from his concern over his daughter. Finally, he concentrated. "We sent the letter of instruction two days ago and I understood they'd transfer the funds that day. Please contact Mrs. Mathers' broker and let me know."

He disconnected. Why was Michele on a boat on a workday? Whose boat was she on and who was she with? Suddenly, he felt fear again and dialed the number she'd called from. A man answered. "This is Michele's father. Is she still with you?"

He could hardly hear over the roar of the out-board motor, the slap of water against a hull, and the wind. RPMs dropped, and then he heard, "Michele, it's your dad."

"Hi, Dad. I'll be there in about ten minutes, I think. How about you?"

"The same."

Questions swirled in his mind when she'd clicked off. Who was she afraid could be tracking her? What could possibly have happened this morning?

******

Kim tapped the blonde girl's shoulder again. This time she moved.

Honesti said, "I gotta pee. I can't believe we're locked in here with no place to go."

Kim looked around the dim space and spotted a little bucket on the floor. She pointed with her chin. Honesti looked horrified.

The blonde girl said, "What's going on? Is the party over? How'd I get so fucked up?"

Kim put a hand on the blonde's shoulder. "We don't know what's happening, but they've locked us in here, and now we appear to be at sea."

The blonde blinked her eyes rapidly. "In the ocean? Going where?"

Honesti, still seated on the bucket, shook her head. "We don't know."

Kim jumped at the ominous sound of the door lock rattling.

As the door opened, a balding, uniformed, armed, security guard, with a pitiful mustache and bushy eyebrows, popped his head in. "Good morning angels," he said smiling.

"What the hell?" said Kim.

Still smiling, he said, "Such bitterness. That's unladylike." His lecherous gaze raked over Honesti, still sitting on the bucket.

She scowled, trying to cover herself with her hands. "Get outa here y'old perv."

The guard grimaced. "Ms. Kim Armstrong, I've been sent to fetch you."

Kim hesitated, but the guard gripped her arm and pulled her toward the door. The other girls glanced at each other, looking shell-shocked.

Honesti said, "Please don't forget us, Kim."

The security guard ushered Kim along multiple hallways, pushed her into an empty room and slammed the door. She paced around the table and chairs, wondering what was next. It suddenly occurred to her that she worked for a company without a single female supervisor. Here she was, truly believing in equal rights in the workplace for women but accepting that situation without question—until now.

Mr. Brown entered the interrogation room and sat across from her, his smirk making her skin crawl. "Miss Armstrong," he said in a condescending tone. "Are you ready to begin helping the company? We know you are trained and talented and can do what we need."

Her fists clenched beneath the table. "What is going on, Mr. Brown?" she demanded.

"You have an opportunity to avoid a poor future, Miss Armstrong, unlike those girls in the room."

Anger welled up. "What's planned for those girls?"

He smiled. "Well, they're young, cute, weak, and desirable. They have party futures in front of them."

"Are you fucking serious? What is this all about? This company is a strong, well-established business. Why would it also be involved in some seedy stuff like that? And why am I different?"

He put on a resigned, fake, caring face. "Miss Armstrong, you have knowledge and abilities that they don't have. And, I hate to say it like this, but, Miss Armstrong, you're kind of old."

She glared at the asshole.

He continued, "Those girls are very valuable because of their youth and innocence. What are you? In your mid-to-late thirties? You have mental talents though."

She avoided screaming epithets. She needed to be calm. She needed to learn more, to try to forge a plan to save herself, and the girls, for whom she now felt responsible.

She glared at him. "What are the company's plans with me?"

"Some computer and internet work."

"Like what?"

"You'll see, if you agree to perform the duties."

"How can I agree to do something when I don't know what it is?"

"Alright, Ms. Armstrong, shall I return you to the locked room with the girls?"

She hesitated. Thoughts muddled through her brain. There was no way out. It was probably best to cooperate as long as possible. "I'll do the work," she said, fearing what that would entail.

******

Now that Tad was receiving instructions to create tasks for the less-qualified workers, he hoped any investigation he performed would not be noticed. He did what he was told but occasionally typed in common commands attempting to verify whether paths through the server he was operating were open or restricted. His searches often resulted in conflicting results. He probed, glanced through folders, and saw connections to other servers and beyond.

He nervously glanced around the room after finding his way into a VPN. Even if guards didn't catch him, probably the tech people could see what he was doing, especially if the VPN was owned and managed by the company. He searched programs for a means to communicate. Click after futile click he tried to enter Facebook messenger and other social media sites. He couldn't

GIGA TROUBLE

open his WhatsApp account without his phone to click on a QR Code. Certainly, the yacht was out of range for a regular phone connection.

Then, he had an inspiration. Since he'd been the one who'd set up and maintained the computer system for his and Kim's fathers' company, Roasted Oak, he could enter the system and leave a message directly on his father's PC desktop, and his father could answer him. Observing his surroundings again, he input the necessary data and links, and typed, "Dad, I'm OK, but in trouble, on a boat of my bosses. Write back."

He surveyed his surroundings again, but didn't see any attention. He left the link open and continued working on the tasks he'd been relegated to perform. Occasionally over the next twenty minutes, he'd check the link for an answer, but none came.

After a while, a message appeared on his screen. "You think you have escaped being observed as you hacked into a system, but you have not. You have now jeopardized the system of your father's business. This computer system misses nothing. You should log out of that system now and remember that you have provided us a link into it."

Tad sat back, vibrating with dread. *Oh no. Who or what had written him? If it was a person, they would have come and taken him away. Was it a computer?*

He logged out of the Roasted Oak system and tried to concentrate, still silently defiant.

Chapter 4

Zipping across the water toward the marina, Michele combed the sparkling, endless expanse of blue searching for any sign of Giga-Blue. Dread about the futures of her co-workers tortured her, but she also saw a horrible future for herself. At age thirty-nine, she cringed at the thought of crawling back to her parents' doorstep like some pathetic failure, jobless, directionless and penniless. When she'd returned home after breaking up with that arrogant, chauvinistic Marco, she'd insisted on paying rent, utilities and expenses while occupying the separate dwelling on her family's property.

Veering into the small channel that led to the marina, Butch throttled down. Michele spotted the M&M at its mooring. The sound of gears winding down made her look up as her father's vintage, silver Porsche 911 moved toward the dock. She smiled, thinking that at her dad's age, he was still driving that quasi-racecar. When asked why he didn't buy a new car, he'd say, "Why? This car is in perfect condition, and we know each other so well."

Gravel and dust spread as Franklin spun to a stop just as Butch slid the boat alongside the dock. Michele jumped off the boat and ran to her dad. They hugged and kissed, Latino style, on the cheeks. They walked back to the dock, her dad resting an arm on her shoulder. She thanked her rescuers, and her dad did as well, also offering money for gas.

Jorge spoke up. "No sir. It was our pleasure to help. You are the attorney for my parents ... Jorge and Katia Arias."

Franklin smiled. "Ah, yes. Fine people. Cubanos like us."

The guys casted off and departed as Michele and her dad climbed into the car. Michele said, "Can you turn your phone off?"

He slid his phone out of his pants pocket, pushed and held buttons and slid the digital slider. As he started to put it back in his pocket, Michele realized it was the old kind that had a removable battery. "On second thought, let's remove the battery and put the phone in the trunk."

Her father looked at her, eyebrows raised, as he handed it over. She removed the battery. Her dad climbed out, walked to the front and placed it in the trunk, or 'frunk' as he called it, for front trunk. She thought it was safe unless a tracker was built into a non-operating phone. She'd heard that it was possible, but most experts said it was not.

As he reentered the car and closed the door, Michele glanced at the car's dashboard. She had heard of the wi-fi of household appliances being accessible. Why not a car's navigation system? But his car and its technology were quite old. No Bluetooth connection, no satellite radio, no smart assistant to ask for help. She glanced at his wrist and reminded herself that like the non-digital car, he wore a non-digital watch.

Feeling assured, she said, "You know that Giga-BATS moved me up and into other divisions several times, and they did the same with Tad and Kim. The company has more subsidiaries and related businesses all over the world than probably anybody knows. We've all become concerned about the scope of work of the various businesses."

Her father downshifted, slowing the car, and turned onto an adjoining street. He glanced at her as he shifted back up. "Like what?"

"Many of the related businesses offer security programs, cell phone applications, security cameras and smart home devices … various ways to track people, listen to conversations, and spy. We think they may be passing information back and forth to their other businesses and may be participating in illegal activities, like scams and theft. Nobody would realize that these companies are related. They keep our phones during the day while we are at work and probably obtain our data. Last night, we met with Pedrito to express our concerns. He's a security officer but he got us all hired."

Franklin grimaced and stopped at a red light, then clicked back into first, turned the corner to the right and pulled over into a small, empty parking lot. "What happened today?"

Michele explained all the surreal events of the morning, up to her daring jump into the sea. Her dad continued driving as he listened and soon arrived at the family home in Coral Gables. Franklin pressed the button to open the black, wrought-iron gates and slid through. He drove along the pavers, past well-manicured flowers, bushes and trees, which were being trimmed at the moment by two workers in uniform. He parked near the front door, and they exited. "Let's go talk to your mother."

Walking in, Michele grabbed her dad's arm. "Dad let's talk outside. There's too much smart equipment in the house, and I'm not sure it's private."

Michele's mother ran from the living room and embraced her. "Oh my God, Michele, what has happened? What's the matter?" She backed up, holding Michele's shoulders. "Your blouse is damp. What happened?"

Michele turned and motioned for her parents to follow. Outside, they sat on chaise lounges near the pool. She gave her mom a quick version of what had occurred, how Kim, Tad and Pedrito seemed to be in trouble, and her escape by diving into the water.

Her mother's eyes grew wide as she clasped a hand over her mouth. "Does Elena know about Pedrito?"

Michele shook her head. "I haven't talked to anybody. They took my phone. I'm worried about being tracked and causing others danger. They probably have the phone numbers of everybody in my contacts, including Dad's."

Michele's father sat in silence, shaking his head, frowning and ringing his hands. Finally, he spoke. "We've got to get to the bottom of this and warn the families. Diana … you're going to think I'm crazy, but I think I should take Michele by boat to Havana. There's no safer place. We don't use our cell phones there. There is probably less technological access there than anywhere. You know I have plenty of family and close contacts there who can protect her. And Diana, I don't think you should be alone here. How about staying with Miguel and Jordan?"

Diana shook her head. "I don't want to endanger them … or Alisa."

Franklin nodded. "I'll talk to Miguel when I get to the office. Are you all right with my suggestion about going to Cuba?"

Diana said, "Yes, I think it's the best. Michele, go get changed and grab some things. Franklin, let's pack you a duffel too."

Within minutes, Franklin and Michele were racing toward Morales & Morales to use the safe phone and prepare for the journey to Havana.

******

Pedrito's head pounded as he struggled to sit up. Every time he moved, the room spun around him like a dizzying kaleidoscope. Bile burned his throat. The acrid taste of vomit filled his mouth. *Oh God, help me.* He fell back onto the narrow cot, waited a moment, then tried again to rise but leaned to the left and fell to the floor. The metallic clang and vibration of his impact reverberated like the sound of a heavy object striking aluminum. He suddenly remembered he wasn't in a building at all, but aboard a boat.

He tried to get up. Looking around the dimly lit space, he saw only light-colored walls and floor. Other cots in the room seemed to be occupied. *Where is the toilet?*

He crawled across the floor, his limbs heavy and uncooperative, desperately searching for a toilet or other receptacle. Seeing a plastic bucket against the wall, he crawled and rolled toward it. Before he got there, puke overwhelmed him and poured from his mouth in a torrent. He gagged and choked as it burned his insides. He tried valiantly to wriggle out of the path of the foul liquid as it drifted along the floor. His supervisor shirt, which he now realized was lacking his security insignia, absorbed the putrid liquid.

Memories of the previous night flickered through his mind—Michele, Kim, Tad, interrogating him mercilessly. The company must have learned about the meeting. That was the only reason they would have beat him this morning.

He remembered that they'd made him drink something, which was definitely tainted and made him completely loaded. Kim had been next to him in the same condition, but then Michele, looking normal, had called up to him from an abyss.

He started worrying about never seeing his beautiful daughter, Elenita's, face and innocent smile. Tonight was his weekly visitation night with her. His ex would raise hell about his not showing up to retrieve her.

Well, at least his mother would learn that he was missing. And she would call Franklin.

He thought of his recent meeting with Mr. Doolittle. Could Doolittle know what was going on here or about the meeting the previous night and how he was being treated here? Doolittle should remember the favor he'd done for him recently. How could he reach him for help? Or had Doolittle ordered his imprisonment? Pedrito finally dragged himself to the door, and, without rising, started banging on it. "Hey, open the door," he yelled.

A voice came from another cot, saying, "Shut the fuck up!"

Another said, "Jesus Christ, you puked on the floor, Dude. What a fucking stench."

And yet another said, "You're a fucking boss man. What are you in here for?"

He lay on the floor, immersed in dread, despair and the stench of puke, hoping he'd survive.

******

Kim walked in front of Brown along hallways. His hand brushed against her behind, the unwanted contact sending shivers of revulsion down her spine.

Her skin crawling, she whirled around. "Listen, Brown," she hissed, her voice full of fury. "You can force me to work, but you keep your filthy hands to yourself. Touch me again, and I'll make sure you sing soprano for a week."

His face reddened as he looked away.

Kim stopped and moved to the side. "You lead the way and dream that I'm ogling your rank ass."

He shyly took the lead, led her into a large room with multiple workers sitting at computers and directed her to a space. She sat, glanced around the room, and viewed the screen on her desk. The other workers in the room appeared to be busy. Some were banging keyboards so hard they reminded her of heavy-duty hackers. Privacy filters protected other workers' screens.

As she settled in front of a computer, a pop-up appeared. "Click on the supplied link and when it opens, input this data." It provided what appeared to be a username and password. She did as instructed.

After she clicked, a page in a foreign language popped up. What the hell was it? Russian? She didn't even know what to do, but the bubble was not instructing. She opened Google Translate and copied in the words. She realized immediately that this was a Russian government site. She caught her breath. What were they doing? What were they making her do?

She received instructions to click through a series of pages and into another. She had no clue where she was going due to the language issue. Then she got more instructions and pasted English text she received into e-mails to multiple persons who appeared to be in the United States.

The language she was given gave a sob story to the recipients, that a family member was traveling and had no money. She then pasted in a link that, when clicked on by recipients, surely was placing malware into their computers. Then, she pasted instructions. She realized that the intent was to make the hack appear to law enforcement that it originated in the government of Russia. She hit the final send button, regretting the huge falsehood.

The next instruction said, 'Now, copy and paste the attached link.' Thank God she was not using her personal identity, computer or device.

Now she was somewhere else in the Russian system, again unsure what she was looking at. She was given a connection to an Instagram account within the server and instructed to insert data. She glanced through language in the link and became convinced that it was a real or made-up leak about a U.S. presidential candidate. Here she was, on a ship from the U.S., working for a seemingly U.S. company, but with international tentacles, using an internet satellite owned and operated by one of the related businesses she worked for.

The screen seemed to mock her, a portal to a world of secrets and lies. Pop-ups and instructions bombarded her. Foreign languages, government sites, military secrets–it all blurred together in a dizzying web of deceit as she followed orders like a puppet on strings. Sob stories, malware, false flags–each new task made her feel more complicit.

Time blurred into an endless cycle of clicking, copying, pasting, each new link dragging her deeper into the abyss.

A pop-up stated, "A toilet and refreshment break is coming up. Each person will have five minutes. The breaks are separated. You will receive a notice when it is your time. You must not be late returning." It showed a schedule with seat numbers and times.

She thought for the first time that her period had started this morning and should be dropping by now. She had an extra pad in her purse. How long was she going to be on this boat? Her flow would only increase, till it ended. She'd have five minutes to take care of everything.

After more strange forays into dark sites, she realized she was in a Russian site again, and it contained communication with a government entity in Cuba. She was directed to drop an IP packet, but fortunately the site wouldn't accept the drop. How deep did this rabbit hole go?

Her break was about forty-five minutes from now. Thank God the computer had a clock since she had no watch, no phone, and no window to gauge the time of day. Another pop-up announced, 'Click on this link, and when connected, click on this.' She did. Oh no. The United States agency called Homeland Security. Are these people idiots? Surely Homeland Security can discern where entry originates. Maybe the yacht would be bombed. Well, then she wouldn't have to worry about blood staining her pants. She smiled at her dark humor. *Sicko*.

She hit the second button and dove into a world of security memos and weirdness. Three-letter acronyms, references to armed forces, world leaders and enemies seemed to surround her. *What the hell am I doing in here?* She kept trying to convince herself that there was no way Big Brother could figure out that little Kim Armstrong, as a person with a name and identity, was the one in the depths of their system.

She recoiled as a fiery orb filled her screen, fixing its searing gaze on her. She realized she was in front of a camera. Had she been identified by facial recognition? She knew she was going to die, or at least go to prison, maybe not right now, but some time.

A pop-up sent by whoever was controlling her said, 'Ignore that attempt at humor. That's how techno bureaucrats amuse themselves. It's not real.'

She zoomed out of the depths of government scariness and sat, stunned, without any hope.

******

Tad stared at the monitor as the endless stream of pop-ups and instructions flooded his screen. Who was pulling the strings behind the scenes? Were they even on this godforsaken yacht? And was that damned message from a person or not?

A new message blinked into existence. "Search for articles about proposed government financial benefits for individuals and businesses and acquire criteria for targets to seek aid in the form of cash payments, loans, and similar financial aid to circumvent possible financial crisis arising from the novel coronavirus."

Almost immediately, he located U.S. government social service and loan agency sites, legislators' pages and independent parties talking about proposals to help people and businesses if the coronavirus became a pandemic. He downloaded significant articles, correspondence and other communications and placed them in a folder.

He sat back, hands on the table, considering how anybody could think that the new coronavirus is going to cause such an effect in the country. From news reports he'd seen, many thought the fears of being a pandemic were a bit irrational. Even President Trump and his followers seemed to have no concern after a couple of days during which it seemed they did.

Governor DeSantis seemed to be concerned too and was talking of imposing restrictions. But all was unclear. With just a few cases in the United States, why would the government propose giving financial support to victims of the illness? It was too early for that, wasn't it? Even today, Miami had few cases. The biggest problem was in New York City. It was unclear whether moves would be created by the national government or individual state governments. Would states handle it in the same way, or would each handle things differently? Was political party affiliation of governments going to play a key?

How could the federal government be moving so fast? Was it even real? They were talking of stopping the Chinese from visiting. If they'd just do that, it would be over, wouldn't it? That's what Trump was saying about what he was calling 'Kung Flu' or 'China Virus.'

Tad found drafts of proposed loan or grant application procedures to be implemented if businesses and individuals suffered because of the virus. He reviewed further and found the proposal for banks that had existing relationships with the Small Business Administration and similar government agencies to issue loans, which may be forgivable in whole or in part.

He dug into the SBA sites and then media interpolation of what was occurring and what would occur. He returned to U.S. congressional communications. Then, he began searching worldwide scientific and governmental sites for international plans on addressing the virus and money-making possibilities in numerous industries. Finally, he searched multiple sites to gather information about possible vaccine studies.

He was instructed on how to link all pertinent information into a private application that sorted, combined and expanded on the data. And all these research sites would be also recipients of IP data packets that would continue to share new materials with this application. Again, he was amazed at the vast circumlocution of the combined information and his employer's ability to grasp and use all of it to its benefit.

A message popped up. "Create a process for an individual worker to seemingly assume control of an existing company of any type that has annual gross income between 1.5 and 3.5 million dollars. Then create a process for workers to locate qualifying businesses and to create loan applications in their names. The workers must clone the companies' internet access, alter the identities of principals and create fictitious executives and departments, close enough but slightly different so a loan or grant can be acquired. When you have the full process in place, we will have multiple workers running the procedure on various companies. And AI will impersonate leaders of the businesses for whom we make applications seeking aid."

He shook his head. He was doing exactly what he feared they would force him to do. And giving other workers tools to complete the work. They'd all be implicated in this giant crime scheme.

He started outlining the process for the general workers to perform as instructed but kept getting interrupted by an artificial intelligence program that tried to impose its ideas. Maybe he should just let it create the outline instead of trying to do it himself. Why were he and other humans even involved?

He couldn't just sit back like a puppet dancing on strings. How could he sabotage the many schemes? He had to avoid detection, but couldn't just give in.

Chapter 5

After hugging her mom goodbye, Michele squeezed into the passenger seat, tossed her bag behind her, and sighed. Her dad slid through the gears and zipped along the canopied Coral Gables streets. The purring melody of the Porsche's engine rising and falling with each gear change enchanted her, as she knew it did her father.

"Listen, Dad. Your law firm uses services like those offered by Giga-BATS. Other types of businesses, like banks, use various programs and services specific to the type of business for protection also. You input client data into legal research, timekeeping, billing, financial records and organizational software. You might even use document creation software. Lawyers have fiduciary obligations to keep clients' data secure. But is it secure?"

Her father looked at her, a bit of concern rising on his face. "How do you know so much about this?"

"Because, Dad, my friends and I have shared with each other what each has been involved in. In fact, to me the scariest one was banking and financial institutions. Giga-BATS has taken over at least one well-known and well-respected, licensed international bank and financial services operation. Perhaps regulators do not even know that ownership or control or whatever it is has changed. Maybe it hasn't even changed."

Franklin said, "I can't believe regulators in the United States would approve acquisition of a financial institution without severe scrutiny. And

I wonder how Giga-BATS could convince executives of a well-respected financial institution to sell its assets to illegitimate people."

Michele said, "Perhaps the institutions they've acquired are regulated by other countries, so there would be no requirement to file anything in the U.S."

Her dad pursed his lips. "OK, but how is owning and operating an international bank or financial institution going to help them?"

Michele said, "In the banking and finance operation, I was ordered to hack into other financial institutions to learn how each handles transfers of funds and to search for data about every employee. I didn't even know how to hack into a system, but they led me through it with step-by-step instructions. You may know that the word "hack" isn't always bad, and in this case, they didn't have me install malware or anything like that; it was more like a surveillance effort. I was told that the research was being done to protect Giga-BATS' bank. I saw instructions, memos, procedures, etc., about wires and other digital money transfers and shared them with the people who were instructing me. I saved everything I found in folders, as instructed."

They arrived at her dad's law office building on Biscayne Boulevard, across the street from Bayfront Park and Bayside Marketplace, and cruised up the levels of the parking garage. Franklin parked in the spot below a sign that stated, "Reserved for Franklin Morales."

Her dad held a card up to a reader, which unlocked the door, allowing entrance directly to the rear hallway of the law office. They walked down the hallway, passing under several ceiling cameras blinking and turning. He held up his card again, and when a door opened, they entered his personal office through the back door.

She whispered, "That entry system, those cameras ... who owns and monitors them? And through what services?"

"I have no idea," he said, as he shook his head, and looked at her with—what—dread?

She walked to the window and gazed out, grasping a full view of where she had boarded the yacht in the morning, where she had jumped and been rescued, and the route from there down to the marina. She gazed along the wide-open ocean horizon toward the Bahamas, wondering where the yacht could be.

Franklin punched a button on the desk phone and asked Miguel to come into his office. Miguel entered an instant later, rushed to Michele and kissed her on the cheek. "Michele, what's going on? Are you all right?" He moved back and examined her. He handed Franklin a bag. "Mom called and asked the front desk to order you two a couple of Cuban sandwiches."

"Wow, great thinking. I forgot it's lunchtime and we have a long trip in front of us," Franklin said as he pulled out the two sandwiches and handed Michele one. "Miguel, please take your cell phone back to your office." Miguel glanced at the two of them like they were a little odd.

Franklin said, "Michele, do you think we can safely talk here? I don't know of a more private place in the building."

She glanced at the ceiling. "No cameras in here, right?"

Her father shook his head.

Michele marched to his computer and affixed a small, yellow Post-it over the camera. "Dad, do your systems have virus protection and firewalls?"

Franklin shook his head and shrugged his shoulders sheepishly as he nibbled on the sandwich.

Michele looked at him askance and had him log in to his computer. She sat at his desk, opened settings, glanced around, clicked something and stood.

Miguel returned and stood, glancing back and forth at them. "What's going on?"

Franklin gave Miguel a brief explanation of what had occurred during the morning.

Miguel said, "Your fears seem a bit farfetched."

Franklin glared at his son. "I also was skeptical when Michele first started describing what occurred, but she has convinced me. I'm taking her by boat to Havana to hide her ... to get her away from technology, without any cell phone or anything similar."

Miguel silently watched them like they were a pair of loonies.

Franklin called his cousin in Santiago de Cuba. She answered with, "Franklin, is something the matter? Why aren't you calling with WhatsApp?"

Franklin said, "I'm sorry Luz. I couldn't. But I'd like to ask you please to go to the business apartment in Havana. I'll talk to you further when you are there."

After a hesitation, she said, "This is strange Franklin. Can you tell me more?"

"No. Sorry. Please just go."

She said, "All right. I'll leave soon."

Franklin then said, "I'm calling Roosevelt and Jude and telling them to come to the office. Michele's employer may have data from the phones of every employee."

Miguel again looked unsure. Michele explained that employees were required to leave their phones in the employer's control during the workday, and that information was probably gathered. Miguel started shaking his head again, until his dad gave him the look.

Their father continued. "After we leave, please go to our home in person and talk to your mother about where she can be safe. I'm concerned about leaving her alone, but she's hesitant to put you and your family at risk. Also, have your Aunt Elena meet you there. Talk outside, not in the house. Turn your cell off and leave it in the car. Make sure Elena doesn't take her cell phone into the house or the yard.

Bring your mom and Elena here when Roosevelt and Jude have arrived. Tell them all to call everybody their kids know and ask if they've heard from them. Call our law enforcement contacts and file reports. They won't act on a missing persons' report this early, but we've got to raise a flag and maybe get agencies talking. Telephone our contacts at the Coast Guard also."

Michele said, "Also tell the agencies that many workers were forced to drink something, whether alcohol or drugs or both, and some were removed from the yacht immediately prior to the yacht's leaving the dock. Where did they go? Home? Are they being sequestered at the office building or someplace else? As the day closes and employees don't return home, people will start questioning. When enough start calling, the agencies will surely take notice."

Franklin opened the office safe and stuffed a plastic garbage bag with cash from the stack he regularly delivered to support the Cuban people on the Island as part of the efforts of a non-profit foundation his father had created. Since credit and debit cards from the U.S. were useless on the Island and not knowing how long he might be there or what might be necessary, he kept thinking of reasons to take more cash.

As Franklin zipped around his office, rustling through drawers and gathering money, Michele said, "Miguel, can you please take my phone and maybe even mom's and dad's phones, to that guy that sells used phones at that company on Flagler Avenue … and see if he can search for spyware?"

Miguel nodded and said, "Okay, Michele. Wow, you guys are really paranoid."

"I have my reasons," she said.

Looking back at Miguel, Franklin said, "We'll stop overnight at one of the yacht clubs in the Keys … probably Marathon … and cross the Gulf Stream in the morning. We'll call the office landline phone tonight and in the morning."

Miguel said, "By the way, two FBI officers called you while you were out, inquiring about Braxton Doolittle."

Franklin said, "Why could they think I'd have anything to do with that bastard? We fired him so long ago."

Miguel shrugged.

Michele said, "That's the lawyer you fired for stealing money? Did you know he's the guy that got Pedrito into Giga-BATS?"

Franklin's jaw dropped. "Are you serious?"

Michele nodded.

Miguel said, "Dad, Teresa says she told you that a deceased client's jewelry and funds are missing."

Franklin said, "Please get the info from Teresa and do what she needs. File reports. I trust you all to take care of things. We must get moving. It'll take us an hour to get to the boat and between three and four hours to get to Marathon. The sun will be setting when we get there."

Miguel shook his head, still looking at them as though they were crazy. Michele knew danger was not far away and hoped they were making wise decisions.

*****

Jude Armstrong was nearing the end of his daily pre-lunch five-mile brisk walk on Daytona Beach, listening to an audio book, *Our Man in Havana*, by Graham Greene. He'd walked a block to the Starbucks on Ocean Avenue where he met Irene, the woman who for years had lived on the beach, in a nearby park when the tide was high, or wherever it was safe. Sometimes during the daytime she'd venture along the streets, slowly moving her two-wheeled shopping cart with one hand and dragging a beat-up suitcase with the other. She sat at a table outside the store, brittle fingers surrounding a brown vintage ceramic Starbucks cup he'd gifted her.

"How are you today, Ms. Irene?" He handed her a five-dollar bill and clicked on his phone to top up the Starbucks gift card he'd gifted her a few years ago.

"I'm fine, thank you, Mr. Jude."

She insisted on putting 'Mr.' before his first name so he addressed her in the formal manner as well.

As he departed, she said, "Have a blessed day."

He set his watch to capture the data of his walk and headed south, passing the Ocean Deck restaurant, as reggae played. Walking vigorously, he laughed inwardly at the silly plot of the story he was listening to, wherein the character named Wormald created a fake report of a foreign power's missiles being installed in the mountains of eastern Cuba. Rather clairvoyant considering that the story was written before the Cuban Missile

Crisis. Since Jude had visited many areas of Cuba over the years on behalf of the Roasted Oak restaurant chain, he pictured the probable scene.

Several times, he leaned down to snatch interesting seashells to add to his collection. At Silver Beach, he turned and headed back to the north. Two shrimp boats slogged along the horizon. A couple of surfers worked the small, but nicely formed, crisp and clear waves.

Groups of friends, families and lovers sat sun-bathing on the sand, played games or threw balls or frisbees. He appreciated the racially and culturally diverse groups enjoying the beach. He approached the ocean pier, on which was perched the building that for years was a dance and concert hall and now was a restaurant. At about two and a half miles of his route, he continued north, past the coquina-rock structures that had been built after the great depression.

The story was interrupted by a phone call. He glanced at his watch and saw that it was the law offices of Morales and Morales in Miami, his company's attorneys. He clicked 'accept' and said, "Hello, Jude here".

"Hey, Jude, it's Franklin. Sorry to call your cell but couldn't reach you on the office phone. I think our kids are in danger. I need you guys to come immediately to Miami."

Jude's heart pounded as he listened to Franklin's cryptic warning, each word a dagger to his soul. "What?" he croaked, his voice barely above a whisper. "What do you mean? Where are they? What kind of trouble?"

Franklin said, "I'm sorry. I can't speak, Jude. You and Roosevelt come straight to my office and bring your passports."

"Our passports? Why?"

"I gotta go, Jude. Can you be here by nine or so tonight? Don't use cell phones because you may be monitored."

Monitored? The sinister word echoed in Jude's mind. He took off running, his heart hammering against his ribs. "All right, Franklin. We'll be there," he managed, his breath coming in ragged gasps.

Jude felt like puking. What in the world could this be about? Visions of his daughter flashed through his mind–her innocent smile, her inquisitive eyes, the way she'd grown into a beautiful, intelligent woman. He was petrified by the thought of her being in danger.

"What the fuck ... what the fuck!" Jude exclaimed aloud as he ran.

He was about to call Roosevelt but then remembered–no cell phones. He entered the office building of Roasted Oak Holding Company, the restaurant enterprise that Jude's father had created, ran to the second floor, yelled as he passed by his partner Roosevelt Harris' office, "Roosevelt, I need to talk to you. Come."

Roosevelt zipped out of his office and rushed down the hallway behind Jude.

Winded, Jude said, "I got a call from Franklin to tell me our kids are in danger ... We're supposed to go to Miami right now. And not use cell phones."

"What do you mean danger? What happened?"

"I don't know. He wouldn't say. He said it's not safe to talk on the phone."

Arriving in his office, Jude buzzed his son Mark on the intercom and beckoned him to his office. Jude ran into his private shower, leaving the bathroom door open, pulled off his clothes, flipped open the faucet and jumped in. Mark rushed into the office and yelled, "Dad. I'm here. What's going on?"

GIGA TROUBLE

Jude repeated the explanation to Mark. "So, Mark, you're in charge, along with Gloria. And Franklin said no cell phones. Roosevelt, he says to bring our passports."

Roosevelt said, "Let me tell Gloria. We'll have to stop at my house for my passport."

Jude said, "I will too," as he ran out of the bathroom, still soaking wet, clothes at various stages of being put together. He hit speed dial on the office phone to contact Kim. No answer. He told her voice mail to please call. He went into his computer and tried to write on Messenger, but she was offline. He wrote, "Contact your mother or Mark."

He buzzed Roosevelt's office. "Try to call or text Tad, or both. And try social media, but via your computer, not your phone."

"I already tried all that. Nothing. He's not on-line."

As Jude buttoned his shirt, tucked it in and sat to put his shoes on, he dialed his ex-wife and mother of his kids, who was living near Atlanta, Georgia. She came on speaker phone.

"Listen, Joyce, I got a call from Franklin. Something's going on with Michele, Kim and Tad. He ordered me to drive immediately to Miami and not to use a cell phone."

Her voice choked with a sob. "What? I don't understand. What's happened?"

"I don't know. When I get to Miami, I'll contact you. If you can call that husband of hers ... uh ... Denver ... see if he knows something. We'll talk. Bye."

Jude rushed down the hall and found Roosevelt's wife, Gloria, staring at Roosevelt in disbelief.

"Come on, Roosevelt....We gotta go," he yelled as he continued toward the door. "We'll call from Franklin's office phone when we get to Miami. You two decide what to do about the virus."

******

Kim finally got her break. She rose and stretched, feeling stickiness on her thigh and grabbed her purse.

A guard appeared. "You may not take your bag."

"What do you mean? I need something personal that's inside."

"What do you need?"

Kim's skin crawled as the guard's eyes raked over the contents of her purse, his gaze invasive and unwelcome. She snatched the pad, her cheeks burning with humiliation, and shouldered past him.

She had no way to know how long she'd been in the restroom as her watch and phone were no longer with her. But, when she exited, she found half a sandwich and a soft drink on a high table. She grabbed them and returned to the room.

As she recommenced work, she received another message. 'Log into attached link #1. Click on the email icon. Copy address #2 as the addressee in the email. Copy the entire string of addresses and paste them into the blind copy recipient area of the email. Copy and paste this link into the body of the e-mail.'

We know you have been suffering since losing your employment. We are an agency sponsored by the United States government to help distressed citizens by giving them useful means of legitimately earning money. The job is to provide us your data and execute documents to assist

GIGA TROUBLE

in providing help through agencies. And every time you sign your name, or allow funds to flow through your account, we pay you $500. This can occur several times per week. Simply click on the below link to apply. If you have questions, please reply or call....

And it gave a toll-free telephone number.

After an exhausting and overwhelming afternoon performing the same frightening tasks and even more terrifying intrusions, she just felt ready to cry. How could she escape?

******

Tad's eyelids grew heavy as he sat motionless, desperately needing his normal rush of caffeine and exercise. He glanced at the clock at the top of the screen. Two in the afternoon. Of course he was dragging. He navigated through the labyrinth of code and commands as instructions kept coming.

He questioned the necessity of his role. He and the others received instructions and then instructed the general workers how to input data into forms. Perhaps that was effective, just because there was probably one group leader for numerous underlings, who were digging into numerous sites, applications and dark web areas. He imagined that the multiple workers may soon be substituted with the company's artificial intelligence programs, which were certainly learning from the activities now performed by people, as they had sometimes overridden his own decisions.

A pop-up directed him to hack into a site with character-based symbols that appeared to be an oriental language, like Chinese or Japanese. He grabbed some lines and popped them into Google translate, with detect language setting on. It was Mandarin. Google Translate provided the English translation: "... United States of America denigrates officials of the Republic of China with accusations about the virus beginning in Wuhan, alleging the virus was created intentionally...." He grabbed some more, which said, "... actually the United States invented the virus and planted it in our Republic...."

The site appeared to be governmental. A pop-up appeared, instructing him to create procedures for workers to send a series of communications to international media. A response to the first comment was also in Mandarin. He popped it into Translate and read it.

The Wuhan virus was created by our scientists as a weapon of biological warfare against the west. The infection of people in the Wuhan province was unintentional.

It was a confession–a false confession. It could lead to World War III, and he was posting it. Could both countries be paying for spoofed communications? And why? He no longer knew which communications were true and which were not, or how he could escape from that surreal universe.

He was directed to hack into different government sites in multiple countries, this time addressing subjects beyond the coronavirus. He saw pages in which Russia seemed to criticize a country, and then the other country seemed to criticize Russia. He believed neither country was the true source.

It seemed his employer had contracts with different parties to engage in opposing communications about other parties. Giga-BATS itself manipulated information and also was paid by customers to post negative messages. It appeared that Russia was shown as performing acts that it wasn't, while Russia was also paying Giga-BATS to manipulate on its behalf. *Oh my God*, he thought; there was no end. It was all one giant circle of subterfuge and circumvention.

He decided to peruse systems again, looking for other means to communicate with the outside world. He didn't know if his father had responded but was afraid to log into Roasted Oak server again. He tunneled through one server after another.

A pop-up message froze him in place, his heart stuttering in his chest. "Mr. Harris, remove your hands from the keyboard and rise, with your hands in the air."

Pain exploded in his skull and stars danced before his eyes as the butt of the guard's pistol pounded his head. He crumpled to the ground, his forehead colliding with the table in a sickening crunch. Rough hands hauled him to his feet, dragging him from the room like a rag doll.

As the door to the white room slammed shut behind him, he lay on the cold floor, his head throbbing. He was trapped, utterly alone, with no way out of this nightmare.

Chapter 6

Franklin rushed out the back door of the office with Michele following and drove rapidly down the parking garage ramp. A silver Camry with two men in it pulled onto the ramp at the second level and followed. He drove to the exit on the west side of the building since the one-way road went south on that side. Seeing that it was still following, he said, "We picked up a car. I'm going to try to lose it."

He turned right onto Northeast First Street and then left onto Northeast Second Avenue. Then, he turned left onto Southeast First Street but still couldn't lose the tail. "This is bad," he muttered. "I'm going north on Biscayne and then I'll loop around and go south."

Becoming more anxious, he continued south on Biscayne as it curved to the right across from The Intercontinental Miami. The car had dropped behind just a bit. "When I get near Vizcaya, I'm going to try to shake them."

At Southwest 32nd Avenue, he leapt into action, downshifting, turning to the right, and flying through gears as he neared fifty miles per hour, well over the residential speed limit. He passed under I-95 and roared along tiny residential streets, with the Camry right behind.

Michele gripped the hand rest, her nails digging into the soft leather. Houses and buildings were a blur as her father raced around corners and tires screeched.

Lights of two parked city police cars lit up as they slid around a corner. Her dad said, "This is a good thing," as he slowed and pulled to the side. One police cruiser stopped behind Franklin while the other paced the still fleeing Camry. Her dad pulled his wallet out and withdrew his license as Michele retrieved the registration and proof of insurance.

The officer stood at the window. "Franklin Morales? I'm shocked. What in the world…?"

Franklin had always believed that performing free legal work for law enforcement officers, besides being a good deed, could help in a tight situation.

"I'm terribly sorry to have done that, Jim. But that car had been chasing us ever since we left our office, and I could not elude them."

Jim leaned in and glanced at Michele. "Miss, do you have some ID?"

Franklin said, "This is my daughter, Michele. She's had a very harrowing situation today and that's why those guys were chasing us."

"What happened young lady?"

"Uh, well, we aren't really sure what they're up to. They've been chasing me all day."

"Franklin and, uh, Michele, would you like to come to the station and give a report?"

Franklin responded, "Jim, we really do not have evidence or knowledge of who these people are. It would be a waste of time for all of us. We'll certainly do it if something else comes up. Please just give me the speeding or reckless driving ticket."

Jim returned to his car, picked up his radio microphone and spoke.

Franklin said to Michele, "I think it's best to get out of here. It won't be helpful or safe to stay here and get police involved at this point."

Jim returned. "Well, I don't know how they managed it, and Officer Burns is pretty burned about it ... heh heh heh. But they knocked him into a tree and got away."

Franklin asked, "Is Officer Burns all right?"

"Yep, he's fine. Just burned." And he laughed again. "Go on now. No ticket this time." And he roared with laughter again. "Good luck, little lady."

She frowned. *Little lady?*

******

As Jude drove toward Miami, Roosevelt sat in the passenger seat and tried to grasp what could be going on. His mind was a whirlwind of memories and emotions. Tad's face flickered before his eyes—a child, a teenager, a man—each image making him more worried. He thought of Tad's mom, Tara, her beauty and her demons. Having met in an N.A. meeting while trying to kick hard drugs, he should have realized their relationship would always be on shaky ground. Tara had never been able to hang on to sobriety, so finally he'd had to distance himself, for Tad's sake. Roosevelt couldn't let Tad experience the sad history he himself had suffered when his own mom had ultimately died of an overdose.

He recalled the beautiful night when Tad was about five and Roosevelt decided Gloria was the woman for him. He'd invited her to walk with him and Tad on the beach in Daytona in the moonlight. At one point, Tad let go of Roosevelt's hand, ran behind him and slid between the two, grabbing a hand of each as he said, "She's pretty, Dad."

Roosevelt almost choked up over the memories, and suddenly the dread was back. But then he convinced himself that whatever was happening, it was going to be Okay.

Roosevelt glanced out the windshield and said, "That's the third time I've seen that helicopter flying up and down the highway. I wonder who or what it's looking for."

Jude replied, "Franklin said we could be followed. Oh no. Is your phone on? And is that a smart watch? Dammit. Turn them both off right now." He pulled off I-95 at Wickham Road and stopped at Starbucks. "All phones and watches off and in the trunk. Coffee and piss break."

But just as Roosevelt began to power down the devices, a text message popped up. The first one said, 'Roasted Oak computer system is now closed down and you must pay ransom to restore it. Click on this link.' He struggled not to choke as he waited for Jude to emerge from the toilet.

He showed it to Jude. "What do we do?"

Jude stood, dumbfounded. He finally said, "We cannot click on that. Man, I wish we were back in the days of payphone booths. I think all we can do is wait till we get to Franklin's office."

But then, another message came in. Roosevelt held it up. "Hi, I'm changing plans. Please go to this sandwich place in Miami instead. Franklin."

Jude shook his head. "Nope. Ignore it. Shut both devices off now."

Roosevelt turned off the watch and phone and placed them in the trunk of the car.

Back on the road, Roosevelt sipped his drink and reminisced about the long-ago occasions that he'd met Jude. The first time, they were about ten years old, fishing on the street in front of the yacht club, while Jude threw a cast net from the yacht club docks, which only allowed white people as members. Roosevelt's aunt had started yelling at Jude, saying he was stealing all the fish with his cast net. Then, the two boys had run across each other near the same place as Jude and two white friends staggered out of the bushes, high as kites on weed. Then they'd run across each other on the street outside the ballpark as they chased foul balls that had bounded over the fence, when Jude's friends had made racist comments, and Jude had looked so embarrassed. The next time, Jude had shown up on Campbell Street in Daytona, the only white kid who would ever do that, to cop heroin from Roosevelt's friends.

After that, they'd both ended up in the same boat, for a long bout of addiction, arrests, prison (or at least he had gotten prison while Jude got a little slap on the wrist). But in the long run, Jude's father had saved both of them and put them in the business they now operated. Neither of their kids had ever seemed to have any inclination to abuse alcohol or drugs like Jude and Roosevelt had.

Jude said, "I just can't quite imagine what's going on with the kids, but I'm petrified."

"Ditto," said Roosevelt. "All I keep thinking about is that it must have something to do with the company they all work for. Tad's been a little hesitant to talk about his work lately."

"You're right. Kim has too."

They cruised the rest of the route in silence.

******

Kim sat up on the stiff cot, feeling drained of energy, knowing that in front of her would be a day sprinkled with fear and strange goings-on in the internet world in which she was mired. She coughed and tried to clear her throat. Her daughter's face flashed in her mind. A sob caught in her throat.

"Open up!" a gruff voice commanded, followed by a sharp knock. "Food and toilet break. Ten minutes."

Kim stumbled to the door, her legs shaky. As she retrieved the tray, her eyes fell on the unappetizing meal. Her stomach turned. She forced herself to eat.

The ten minutes ticked by all too quickly. As Kim was escorted to the shower, she caught a glimpse of another haggard face. She felt a bit off. Was it just fear and depression or could she have acquired the coronavirus?

She arrived at her seat at the same moment that Honesti arrived and was seated next to her.

Honesti's eyes widened. "Oh my God, I'm so happy to see you."

They embraced.

"Thank God you're all right, Honesti. Do you have experience in computer work?"

Honesti nodded. "Depending on what I have to do."

A voice came over a loudspeaker. "No touching. No conversing. No communication of any kind."

The two looked at each other. Honesti was so much younger than Kim, probably eighteen years old. Kim hoped that they would live through whatever was going to happen. Kim sat down and waited for an instruction. She could feel Honesti's presence at her side. She had to be so frightened.

A pop-up instructed Kim to enter a site. She was able to read this apparent sales site because she'd learned Spanish. It spoke of delivery of products with a shelf-life not exceeding nineteen years. What kind of product could that be? She received another instruction. She hesitated. She hit the next link.

Oh no. She realized the shelf-life language did not involve a product at all. Kim's head swam as she stared at the screen, the images before her a nightmare of lost innocence. The images were of young girls, their eyes haunted and vacant, their bodies exposed and vulnerable. She immediately clicked out. Beside her, Honesti's silent, shocked look told her she was seeing the same. They and all the workers knew too much, had seen too much.

******

Tad's head throbbed as he blinked against the sudden light. A guard opened the door and stood above him. It was impossible to even guess the time with no device.

The guard said, "Do not search again outside the scope of your orders. Let's go."

The guard's voice was a distant buzz in the fog of Tad's pain and confusion. Tad reached to the back of his sore neck tendons and squeezed.

He stumbled to his feet, his legs unsteady beneath him, and followed the man back to the server room. *One step at a time. Think positive.* He would act like he was Okay. *I feel fine. I feel fine.*

As he settled into his chair in the server room again, he could feel the fear his colleagues were experiencing. But he couldn't focus on them or let his guard down for even a moment. The instructions kept coming.

This time, he was directed to enter bank and brokerage sites in order to study the particulars of obtaining approval to transfer funds to an account at a different institution and to search for identity information regarding employees, including their social media presence, any recordings or copies of their voices, photos and videos. Individual and business customers of the institutions he searched had accounts in the exact same name as existed at the Giga-BATS institution so it would appear that a customer of one institution was merely transferring money to the same person's account in another institution.

Then, he created a procedure for entering and locking financial institutions' sites and encrypting all data until ransom was paid. And then he created procedures for ransomware attacks on hospitals, large companies, government entities and schools.

He vibrated with tension as he considered his part in helping the criminals.

Chapter 7

Franklin pulled into a parking spot at the marina, grabbed their bags and headed for the dockmaster's office. He stuck his head in the office door. "Hey Fred."

"Oh, hey, Franklin...." Then he saw Michele. "Hi, Michele."

She nodded and smiled.

Franklin glanced around. "Seen anything weird today? Anybody looking around our boat?"

Fred quizzically returned the look. "Nope. Nothing. Why?"

"Just curious. We are taking off for a while. If anybody snoops around, or looks at my car, or asks you anything, could you call Miguel at the office?"

"I will. Ya'll need gas or supplies?"

"I'm gonna check, but I doubt it."

"All right. I'll accompany you and help you cast off."

As they walked, Franklin noticed a Sheriff's car and trailer. "I see the law is on the water."

"Yep, maybe trying to track down the coronavirus on the high seas." The dockmaster laughed loudly.

Franklin smiled. "Well, I hope he captures it."

They rushed to the boat, followed by the limping old Fred. Franklin bounded aboard, checked the gas and fired up the engines. Michele found herself smiling with nostalgia. She loved this boat and the times she'd spent on it. The not-so-great musty odor came out of the closed-up cabin as her dad opened it up. Well, that was part of the memories too.

Fred untied the lines and casted off. Michele caught the lines, coiled and dropped them on the deck with a thud. Franklin idled toward the protected channel and the open water. Michele caught a glimpse of a small wooden boat speeding at them. "Dad," she yelled, pointing.

Franklin's eyes widened as the boat aimed straight at them. He suddenly charged to the starboard, putting the stern in the line of the other boat. The charging boat turned sharply but glanced the port side of M&M.

Franklin maneuvered around to the starboard again, still idling, as the attacking boat sped up and veered back to port. Franklin heard a siren and noticed the sheriff's boat racing toward the attacker, which flew off north on the river, with the sheriff following, yelling into his radio mic the whole time.

Franklin smiled at Michele. "Two lucky breaks, or mistakes by the other side. Hang on. Here we go."

The bow planed up and leveled as they hurtled toward the Florida Keys. Father and daughter were in their element as M&M maneuvered the slightly swelling sea. The deep blue water invited them, sometimes throwing sprinkles of white froth onto them.

Michele again glanced out to sea, looking for the yacht, carrying people she cared about.

And could those people who kept chasing her find them again in the middle of the Florida Straits? They'd have little protection, even if her father had a weapon.

******

Tad kissed Michele passionately. She whispered, "I told you, not now, Tad."

He placed a kiss at the nape of her neck, whispering back, "You seem to like it."

She shook her head. "Just not now, Tad."

He heard a noise, a muffled scream. Michele's voice, weakly saying, "Help me, Tad."

He jolted with fear. *Where are you, Michele?* He heard the hollow vibrations and remembered he was on a boat. He sat up quickly, realizing he'd been dreaming.

Dizziness overpowered him. He collapsed. God, he felt awful. What was it? Why was he so exhausted and weak? Lack of good nutrition? Lack of exercise? Effects of whatever he'd imbibed? Were they spiking his food and drink? He shivered. His throat seemed to be getting sore.

Michele. Where was she? Was she in trouble? Did one of them give the other the coronavirus? It was only a single kiss.

He tried to sit up more slowly. His body was so heavy. He wrapped his hands around his aching forehead and squeezed. He felt a lump on his forehead and another on the back of his head. Maybe he should just stay here and sleep. He collapsed again.

*****

Franklin said, "I gotta hit the head. Can you take the wheel?"

Michele nodded and moved enough to grab the wheel. The sun had begun its decline, tinging the cirrus, cloud-laden sky orange. She gazed at the beautifully toned and ever-changing hues of the water, changing based on the depth and makeup of the bottom.

After passing Pennekamp and the southern point of Key Largo, she spotted Plantation Key. As they had no phones or other equipment, determining the remaining distance was difficult. But she and her dad knew the entire route well. As always, she felt free zipping over the smooth, translucent sea, but its usual soothing effect could not calm the worry within her.

They discussed the cut they'd take to cross to the other side of the key to reach the yacht club. He asked if she'd like him to take the wheel again, but she said no, that she loved steering.

Her dad said, "I'm glad we left phones behind. I'm sure the criminals could have found us. Even if they know we boarded a boat, they probably have no knowledge of where we went."

Michele slid into a slip at the yacht club at eight in the evening. Her dad leapt onto the dock and tied off. They hurried to the clubhouse, fearing that they'd missed the chance to get a snack. Robert Morris, the assistant manager, greeted them. "Franklin, Michele, it's great to see you two. The kitchen just closed, but I kept you plates of tenderloin, mushrooms, potatoes and asparagus. I hope that will suffice."

"Wow, Mr. Morris, thank you so much," Michele said. "How did you know we were coming?"

Mr. Morris smiled. "Well, Michele, your brother Miguel put a little bird in my ear. As a matter of fact, he wants you two to call him right away. I set you up a room with a phone, over there. I'll bring the food in. Ya'll want beer?"

Franklin nodded. "Sure. Thanks. That's all great, and ice water please."

Franklin dialed the office, leaving the receiver in the cradle.

Miguel picked up immediately, saying everybody was in the room, including Aunt Elena.

Elena's screeching voice stood out. "Franklin, where's Pedrito? What's happened?"

Franklin cleared his throat. "We're trying to figure it out. Our kids had a meeting last night with Pedrito about fears their employer was up to something. Their discussions may have been monitored. This morning all workers were forced to board the company yacht. All that occurred on the yacht was very strange. Some workers seem to have been drugged. Michele never saw Tad after arriving at the yacht, but Kim and Pedrito appeared intoxicated."

"Oh my God," said Roosevelt. "What can we do?"

Elena screamed, "What do you mean intoxicated?"

Jude asked, "How did you get off the yacht, Michele?"

"I jumped overboard and swam. I was that afraid. I'm sorry, *tía*. I would have taken them with me, but I couldn't, so I decided if I got away, I could get help for them. Pedrito was stripped of his credentials. He wasn't working."

Elena sobbed.

Franklin said, "Miguel, did you have any luck with our contacts at the Coast Guard or law enforcement?"

"As you suspected, *papá*, the police said it's too early. I tried to explain that it's not one person and we have evidence that these people were involuntarily taken. They said that's generally not enough, but they would investigate. I got our Coast Guard contact on the phone as a conference call with the police. He said he'd talk to superiors about sending a boat or two for a search. I urged them. I said if you don't find that yacht now, you might not."

Franklin grimaced. "All of you ... call all the contacts you have for the kids. You won't be able to contact the kids directly. Their phones have probably been taken. In fact, don't call or text them. I'm sure you already have, but don't do it more. Turn your phones off and leave them at the office. Make any calls from the office land-line phones. Michele and I will mull all this over tonight and call the office early. Can you all be there by seven-thirty a.m.?"

They all acknowledged that they'd be there. After disconnecting, as Franklin and Michele gulped down what was probably delicious food without noticing, Franklin asked whether all the Giga-BATS businesses were domiciled in Miami, or Florida, and she responded that at least some were international.

Franklin said, "International and even interstate is good. It gets federal law enforcement involved."

Michele said, "By taking the kidnap victims into international waters, they've also made it federal."

He downed the last of his water and glanced at his watch. "Let's get some shuteye. Tomorrow's going to be a long, long day. Turn your mind off till the morning."

Tuesday, March 17, 2020

Chapter 8

Michele and Franklin sat before a banquet of fruit, orange juice, Cuban-style espresso with a touch of frothy milk, eggs, ham and pancakes. Michele forced a forkful of eggs into her mouth, chewing mechanically.

Franklin watched his daughter with concern. "You need to eat, sweetheart. We've got a long day ahead."

Michele nodded, her eyes distant. "I know, Dad. It's just..." She trailed off, her voice catching.

The phone rang. Franklin answered, putting it on speaker.

"Any news?" Miguel's voice crackled through the line.

"Nothing yet," Franklin replied, his jaw tight. "But we're not giving up. Please call the cops and Coast Guard again, and the FBI and CIA. Elena, do you still have that contact at the Coast Guard?"

"Carlos Martin," Elena confirmed. "I'll reach out to him right away."

"Good," Franklin nodded. "And listen, all of you. Go to the Giga-BATS office building. Make a scene if you have to. Show them we're not backing down."

Miguel said, "Consider it done."

"Then, Miguel, we'll contact you on the office line when we're able. We should be there between eleven and noon. You can set up any law enforcement agency to talk to us."

As the call ended, Michele pushed her plate away, having eaten very little. "Dad, what if we're too late? What if….?"

GIGA TROUBLE

Franklin grasped her hand. "We can't think like that. We'll find them, Michele. We'll bring them home."

She nodded, blinking back tears. With a deep breath, she stood. "Let's go."

They downed the last of their coffee, juice and water, made their last pit stops and headed for the boat.

Michele steered under a bridge to the south-east side of the island and cut through the growing swells, wishing the sea she loved so much would sooth her concerns. "Where could that boat be?" she muttered, scanning the horizon. "It's too big to just vanish."

Franklin placed a hand on her shoulder. "We'll find it, Michele".

*****

Elena's SUV screeched to a halt outside the Giga-BATS building. The group piled out, looking determined.

"Remember," Miguel said. "We're just worried family members."

The tense group slowly approached the entrance. Elena pressed the intercom button.

"State your names and purpose," a monotone voice crackled through the speaker.

One by one, they introduced themselves. Jude, his voice thick with emotion, added, "We're here to see our family members."

Silence stretched for what felt like an eternity. Finally, the voice responded, "Those individuals are working off-site today."

Elena's composure cracked. She surged forward, her face inches from the camera. "Where is my son? None of our children came home last night!"

"Their positions are classified," the voice replied, maddeningly calm.

Roosevelt slammed his fist against the wall. "Classified? They're our family, not government agents!"

Miguel stepped forward and firmly stated, "We need to speak to someone in charge. Now."

Another pause. "You are speaking to a chief of security."

"Listen here," Jude snarled. "If you don't give us answers, we're going straight to the police. Do you understand?"

The intercom remained silent.

"Fine," Elena spat. "Let's go. Straight to the authorities."

They stormed back to the car and headed for the combined Coast Guard and Homeland Security offices on Biscayne Boulevard.

On arriving, they entered through the unlocked front glass door and stopped in front of a desk with armed officers in uniform and a metal detection machine. Elena said, "Good morning, can I see Carlos, please?"

The blond Caucasian officer said, "Of course, ma'am. But as you know, I need to log in your ID. And if you all are together, I need all of them please."

All handed their driver's licenses to the officer.

"I also need each of you to step in front of the camera." As he took one shot after the other, another officer requested that Mr. Martin be sent to the reception area.

A dark skinned, rather chubby man entered the secure area, winked at Elena and looked at a screen over the security guard's shoulder.

"They're all clear," said the guard.

Carlos Martin walked out through the metal detector entranceway, hugged Elena and kissed her on the cheek.

As she mentioned the names of the others, he reached out and shook hands with each of them, saying, "If the virus continues, within another day, handshaking will probably be forbidden, and we'll have to wear masks."

A tear dribbled down Elena's cheek. "Carlos, can we all talk to you a minute?"

"Sure," he said. "There's a secured room right there." He approached the door and held his credentials in front of a digital eye.

Inside, Elena tried to keep from bawling. "Carlos, I'm not really sure what agencies do what, but I think you can connect us to the appropriate one."

He nodded. "Go on."

She sniffled and made a face, like she was trying to keep it together. "My son, Pedrito, and the sons of these two and my niece, the sister of Miguel here, all work for a huge company called Giga-BATS."

He nodded. "I know of it."

She explained the situation, trying to be as clear as possible.

Carlos said, "I'm rather shocked to hear of these suspicions about a seemingly reputable international company."

"So are we," said Jude, "…and maybe that's part of the reason no agency is paying any attention to us. But many families must be raising alarms by now."

Miguel said, "I called an acquaintance at the Coast Guard yesterday but didn't get any interest in even looking for the yacht."

Carlos nodded. "That's not surprising if you called the regular Coast Guard, which is not connected to the investigative services arm. The basic Coast Guard's responsibility is in finding people lost at sea, not kidnap victims or criminals. In my division, we do investigative work, in collaboration with a number of other agencies. Let me go upstairs a bit and talk to others about what to do."

Carlos returned minutes later and escorted them back to the front desk, where they were issued identification stickers and bracelets; then he led them through the metal detector and to the elevator. Arriving at the designated floor, Carlos led them into a large room containing a long table, around which stood five men and two women. Carlos said, "Allow me to introduce our visitors. I've been friends for years with Elena Morales here. I'll let the others identify themselves."

After the visitors stated their names, he waved his hand toward the officials, stating each name and indicating that two men and a woman were from the Coast Guard Investigative Services, with the acronym, CGIS, and the other man and woman were from Department of Homeland Security, with the acronym, DHS.

After everybody sat, a CGIS man said, "Please give us a synopsis of what you are here for."

Elena suggested that Miguel make the presentation.

Miguel began, "We are here seeking help because all of us have family members whom we strongly believe have been taken against their will on the yacht of their employer, Giga-BATS - All True Solutions. There are probably over a hundred other employees there as well. This is not only about our loved ones."

A CGIS man said, "What is the basis of your beliefs?"

Miguel said, "My sister Michele was one of them and escaped. She informed us about the kidnapping. She said the yacht headed southeast, perhaps toward the Bahamas, as it entered the open sea. She also said some workers were removed from the yacht just before it left. Somebody must be reporting missing people by this time."

The CGIS man said, "We need to interview Michele. Why isn't she here?"

"Out of communication," said Miguel.

"Well, you need to reinstate the communication," the man answered. "We can't go on third party hearsay."

"I'm sorry," Miguel said, "...but that's not possible, yet. She and our father left town without their phones because they were being pursued by men who seemed to work for Giga-BATS."

The other CGIS man said, "We can certainly do air reconnaissance between here and the Bahamas and farther east and south, perhaps into the Gulf of Mexico and the Keys."

The DHS woman asked the DHS man to leave the room and call Miami police and Miami-Dade County Sheriff's department to inquire as to missing persons reports.

The CGIS woman looked at the remaining DHS officer and said, "We need to act. The kidnap victims are obviously in danger."

The man who'd previously made positive comments nodded. "I agree."

The man who'd left to make calls returned. "The city police and the county sheriffs' department have both received numerous calls, and they are just now trying to figure out what to do and whether to get federal agencies involved."

The CGIS woman nodded. "Implement search mode, by air and sea. If the vessel is located, the agencies will determine the next course."

The DHS woman ordered her colleague to arrange a conference call among all the police departments and other agencies.

Carlos said "We will be in touch. Try to find out where Michele is and how we can interview her, even if by phone. Leave us all your phone numbers so we can contact you."

When they left, Jude asked if they could stop at an address that seemed between where they were and where they were going. "It's my daughter's apartment. I don't know how to reach her husband. One issue in the modern world with no home phones. But I have been there before and have the address." Elena followed his directions.

When they arrived, he got out, rang the doorbell and waited. Nobody answered the door, but a car pulled into a parking space and Kim's husband got out, released Neveah from her car seat and climbed the stairs to the apartment. Jude said, "Denver. Kim seems to be in danger. I wasn't sure if you were aware."

Denver glared at him. "Where is she? I've tried to reach her all night and all today. She went to work yesterday morning and never even called."

Jude stood mute, realizing that all did not seem well on the home front. "Denver, are you concerned that she may be in danger?"

He sighed. "What kind of danger?"

"We have heard that the workers were sent to the company yacht, which left port with numerous workers onboard. No agency has found the boat, and nobody can get through on any phone."

Denver stood, mouth open, eyes wide. "God-damn it. I told her to run from that company."

Jude stared. He touched Neveah's foot and said, "Hi Neveah." Neveah looked at him, a little unsure, it seemed. He looked back at Denver. "Give me your cell number and I'll let you know what I learn."

Denver gave it to him. "Yeah, let me know."

Back in the car, Jude said to the others, "I don't have a good feeling about the marriage of my daughter to that guy."

*****

Bam. Pounding on the door of the tiny cabin where he'd slept felt like hammers in his skull.

A voice came through the door. "Get up. Your breakfast is here on the floor outside the door. You have a bathroom and shower appointment in five minutes."

Could he move? Could he walk? He stood, slowly. *Oh, God.* He slumped to the floor. So weak. He crawled across the floor toward the door and reached up for the handle but couldn't reach it. He sat up. Again, exhaustion pushed him. He swayed. He opened the door and pulled the plastic tray into the room. He grasped a tiny, sealed plastic cup with what looked like canned fruit pieces in a fake juice concoction and yanked on the tab, trying desperately to remove the sealed lid. Thank God there was a cold canned espresso. He managed to flip the metal cap open by slipping the silver-colored plastic knife under the flap and moving the tab enough to get his finger under it. He downed it.

He struggled to twist the top off a plastic bottle of water and finally succeeded. He sipped the water and yanked the plastic wrapping off a sealed honey bun that looked like one from a convenience store. It tasted like absolutely nothing. It might as well be cardboard, and likely it was. Then, thinking back, he didn't recall even noticing a flavor of the canned espresso.

His body wracked with exhaustion and nausea, he crumpled onto the cool, hard floor. But seconds later, the guard yanked his arm and said, "Get up. Let's go." He struggled to his feet and stumbled into the hallway, his vision blurring under the bright fluorescent lights. In the bathroom, Tad collapsed again onto the shower floor, letting the warm water wash over him.

The deep angry voice of the guard yelling, "Times up," and pounding on the door jolted him back to reality.

******

Franklin pointed ahead. "I think that indentation ahead is our destination, Marina Hemingway. We're in Cuban waters, so expect company soon. Take the wheel so I can hit the head before we get tied up with bureaucracy."

As he popped back up from the cabin, he said, "Here comes Cuban Border Patrol." The boat came at them hard, white spray exploding beneath the bow as it forged its way through the swells.

Franklin said, "Get out our passports," and Michele went below.

As Franklin dropped RPMs, the border patrol vessel did as well, causing the bow to drop, spraying white foam straight to the sides. Two young, uniformed men stood, hands on holstered weapons, flanking a fixed machine gun pointing downward. Franklin had already slowed to an idle, but the men motioned for him to halt. As he did, the official boat slid to the side and two of the men grabbed the gunwales of M&M.

"What's your destination and purpose?" one armed officer barked in Spanish.

Franklin responded smoothly, "We're frequent visitors to Havana. Contact Mario Rodríguez of the police. He'll vouch for us."

The officer's eyes narrowed. "Passports and visas."

As they handed over their documents, Franklin added, "We had to leave suddenly. A group of criminals have kidnapped people. My daughter here escaped, but they're chasing us."

The officer's hand moved to his weapon. "Kidnapped? By whom? Your CIA?"

"No," Franklin said quickly. "A private company."

GIGA TROUBLE

The officer stared at Franklin, working his jaw, finally stepping back into the pilot area, where he grabbed the receiver and spoke. A few minutes later, the officer leaned out of the pilot house and motioned for Franklin to enter.

One of the other officers entered the cabin of M&M and looked around. He asked Michele, "Do you have anything to declare? Do you have any drugs, cash, gifts, electronics?"

Michele said, "No," thinking that she only had to mention cash over five thousand.

Franklin said into the microphone, "Thank goodness you answered, Mario. Sorry for not announcing our trip and arriving in this unusual way, but I've brought my daughter here to protect her."

"*Bienvenido, amigo*. Why does she need protection?"

"She's a victim of a possible international crime. People were trying to harm her. And her friends are in danger. Mario, I'd rather talk in person."

"*Bien, hermano*. I'll head to Marina Hemingway to pick you up."

Mario spoke to the officer as Franklin exited the cabin.

The officer hollered from the pilot house window, "Follow." The military vessel backed away, veered around, and headed toward shore.

Michele popped the engines into gear and followed, in the slight wake of the military vessel. Ripples popped against the bow. Slight rolling waves from the northwest tapped the stern regularly. Michele noticed a huge yacht approaching from behind and grabbed the binoculars. Her eyes widened as she took in an impossible and terrifying vision.

Chapter 9

Michele slid M&M into a slip at Marina Hemingway as directed by officials at the gas dock. "It's amazing how close Marathon is to Havana," she murmured, her eyes darting around the unfamiliar marina.

Franklin stood beside her, nervously scanning the docks for Mario. "So near, and yet so far…," he muttered, his voice trailing off as he spotted three uniformed figures approaching, "…in many ways."

One of the officers, a young woman in a crisp blue uniform, strode forward, her nightstick swaying ominously at her hip. Flanking her were two men—one in matching blue, the other in green with a red cap. Their hands rested casually on their holstered weapons.

"State your names," the woman ordered in Spanish.

"Franklin Morales and my daughter, Michele Morales," Franklin responded.

The woman pulled out a pen and scratched notes in her tiny notepad. The man in green stepped forward, his face impassive. "Passports and visas," he demanded, extending his hand.

Franklin swallowed hard. "We have our passports, but … no visas. Not yet."

The officers glared menacingly. One said, "Where is your home port and why are you here?"

"We came from Florida," Franklin responded. "We're here to meet Police Chief Mario Rodríguez. He's on his way."

The officials exchanged glances. The man in blue stepped away, speaking urgently into his radio. When he returned, expressionless, he said, "We'll wait for him to arrive."

Franklin glanced at his watch. How long would it take Mario to get here? The marina was at least half an hour west of the city. He forced a smile, hoping it didn't look as strained as it felt. "Let's get something to eat," he said to Michele, then turned to the officials. "We'll be in that restaurant just there, waiting."

As they walked away, Franklin could feel the officials' eyes boring into their backs. He leaned close to Michele, whispering, "Stay calm. Mario will sort this out."

They settled at a table, the smell of roasting chicken doing little to ease Franklin's nerves. Michele picked at her *pollo asado*, topped with grilled onions in a mojo sauce, and accompanied by *col, congrí,* and *plátanos maduros*. Franklin ordered a Bucanero beer for each of them.

Michele said, "I'd forgotten how rich this beer is. It reminds me of Killian's Red. So tasty."

A van with police markings turned on the street, slowed and stopped. Mario jumped out of the van from the passenger side and strolled toward them. Michele and Franklin rose. Michele recognized the short, white policeman with greying hair and a look that seemed like a constant smile, from her prior visits to Cuba. Mario embraced Franklin and kissed Michele on the cheek. "*Bienvenidos a Cuba, amigos*," he said warmly. Continuing in Spanish, he said, "What brings you here?"

Franklin relaxed slightly, but the tension didn't leave him. "Mario," he said in Spanish, "We've got trouble. Big trouble. And some interesting developments to share. Can you take us into the city, help us acquire visas so we're legal, and take us to the apartment in Habana Vieja? In fact, I asked Luz to come up from Santiago de Cuba. She should have arrived in Havana by now."

"Oh, it will be great to see your cousin. She hasn't worked for us for a while. Let's get you into the city and sort out those visas. Then we'll talk."

Franklin and Michele grabbed their backpacks. As they approached the van, Franklin gestured to it. "Nice wheels. It seems you're moving up in the world. No more choking on exhaust fumes like in that old rattle trap vehicle you had in the past."

A young, dark-skinned officer sat behind the wheel, watching them approach. Mario made quick introductions: "This is Álvaro."

As Álvaro started off, he glanced in the mirror and smiled. "A pleasure," he said in Spanish.

Álvaro navigated his way out of Marina Hemingway and turned left on Quinta Avenida, heading toward Havana. Michele and Franklin sat in apprehensive silence as the van passed the signage promoting the unusual Fusterlandia and the opulent former mansions of Miramar, now mostly embassies.

Mario's radio crackled to life. With their passports in hand, Mario quickly recited their information and asked that visas be delivered to the apartment.

After passing through the short tunnel that joined Miramar and Vedado, the van hugged the coastline along the Malecón, passing the hotels and weathered former homes of Vedado, and then the more decrepit buildings of Centro Habana. All along the Malecón, Michele and Franklin gazed at the sea, watching for the Giga Blue, which would be enroute to the Havana Harbor.

GIGA TROUBLE

When they stopped at the intersection of Malecón and Prado, Franklin said, "I don't like that new hotel. All the character is gone. I don't like the renovated 'Packard' over there either. But I do like the views from the bar area that overlooks the inlet and El Morro."

They crossed over El Prado and continued along the Malecón. At the corner across from El Morro, the road veered right as it entered the harbor area.

Suddenly, Michele whispered, her eyes wide. "Dad Look! It IS the Giga Blue."

There, gliding majestically through the harbor channel, flanked by Cuban patrol boats, was an enormous yacht. Its sleek lines and gleaming hull were unmistakable.

Mario glanced with a hint of curiosity. "You know the Giga Blue? It's a regular here–home port in the Bahamas."

Franklin shot Michele a look, silently willing her to stay quiet. "Yes," he said carefully, "it's often docked in Miami."

Michele glanced at him, knowing that this was not the time to talk details.

After passing the Giga Blue, and following the directions of Franklin, the driver wound through the narrow streets of Habana Vieja, avoiding potholes, pedestrians, dogs and garbage.

Michele's mind whirled. The Giga Blue's presence couldn't be a coincidence. Were her friends and co-workers truly on board? How could they convince Cuban officials that they needed to be rescued?

Álvaro parked in front of the weathered five-story apartment house. As they climbed out of the van, the portly, disheveled man with a pungent odor who regularly sat on the curb stood and rushed to greet them. "Amigo!" he cried, embracing Franklin. "Let me take your bags. Welcome, welcome!" Then he bowed to Michele saying, "*Señorita.*"

Franklin pressed a few convertible pesos into the man's hand, forcing a smile. As they walked toward the elevator, the old man leaned in close, as Franklin tried to avoid his rancid breath. "You want some of the blue pills?" the man whispered conspiratorially. "Maybe to help you with the *señorita?*"

Franklin felt his face flush, acutely aware that Michele had overheard. "Uh, she is my daughter," he stammered. "And you know I never buy those things you offer."

The man's eyes widened as he glanced at Michele with a sheepish grin. "*Perdón,*" he mumbled.

As the ancient elevator groaned its way upward, mosquitoes flitted around them. Franklin swatted as each came close, saying, "Why do they always hang out here?"

The old man chuckled. "Waiting for good blood."

Franklin said, "Correct, and to infect me with Dengue or Zika, again."

The elevator shuddered to a rough stop on the fifth floor, and the door opened. They turned the corner and walked to the first door. The moment that Franklin knocked at the door to the apartment, Luz snatched it open. "*Hola,* Franklin," she said, pulling him into a tight hug and kissing him on the cheek. She turned to Michele, embracing her and kissing her as well. Then she turned to Mario and kissed him on the cheek. "*Bienvenido. Pasen. ¿Quieren cafecito?*"

As they settled around the tiny kitchen table, Luz bustled about, preparing espresso. She set cell phones and written instructions on the table. "We have wi-fi now," she explained, handing out Etecsa cards. "You know how to use these, right?"

Franklin nodded absently. He took a sip of the strong, sweet coffee, steeling himself for the conversation to come. "Where does the signal come from?"

Luz smiled. "We have a router in here that connects to the unit across the hall, where there is an antenna that reaches the public Wi-Fi of Etecsa at the park at San Rafael and Galiano. You need an Etecsa card, just like you would in the park itself."

Franklin said, "I suppose the signal from across the hall is a direct line to the park, whereas buildings between this unit and the park would interfere."

"Exactly," Luz said, nodding.

Luz settled into a chair, her eyes moving from Franklin to Michele and back again. "What is happening?" she asked. "Why did you rush to Havana by boat? Why all this mystery?"

Franklin met Mario's gaze, then Luz's. He took a deep breath. "It's a long story," he began, "but there are two reasons we came." He recounted the events of the past few days and the growing suspicion that the company was involved in something sinister.

"Michele and her friends believe the company has been monitoring workers' locations and contacts," he continued. "And we believe they may be forcing the kidnapped employees to perform cybercrime activities."

Michele took over. "My friends ... and many others ... are held hostage aboard the Giga Blue. And now Giga Blue is here. It can't be a coincidence."

Mario's eyebrows shot up. "This is serious," he murmured. "Very serious indeed."

"Mario," Franklin said urgently, "does your government board vessels to review passports and visas? What happens if, like us, they don't have the proper documentation?"

Mario answered, "Yes, various agencies board vessels and review such matters, including medical personnel to ascertain that everybody meets our health requirements. Nobody can exit the boat onto our soil without being fully cleared."

A glimmer of hope sparked in Franklin's eyes. "Can we find out which agencies will board? Maybe ... whisper some concerns in their ears?"

Michele glanced around the table. "And remember, none of the workers have passports or even a change of clothes. We all thought we were just going to work yesterday morning."

Mario abruptly stood up, his face set with determination. "Let me go down to the van to make some calls. We need to move quickly."

As the door closed behind Mario, Franklin, Michele and Luz exchanged worried glances. Michele wondered whether Cuban government would really help in light of its apparent connection with the yacht that regularly docked in Havana.

******

Pedrito lay on the hard cot, his eyes fixed on the ceiling. The small space was a cacophony of misery—snores, mumbled conversations, and pained groans filled the air. But it was the stench that truly overwhelmed him. The sour odor of unwashed bodies mingled with the far worse smell emanating from the overflowing buckets in the corner.

GIGA TROUBLE

His stomach growled painfully, a reminder of how long it had been since their last meal. But the thought of food brought a new wave of anxiety. Every time they ate, drowsiness would overcome them, and they'd pass out. The realization that they were being drugged was inescapable.

And then there was the aftermath. The "food"–if you could call it that–seemed designed to wreak havoc on their digestive systems. Pedrito watched as yet another of his fellow prisoners staggered to the buckets, face contorted in pain.

He tried to move, to find a more comfortable position, but every muscle in his body screamed in protest. How long had he been lying here, motionless? Days? Weeks? Time had lost all meaning in this hellish place.

How in the hell could he communicate with Doolittle? He'd done everything for him. And his going to the meeting was really just to learn. He didn't support Michele and her friends. He was going to turn them in. Who could he approach, and how? He decided that his immediate superior, Alex, would be the appropriate one. The next time food was delivered, he'd ask the person to tell Alex he had information to share.

A familiar, dreaded sensation bubbled up in his sizzling gut. Not again, he thought desperately. But there was no fighting it. With a groan, Pedrito hauled himself off the cot, his legs shaking as he stumbled toward the buckets.

The line was long, each person shifting from foot to foot, faces pale and drawn. Pedrito clenched every muscle in his body, willing himself to hold on just a little longer. But as he stood there, a new, terrifying thought struck him.

******

Tad was in a haze of pain and exhaustion. Each breath felt like sandpaper in his lungs, a dry cough tearing him apart from the inside. Every part of his body ached.

"Just a little longer," he muttered to himself. *You can do this.*

But then he wondered—the cough, the aches, the fever—*no it couldn't be the new virus."*

A sharp ping interrupted his thoughts. A message flashed on his screen: "Mr. Harris. You appear not to be working at your full capacity and to be acting a bit sluggish. Is something wrong?"

They were watching him. Always watching. His fingers shook as he typed a response: "Sorry, I have a headache and feel a bit tired. I'll try to do better."

He hit send, then slumped back in his chair, exhaustion overwhelming him. What was the point of all this? Was he really going to make it out alive?

A small voice in the back of his mind whispered, *cooperate, and you may have a chance. At least another day.*

The words repeated in his head as he forced his fingers back to the keyboard. He had to keep going. He had to survive.

After what felt like an eternity, a new message appeared: 'Lunch break. Report to toilet room 5, then break room 6.' Tad's legs shook as he stood, the room spinning around him. He stumbled to the door, each step an agonizing effort. The hallway stretched before him like a funhouse mirror, warping and twisting as he made his way to the assigned rooms.

Finally, he pushed open the door to break room 6. The smell hit him first—a sickly sweet odor that made his already churning stomach lurch. On a high-top plastic table sat what passed for lunch: a sad pile of wilted lettuce, surrounded by limp vegetables and topped with a greyish lump that might have been tuna in a past life. Tad stared at the plate, willing himself to eat. "Vitamins," he muttered. "Need ... sustenance."

With trembling hands, he drizzled dressing over the salad and lifted a forkful to his mouth. The moment it touched his tongue, his gag reflex kicked in. He choked it down, fighting the urge to retch. *Come on*, he growled, forcing another bite. *Eat, damn it!*

But each mouthful was a battle, trying desperately to swallow the tasteless, textureless food.

He choked down a sip of apple juice, but it might as well have been water for all the flavor it had. As he struggled with another bite, a thunderous bang on the door made him jump.

"Time!" a gruff voice shouted.

The door flew open. A burly, impatient security guard filled the frame. "Hey, I said time's up. Let's go."

Tad stared at the man, his mind racing. He had to get up, had to move, but his body felt like lead. Slowly, painfully, he pushed himself to his feet.

As he shuffled past the guard, a wave of dizziness washed over him. The world tilted sideways, and Tad felt himself falling. Then everything went black.

When Tad came to, he lay in a stark, white room. The antiseptic smell burned his nostrils, and a steady beeping filled the air. He tried to move, but his limbs felt heavy, unresponsive.

A figure in medical garb loomed over him. "Mr. Harris, can you hear me?"

Tad tried to speak, but only a weak croak escaped his lips. All he wanted was to lie here in peace.

Chapter 10

Franklin paced the small apartment, his fingers drumming an anxious rhythm against his thigh. He turned to Luz and said, "I really need to call home. How can I do that?"

Luz's brow furrowed as she considered the options. "You could try the cell phone here, Franklin. It has WhatsApp with a Cuban number, so they won't recognize it's you." She paused. "But the Wi-Fi here is weak. It might be better to have Mario connect you via a landline at the police station."

Franklin glanced at his watch, then back at Luz. "I'd like to try here. Now."

Luz smiled. "You can put in your own WhatsApp number even though you are using a phone with a different telephone number."

He logged into his WhatsApp account and tried to contact Miguel. It seemed that Miguel tried to answer, but the connection was too sketchy, and the call disconnected several times before he gave up. "Damn it!" he muttered, trying again. And again. Each attempt ended in failure, leaving Franklin feeling more isolated and desperate than ever.

Mario returned. "Here are your visas, Franklin and Michele. The yacht has docked. Let's go there and monitor from shore."

Franklin hesitated. "Wait, Mario. I still need to make those calls. Luz mentioned using a landline at your office."

Mario said, "Later, my friend. We need to see what's happening at the boat first. Then we'll go to the station. Come on."

The group, including Luz, took the elevator down and piled into the van. Mario said, "It's just a few blocks. Several agencies are arriving. I'm going to try to enter the yacht with the others."

Michele glanced around. "Mario," she said, "Do the other departments or agencies know of our concerns?"

Mario turned around and answered, "Some do. Some don't."

Álvaro drove to the Malecón and turned right, passing deeper into the harbor area. And there, not far ahead, was the yacht. It looked so innocuous, dwarfed by the massive cruise ship pier. As they pulled up, other official vehicles arrived and parked in front of the building that sat between the pier and the road. Men and women in police and military uniforms as well as some in medical garb hurried about, some carrying briefcases, others wheeling carts laden with equipment.

Mario turned to them. "Stay in the van for now. If they let me join the inspection team, you can watch from the wall once we're on the dock. But when we come back, get back in the vehicle immediately. I don't want any trouble for bringing you here."

With that, he was gone, jogging to join the group of officials gathering near the pier. Franklin, Michele, and Luz watched in tense silence as the Cuban welcoming committee marched toward the yacht.

Unable to stand it any longer, they slipped out of the van and made their way to the seawall. The stone was rough under their hands as they leaned forward, straining to see what was happening.

Pacing nervously, Michele strived to talk. "God, I'm so afraid. What if they're hurt? What if they're not even there?"

The sun beat down mercilessly as the group waited for what seemed like an eternity. Michele could only hope and pray.

******

Elena, Roosevelt and Jude sat in adjoining small conference rooms at Morales and Morales making phone calls on land-line phones. Roosevelt called Gloria and updated her, as Jude called his ex. Both women asked if they could go to Miami to help, but Roosevelt and Jude explained that they were about to leave for Cuba. The family members compared notes about who had called which friends and acquaintances of their kids. Nobody had gotten any leads from the calls. Law firm staff members stopped in from time to time to offer Cuban coffee or other refreshments.

Miguel had brought his mother into the office. She sat morosely and silently, but finally said, "God, I'm worried. They should have gotten to Havana by now. Why haven't they called?"

Miguel said, "I know they've arrived because Dad just tried to call several times, but the connection wasn't good. They'll call again when they have good coverage. I'm sure."

The receptionist told Miguel that Mr. Carlos Martin was on the line. He tapped the speaker button and said, "Mr. Martin, I have you on speaker. We are all here in the room."

Mr. Martin answered, "Hello, I just want to report to you that one vessel and several aircraft have departed on a search effort, and DSH has brought in FBI, CIA and others to work with local police agencies. They are interviewing families of workers that we've been able to pinpoint. We have not yet located any workers that Michele said were removed from the boat. The federal agencies are seeking search warrants for the Giga-BATS company office to see if they are there and to obtain data and information."

"Very good," said Franklin. "I'm so glad you and your agency were able to get this ball rolling. Please keep us posted."

GIGA TROUBLE

******

Kim was exhausted. Her body ached. Her nose ran and her throat was a bit scratchy, but it seemed like a little cold. She blew her nose, trying to get the congestion out. She'd eaten as much of her breakfast as she could.

The yacht seemed to be in calmer waters, but where? The door of her room banged open and crashed against the wall. A voice ordered, "Out. It's time to work."

She was so tired of this. Why wouldn't they just leave her in peace? She finally managed to sit up, examined herself in the tiny mirror, saw that her brownish hair seemed a bit oily and disheveled, pulled her hairbrush out of her bag and started brushing.

"Come on. Looks don't matter," the guard said.

She trudged down the hall ahead of the guard, confused again about how hallways and rooms seemed to change constantly. She wondered where the controls could be. A door opened as she passed by, providing a view into a large room with glass-enclosed cubicles where workers spoke on telephones. It must be a boiler room to make scam phone calls.

As soon as she sat down, a message popped up on the computer instructing her to click on a hyperlink, leading to a chat room. The discussion seemed to be among members of a political group in the United States, discussing posting data on social media about opposing political positions.

Shortly, she was given a link to a video and instructed to post it in the group. She popped into a chat room apparently consisting of Republicans and immediately saw multiple negative comments about leftists, communists, nationalities and race. Then, she entered a page that seemed to consist of Democrats, denigrating "right wingers" as being "hate mongers" and "racists." She posted a video in the Democrat chat room, showing a group of middle-aged white men making negative comments, followed by explanations of how harmful the rhetoric was. But then, it showed Democratic members of Congress actually saying the same hateful things that the Republicans had in the other video. That just couldn't be. She concluded that these videos were cut or altered and determined that artificial intelligence could have created the apparent impersonation. She couldn't figure out whose side the leaders of her company believed in because they seemed to promote and denigrate all sides and all countries and beliefs. Could they be paid by everybody to tout every side's beliefs? Was their intent more sinister than just making money?

After that, she was required to sift through what appeared to be communications from various Venezuelan government departments. Then, without warning, she was redirected to a site that seemed to belong to the Cuban military or police. It was difficult to tell which country's communication she was reading, since all was in Spanish. From there, she found a Russian government site that contained a tie to the prior two communications. Finally, with great trepidation, she picked up an email string and began to insert data, on behalf of the three different governments.

Suddenly, a pop-up in Spanish appeared on her screen. She understood enough to know that it said she was an imposter, concluding with "We know who you are, and your life is in grave danger."

Kim's breath caught in her throat. Before she could react, she was simultaneously thrown out of all three sites.

She sat there, frozen, her mind reeling in dread. Whoever they were, they had caught her.

Could any other force realize that all this activity was originating here on the yacht? Could the yacht be attacked, even bombed or torpedoed, by a party that disliked the messages?

******

Tad lay on his cot, feeling miserable, exhausted and achy. They'd let him rest, but it wasn't helping. He coughed again, causing his chest and back to ache more.

He began thinking of Kimeca, a girl he'd been hanging with for a couple of years. Was his relationship with her serious? Would it ever be? Did he want serious? What did he want with Michele, just another Kimeca? Something more? He wasn't sure. Wasn't sure at all. Even if he pursued Michele, he didn't know what she wanted. But he believed she was a serious person, who wouldn't allow him to just have a casual sexual relationship.

Tad was so tired of the crap that was happening on this boat. The tasks he was ordered to perform reminded him of Winston Smith in George Orwell's book, *1984*, working in the Ministry of Truth, receiving instructions from other Ministries via paper submitted through a series of tubes and updating prior written documentation that was no longer approved or favored by dictating into 'speakwrite' and disposing of paper through the memory hole.

It seemed the yacht was stationary in calm waters. He thought again about the computer that had communicated with him. He was certain that all the data they'd acquired was being utilized by artificial intelligence to replace the workers. They wouldn't be needed after AI took over.

Suddenly, one of the supervisors and a guard were in the tiny cabin pushing him. "Damn, man, that hurts. Please."

He briefly tried to push himself up but failed.

"Come on asshole," the supervisor said. "We've got work to do."

Weakly, he managed, "I can't. Sick."

One of the men hit him roughly in the ribs, greatly exacerbating the pain. He groaned loudly. One grabbed him and pulled him to a sitting position.

The other gazed into his eyes. "He might really be sick."

"That's no excuse," said the other. "Let's take him to the doctor to see what he says."

They dragged him to his feet, still barefoot, in his underwear and a t-shirt. They put one of his arms over each of their shoulders, dragged him out of the cabin, then down multiple hallways and finally pushed him into a room.

******

Kim and her fellow prisoners sat edgy and motionless before their screens, awaiting instructions that never came. Suddenly, a voice boomed over the loudspeaker, making Kim jump. "Your work is done for the day." It was far too early for the work to stop. She glanced around, trying to catch someone's eye, but everyone kept their gazes firmly fixed on their screens.

"Row one, stand and line up at the exit door."

As the first row of workers rose in eerie unison, Kim studied their faces. Fear, resignation, confusion—all very evident. She quickly looked away, remembering the consequences of making eye contact.

When her row was called, Kim's legs felt like lead as she joined the line shuffling toward the exit. But instead of the familiar turn, they were met with a straight path where a wall had been before.

A man with an iPad stood nearby, tapping and swiping as he gazed down the newly formed corridors. The gruff voice of a security guard interposed her thoughts. "You will find the same berth you've been sleeping in. This is simply a different route."

As Kim entered her tiny cell, a cough wracked her body. She sank onto the hard cot, her muscles aching more than ever. The yacht seemed still, but in the silence, she could hear faint thuds and feel slight vibrations. Her eyes roamed the meticulously constructed walls surrounding her tiny cell. She thought back to old sci-fi films where beings were entombed in crypt-like compartments.

Desperate for human connection, Kim whispered into the stillness. "Hey, can you hear me?" Nothing. She tried again, louder this time. Still nothing. Finally, she knocked on the wall, her voice rising with desperation. "Please, is anyone there?" A moment passed, and then—a faint tap in response. Hope surging through her, she said as loudly as she thought was safe, "Can you hear me?"

But she froze as a man's voice sounded from a hidden speaker. "These walls are quite soundproof, but you are instructed not to try to communicate, not to make any sounds. Stop."

Kim's breath caught in her throat. They could hear her. Were they watching, too? Her eyes darted around the room, searching for hidden cameras. Even the simple act of using the bucket that served as a toilet now felt like a violation.

She curled up on the cot, trying to ignore her aching body and full bladder, trying to forget about the inability to communicate with one of her own.

******

Franklin paced restlessly beside the wall where the others sat monitoring the yacht, checking his watch for the hundredth time. "Luz, what time is it now?"

Luz's voice was gentle, but Franklin could hear the strain. "It's 2:15. They've been in there about half an hour."

Franklin ran a hand through his hair. "I need to make those calls. Diana and the others must be going out of their minds with worry."

The minutes crawled by, each one feeling like an eternity. Finally, the group was emerging from the yacht, but they were not accompanied by any of the kidnapped workers.

As Mario had instructed, they quickly piled back into the van.

When he finally slid into the seat, his face was grim. "They lied," he spat out angrily. "There are many more people hidden on that boat somewhere. We tried to make noise, hoping someone would hear us, but...." He trailed off, shaking his head.

Franklin again begged Mario to take him to the police station to make a call, and Mario finally agreed. The driver started the vehicle and cruised along the part of the Malecón that ran next to the harbor. After a while, he turned right and entered the interior part of the city. After taking a few turns, he pulled into a parking lot behind a building with a sign in front announcing a police precinct.

GIGA TROUBLE

Inside, Mario took Franklin and the other guests to a room with a phone, dialed the number that Franklin gave him, and punched in a bunch of numbers from a card. He handed Franklin the receiver, waited a moment for the other side to answer, and left the room.

The receptionist said, "Morales and Morales, how may I help you?"

"Hi, Maria Virginia, it's Franklin. Please connect me to Miguel."

After a brief pause, his son's voice came on the line. "Dad? Are you guys all right?"

Franklin took a deep breath, steadying himself. "We're fine, son. Is everybody in the room with you?"

"Yes, they're coming in right now."

"The yacht is here. Don't say where 'here' is out loud, just in case."

He heard a sharp intake of breath, then Elena's voice cut in. "What about our kids? Are they safe?"

Franklin closed his eyes, wishing he had good news. "We don't know yet. The officials boarded the yacht, but … it seems the kidnap victims are hidden away somehow. They're still trying to find them."

Miguel said, "Dad, the FBI agents have returned twice."

Franklin said, "Do you have any idea what they're after?"

Miguel answered, "No, other than they asked at the front desk for Braxton Doolittle every time."

Franklin sighed. "It's been quite a few years since we booted him out of the firm."

Speaking to her aunt Elena, Michele said, "*Tía*, it was Braxton Doolittle who got Pedrito involved in Giga-BATS, wasn't it?"

Elena said, "Yes, as a matter of fact, it was. He seemed to be some kind of executive when that company came together."

113

"Miguel," Franklin said, "tell Elena's Coast Guard contact where the yacht is. And listen, I think it would be good if Jude, Roosevelt, and Elena could come down here. But the government here is considering stopping flights because of this virus situation. Is Diana there?"

"Hi, honey. I was just being quiet while you were talking business. How are you two?"

Michele answered, "We're fine, Mom. Dad was begging them to get him to a phone to call you all and put you at ease."

Franklin said, "Is Florida government shutting down because of the virus?"

Jude answered, "In some ways. Gloria and Mark are handling the Roasted Oak company procedures and preparing for a possible reconfiguration."

Franklin said, "Miguel, take whatever action is needed to protect employees and clients if it gets worse."

Miguel said, "Oh, Dad, I forgot to mention that international news is blowing up about cybercriminal activities, especially ransomware attacks on numerous institutions, medical facilities, utilities, governments, universities and so on. Attacks are rampant around the world. So many types, so many victims. It's non-stop."

Roosevelt spoke up. "And, coincidentally … or not … Roasted Oak's system has been hacked, and we've received ransom demands. So far, we haven't been able to resolve it. I'm concerned about our leaving the country with that huge issue up in the air. We're leaving Mark and Gloria in charge, and our web site and even e-mail communications are out of commission."

Michele said, "I think we know from where all the crimes are emanating, and it's likely you were targeted because they got the data from Tad's phone. Do you have cybercrime insurance?"

Roosevelt answered. "Yes, but we've been reading that maybe that's not the best way to resolve it. There are companies that negotiate."

Michele responded, "Miguel, can you help them in dealing with that?"

"Sure, Michele. I'll be happy to help, as much as I can."

"Thanks," she replied. "And Miguel, did you get mom's and dad's phones checked?"

"Oh yeah," Miguel answered. "Dad's phone had Pegasus on it ... you know ... that software created by the Israeli cyber-arms company, NSO Group. It was supposedly created to monitor criminals but now is also often used for the wrong reasons."

Michele said, "No, I've never heard of Pegasus or NSO Group. Can it be removed?"

"Yes. The guy uploaded all Dad's data to the cloud, then reset the phone to factory settings and then downloaded the data again. Mom's didn't have spyware. Probably they added it to your phone, Michele, manually, and probably they sent dad a text or something with a link in it. I figured they found him because of communications with you, so I had my phone checked too, and it was on my phone too. I'm embarrassed to say I probably clicked on something. I guess you two aren't as weirdly paranoid as I had thought," he added, chuckling.

As Franklin disconnected the call, he and Michele shared a look.

Michele said, "I still feel so much dread and frustration. Mario, will your government do all it can to free the kidnap victims?"

Mario's jaw was set. "I'll see to it that we free them and get to the bottom of this."

Tension filled the room.

Wednesday, March 18, 2020

Chapter 11

Michele jumped at a sharp knock at the bedroom door.

"Michele? Are you ready?" her father said impatiently.

"Just another minute Dad," she called back. She was alarmed at her appearance when she looked in the mirror. She looked pale and disheveled, with dark rings under her eyes.

The fixed phone in the apartment rang just as Michele stepped into the living room. Franklin held the receiver near his ear, with Michele leaning in to hear as well. Miguel said, "Good morning. I just saw your email. I have Elena, Roosevelt and Jude here at the law office on speaker."

Franklin said, "Good morning. What's the status of the travel we discussed?"

Jude answered, "Tomorrow morning, earliest."

That meant their plane would arrive about nine on Thursday morning. "Okay," he said. "And each of you please bring four thousand dollars. Miguel, please get it for them from the safe in my office."

Roosevelt said, "Is taking that much money legal?"

"Yes, you don't have to report under five."

Elena asked, "Do you know anything new about our kids?"

"I'm sorry, Sis. No employee of Giga-BATS has been found on the boat yet. Local officials will probably board the yacht again today."

Roosevelt said, "Please keep pushing the authorities to find and free them. Keep us posted."

Michele and her dad took the elevator down and stepped out into the humid air.

Luz fell into step beside them and suggested they eat at a nearby restaurant. She said, "It's part of the association of restaurants that Jude and Roosevelt's group supports."

They sat on white plastic chairs at the small, open-air restaurant, swatting multiple hovering flies. Franklin ordered a spicy egg and ham combination, with fresh mango frappe and frothy and rich espresso, and Michele and Luz ordered the same.

Just as their food arrived, Mario collapsed into a seat, his face a mask of exhaustion. He signaled the server for a cup of espresso by pointing to Franklin's cup. His voice was low and gravelly. "We kept watch all night. No movement, no one left the boat or entered … at least by way of the dock."

Michele said, "What do you mean, 'at least by way of the dock?'"

Mario drummed his fingers on the table and cleared his throat. "Two teenage girls … fourteen years old … were seen near the boat last night. Now they're missing. We are wondering whether, in spite of the tight surveillance, somebody from the boat could have abducted them. These girls have police records, so at least some of our ranks don't have much sympathy."

Franklin shook his head. "Police records?"

Mario grimaced. "Prostitution … offering services to foreigners."

Michele said, "Oh my. They're so young. How sad. Maybe the yacht has a hidden door at or below the surface level of water for access by a small boat or even a submarine."

Luz said, "Local girls being grabbed would raise the level of inquiry significantly."

Mario sipped his coffee. "Also, at about five this morning, the yacht fired up its engines, casted off and headed for the inlet."

Michele gasped. "Are you kidding me?"

Mario held up a hand, a hint of a smile playing on his lips. "Don't worry. We were ready. Military ships blocked the exit. One banged the yacht in the bow area. It's back at the dock now."

Michele asked, "When do authorities plan to board again?"

Mario stood, adjusting his gun belt. "We're going back in today. Several additional agencies operating surveillance technology will board this morning. We're going to ask for schematics of the boat, because it seems that there's much more space that was hidden. We also are implementing infrared technology that can locate living beings from the sky."

******

Michele, Franklin and Luz climbed to the rooftop of the restaurant where they'd eaten dinner the previous night because of its vantage point over the yacht. Soon, Michele, who was gazing with binoculars that Mario had provided, said, "A number of officials are marching down the dock toward the boat."

Franklin and Luz snatched up binoculars and squinted. Franklin said, "Police, military, medical. Looks like about twenty in total. They seem to have everything but a cannon."

The gangplank was not extended to the dock, making it impossible to board. The Cuban officials in the front of the crowd tapped rifle butts and black clubs on the hull of the boat. Several guards on the yacht leaned over the side, shaking their heads and raising their fists. Officials on the dock also waved fists and pointed to the entranceway. Both sides seemed at an impasse for a considerable time. Finally, a Cuban official held up what seemed to be a document, as other officers waved weapons and banged on the hull again. After another seemingly interminable standoff, the gangplank was extended to the dock. After it was stabilized, the Cuban officials rushed up and onto the main deck and streamed toward the entranceway to enter.

"That's a lot of power," Franklin said. "These Cuban officials aren't messing around."

"I hope they show the same force inside and free the hostages," said Michele.

Luz asked, "Should I go with a car to pick up Roosevelt, Jude and Elena tomorrow?"

Franklin smiled. "Would you ask the same question if Jude wasn't coming?"

Luz's cheeks turned crimson. She looked down at the table. "Of course," she said meekly.

Michele glanced at her dad in horror. "How rude, Dad," she said.

Franklin grinned. "I'm sorry, Luz. I just notice a special brilliance in your face when Jude is around. And he acts like a kid in school when you are around too."

"Enough," said Luz. "Please do not repeat your thoughts to Jude … or anybody else, for that matter."

Michele glared at Franklin.

"I'm sorry," Franklin said, looking back and forth between them.

Luz made a call to arrange the pickup.

Periodically over the hours of surveillance, one of the three would glance at the yacht or pick up the binoculars and scan, but nothing occurred.

******

Confined to her tiny cell, Kim's body was racked with pain. Every breath was a battle. The persistent, painful sensation in her throat seemed to sliver all the way down through the middle of her chest. She fumbled in the blackness, feeling for the toilet paper and blowing her nose for what felt like the hundredth time. A memory flashed through her mind–a violent jerk in the night, followed by a bone-jarring thud.

And now, strange sounds echoed through the yacht–metallic clangs, angry voices in Spanish and English, the ominous thud of footsteps drawing nearer.

A voice bellowed in English, "You are not permitted on this deck!"

Then, amidst a loud cacophony of argument in both languages, a woman yelled in English, "Get your hands off me!"

A male voice shouted in English, "I told you. All these people have paid to be taken to another country. We aren't staying here. We aren't deboarding. Just leave us alone and let us go."

A mechanical whir vibrated the walls. Were they changing passageways again? Were her captors hiding them, or were rescuers finding their ways in?

She stumbled to her feet, swaying as a wave of dizziness washed over her, and collapsing again on the cot. She was terrified by the banging and hollering, which seemed to be nearing. She thought of calling out but decided it was safer to remain motionless and silent.

GIGA TROUBLE

Suddenly, the door crashed open with a bang. She flinched, her eyes widening as two men dressed in green with red berets, and a woman in white, her mouth and nose hidden by a mask, stood in the doorway.

The woman jammed a thermometer into Kim's mouth and then spoke rapidly into a walkie-talkie. Kim was stunned when she heard the word "coronavirus."

The two officers backed away, leaving her in the same position on the hard cot, too weak and scared to move. Two men in white wheeled a mobile stretcher past her cabin. Then, two other men with masks covering their faces parked a stretcher at her door. One of the men and the medical woman grasped her by the arms and legs and carried her through the door. She groaned in agony as they dropped her onto the stretcher.

She recoiled at the horrible sound of rattling, squeaking and clanging of metal on metal as she and others were wheeled through a maze of corridors. When they reached an elevator, they lifted the stretcher at an awkward angle and squeezed it inside, causing her greater pain as the taught straps held her in place and pushed on her chest. She struggled to maintain consciousness.

And then she was on the main deck, squinting against the harsh sunlight, trying to make sense of her surroundings, and hearing the coughs and groans of other ill workers on nearby stretchers.

Was this rescue? It had to be. She couldn't take any more suffering. She closed her eyes and cried.

******

Tad lay on the cold examination table, fighting against the intense pain to inhale and exhale through his constricted lungs.

In the little room he'd been thrust into, a man draped in a white medical coat checked his vitals. The man said, "What do you feel?"

Tad tried to speak, but only a groan escaped his lips. He gestured weakly to his chest, his ribs, everywhere.

Something banged outside the door. Men's voices spoke loudly in Spanish.

Tad said in a faint rasp, "What's going on? Where are we?"

The angry voices shouted louder and louder.

The medical man's eyes widened in fear. "Quiet," he hissed at Tad.

But Tad's survival instinct kicked in. Realizing that this might be his only chance, he lunged for the door handle. The man grappled with him, trying to keep the door closed. But Tad had managed to unlock it.

The person on the other side roughly shoved the door part-way into the room, pushing into Tad's sore ribs. Tad groaned loudly.

The medical man leaned on the door, struggling to keep it from opening all the way. The intruder's hand slid through the gap, waving a pistol. Finally, a brute force burst the door open, knocking Tad down and sliding him across the floor, still groaning and fighting back tears.

Pain shot through him as armed men in olive-green uniforms stormed into the room, knocking the medical guy to the ground. Through the haze of agony, he heard voices shouting in Spanish and broken English.

Soldiers and more medical people entered the room, the medical ones with masks over the bottom of their faces. A soldier kept yelling at him, but he couldn't focus, couldn't understand.

Another said in broken English, "You espeak English?"

He nodded.

The man continued in a funny pronunciation, but he understood, "Identification. Why you hide?"

Tad wearily shook his head.

A new medical person asked what was wrong with him.

The man who'd been treating him said, "His temperature is a hundred and six degrees, Fahrenheit."

The new medical man said, again in broken English, "Forty-one in Celsius. Too high." He put a hand on Tad's forehead, backed off and looked at the female medical personnel, saying something in Spanish.

She leaned in with a stethoscope, listened to his chest, and shook her head, saying something in Spanish.

The new medical man said something to the military men, pointing at Tad and waving a hand in front of the medical man's own face. One opened a cabinet door and tossed things around. He found a box of paper surgical masks and handed one to each of the military men. Looking confounded, they finally strapped the masks over their ears. He pointed to his, and to their mouths and noses, advising them to cover themselves better.

A soldier made an attempt at English. "You came here by force?"

Tad nodded.

"More people like that?"

Tad nodded.

"How many?"

Tad shrugged his shoulders and shook his head.

The man said. "Ambulance come."

Relief flooded through him, quickly followed by a new wave of terror. Could this be another trick?

Chapter 12

Sweating from the roasting heat, Michele, Franklin, and Luz maintained their hours-long vigil on the rooftop, eyes fixed on the Giga Blue.

Michele's leg bounced. "They've been aboard for hours," she muttered nervously. "What could be happening in there?"

Hearing the wail of a siren, Michele leapt to her feet, straining to see around the wall. An ancient ambulance, straight out of the 1950s, rumbled down the street. Its red light spun slowly inside a glass dome on the roof.

Luz said, "Who could it be for?"

The roar of engines drew their attention skyward. A massive four-prop plane that looked like a vintage bomber lumbered through the air.

Luz's eyes widened. "The surveillance plane ... searching for heat signatures."

Michele gripped the railing. "Please," she whispered, "let them find something."

Movement on the dock caught their attention. The ambulance crew was wheeling a stretcher toward the yacht.

Michele's breath caught in her throat. "Oh God," she choked out. "Someone's hurt."

Luz's phone rang, causing all to turn toward her. As she listened, her expression cycled through concern, relief and shock. "*¿Más de cien?*" she gasped. "*¿Estás seguro?*"

She hung up, her face pale. "The infrared showed over a hundred live bodies on board."

Michele's jaw clenched. "According to Mario, only fifteen people presented themselves yesterday. The kidnapped workers are hidden away."

Several officials, two in olive-green uniforms and one in a blue uniform, marched down the ramp and stood on the dock, communicating by radio.

Michele, gazing with binoculars, said, "The stretcher is being wheeled out with somebody on it."

The other two grabbed their binoculars and ran to the wall at the end of the rooftop. Michele kept adjusting the view as the medical personnel, who wore surgical masks, wheeled it into the canopied ramp and onto the dock. She couldn't see the patient's obscured face but finally saw dark skin on the arm. Michele frantically tried to focus better, finally seeing that the lower part of the face was covered by a mask.

Finally, she could make out the eyes and forehead above the mask. "It's Tad!" she cried, her voice breaking. Her binoculars clattered to the table as she ran to the stairwell and hurtled down the stairs two at a time. Reaching street level, she raced down the side street and then recklessly sprinted across the Malecón, narrowly avoiding being hit by vintage American cars amid a cacophony of horns and screeching tires.

As she neared the ambulance, the stretcher was wheeled from the dock into the building that separated the dock from the street. She kept running at the same frantic pace, arriving as the front door of the building opened and the stretcher was pushed out. She ran toward Tad, yelling, "Tad, Tad."

An officer raised his weapon and hollered, "Halt," as she reached Tad and hugged him.

Tad seemed unable to return her embrace, but he managed a feeble croaking sound, "Michele?"

One of the medical men said, in Spanish, "We believe the patient may have the new coronavirus. Stand back."

Michele almost cried as she felt Tad's clammy skin and heard his labored breathing.

He nodded sorrowfully, the simple movement seeming to drain what little energy he had left.

Realizing the potential danger, Michele pulled the top of her t-shirt up over her nose and mouth. Then, noticing she was exposing too much of her midriff, she quickly switched to holding the crook of her arm over her face instead.

Seeing a swollen lump on Tad's forehead, Michele said, "How did you get hurt?"

Tad groaned as he shook his head, his eyes fluttering closed for a moment before he forced them open again, unfocused and glassy.

Michele watched helplessly as the ambulance doors slammed shut, just as her father and Luz arrived. Franklin signaled for a taxi as he put an arm around his daughter's shoulders. "Come on," he said gently.

The taxi tailed the ambulance as it lumbered along the Malecón with its light still spinning.

******

Tad was being jostled along pitifully paved roads as the ambulance swung from side to side and often banged through gaping holes in the asphalt. The intake and expulsion of air was agonizing, resulting in dry, painful coughs.

Tires screeched as the ambulance jolted to a swaying stop, and medics pulled the rear door open. Michele, flanked by her father, and a woman rushed up. Seeing a single tear roll down Michele's cheek, he wished he could reach out and hug her, to tell her everything would be okay.

As his stretcher was pulled out, Tad shuddered violently. The wheels hit the ground with a bone-jarring thud, and he found himself being wheeled toward what had to be a hospital entrance.

A rather large woman with a dark round face, dressed in medical attire, put her hand up, pointed and started speaking rather forcefully in Spanish. The men who had brought him spoke back, all debating heatedly. The woman kept shaking her head and waving her arms. The men shrugged and replied in the same almost violent manner.

Finally, one of the men lifted Tad's head from the gurney, put two more masks on his face and draped a large piece of clear plastic over his entire body. Tad panicked, thinking he might be asphyxiated. Then he realized he couldn't inhale the plastic through the masks. He continued watching the argument through the plastic as straps were strung across him, making his chest feel even tighter.

Inside, he was rolled along a long hallway, between dingy, cracked concrete block walls that showed evidence of years of neglect. One wheel of the stretcher was clearly damaged, causing a bumpy, dragging motion accompanied by a nerve-grating grinding noise.

The stretcher took a sharp turn, banging against the corner of a wall before bumping over a threshold into a large, chaotic room. Tad gazed wide-eyed through the plastic membrane as the stretcher clattered past multiple beds occupied by patients in various states of distress. Family members crowded around the beds, some wailing in grief while others chatted as if at a social gathering, creating a surreal atmosphere of tragedy and normalcy intertwined.

He felt far removed from the sterile, efficient medical facilities of the United States. He half-expected to see chickens or livestock roaming freely, or perhaps some kind of witch doctor making rounds. After rolling further along a maze of hallways. He was jammed into an ancient elevator that jerked and swayed alarmingly as it ascended. Finally, they deposited him in a small, silent room.

The door slammed shut with a finality, leaving him in utter silence, wrapped in a plastic cocoon.

*****

Michele, Franklin and Luz had stood uncertainly outside as the ambulance people, followed by the angry hospital administrator, pushed him inside.

Michele looked at Luz. "Why is the lady so angry?"

Luz's brow furrowed. "This is a public hospital, which offers free care for Cuban people," she said. "Tourists are supposed to go to international hospitals, which are also much better."

As if on cue, the driver and other man from the ambulance that had transported Tad emerged from the exit door.

Michele addressed them in Spanish. "Excuse me. Why did you bring him here?"

The driver replied matter-of-factly, "... because he did not arrive on a plane or a cruise ship. Tickets on planes and ships include health insurance pursuant to Cuban law. He has no ticket and consequently no health insurance, so he can't go to an international hospital."

Michele turned to Luz, her voice trembling, and asked, "Will he get the care he needs here? What would they do for a person sick with coronavirus here? I heard some Italians were in Havana with the virus. Where were they?"

Luz answered. "The Italians were admitted to Pedro Kourí Tropical Medicine Institute … an international facility, which is for very ill patients. Patients who aren't that ill would be fine at La Pradera, which is a medical facility joined to lodging for patients' families. It's mostly used for medical tourism for elective surgeries and treatment."

Michele looked at Luz and the ambulance men. "How do we get him admitted in an international facility?"

The ambulance driver shook his head. "Since he has no insurance, somebody must pay."

During an awkward silence, Michele looked from her father to Luz, her eyes pleading for a solution.

Franklin stepped forward, his voice calm and authoritative. "With whom can we discuss moving him?" he asked. "We will pay for his care."

The driver's eyebrows rose slightly. "Come on," he said, gesturing for them to follow him inside the building. "The woman you met at the door will be very happy to ship him elsewhere."

They entered the hospital and walked down a short, dimly lit hallway. The stern-looking woman who'd argued that Tad should not be admitted glared at them.

Luz took charge, addressing the woman directly. "These people will pay the price of an international hospital. I think La Pradera would be suitable. With his level of illness, would it be suitable?"

The woman's gruff, indifferent attitude was instantly replaced with a broad smile. Nodding exuberantly, she said, "Yes. He does not appear to be critically ill. For basic treatment and rehabilitation, that is fine. Let me call ahead."

As she made the necessary calls, Michele turned to her father and whispered, "Dad, will this La Pradera place really be better? How can we pay for it?"

Franklin put a reassuring hand on his daughter's shoulder. "In cash. The cash I brought, and what Elena, Roosevelt and Jude are bringing. It's money from the Foundation that supports Cuban people … which your grandfather created. We need to take action to protect all the kidnapped workers."

Michele nodded and smiled. "Thank you, Dad."

******

While waiting for Tad to reemerge from the public hospital for further transport to La Pradera, Luz dialed Mario and hit the speaker button.

Somewhat out of breath, it seemed, Mario said, "We've accessed quite a few sequestered people. About six of them appear to have the coronavirus. We are extricating the sick ones first."

After Luz explained what they were doing with Tad, Michele said, "Mario, send all ill or injured evacuees that do not need extensive medical treatment to La Pradera."

As Mario relayed the information to his team, the sound of stretchers rumbling along the dock, punctuated by sharp orders and the occasional cry of distress, came over the phone.

GIGA TROUBLE

The unmistakable staccato of gunfire caused Michele to jump. Horrified, she yelled into the phone, "What was that, Mario? What's happening?"

The only response was the sound of running feet, rumbling, yelling, clattering, and the terrifying rat-tat-tat of automatic weapons fire.

After a brief pause, Mario's voice cut through the bedlam, tight with urgency, "Gunfire onboard. They've pulled up the ramp." He yelled to his comrades, "Run, faster. Get the patients inside the building up ahead."

Michele's face had turned ashen as she leaned closer to the phone. "Mario," she yelled, "What's going on? Who's shooting?"

More banging reverberated through the phone, followed by a loud, ominous rumbling that seemed to shake the very air.

"*Carajo,*" Mario yelled. "They've fired up the engines." He yelled an order, probably into a radio or walky-talky. "Get the cover boats here. They're trying to flee again."

The sound of gunfire intensified–BAM, BAM, BAM–each report making Michele flinch. She could almost smell the acrid scent of gunpowder, taste the metallic tang of fear in the air.

Franklin pressed for more information. "Where is the gunfire coming from?"

"Onboard the yacht. We still have quite a contingent onboard."

"Oh my God," Michele whispered as her words were drowned out by another volley of gunfire and groans.

******

Kim drifted in and out of consciousness. The light tickle had evolved into a wracking continual cough that sent sharp pains through her entire upper body with each ragged breath.

The stretchers clattered down the boarding ramp and then jerked along the dock's uneven planks.

She fought to avoid whimpering as she squinted against the harsh sunlight. And then, her eyes flew open in panic at the sound of gunfire—BAM, BAM, BAM, BAM, BAM. Rat-tat-tat. BAM, BAM, BAM.

Everything seemed to spin around her in a dizzying whirl of motion and noise as the stretcher bounced more rapidly along the rough boards. She fought back a scream.

******

Pedrito huddled on his cot, every muscle in his body tense. The previous silence was suddenly replaced by a cacophony of banging and yelling. He strained his ears, trying to make sense of the commotion. He again recognized that he was hearing native Cuban Spanish. He flinched at the unmistakable sound of gunfire, followed by more yelling in both English and Spanish. He nearly leapt from his cot, his body flooded with adrenaline despite the achiness and agitation that had plagued him for days.

The gunfire grew louder. He hoped the walls were dense enough that bullets would ricochet off or be embedded. Then, he jolted at the unmistakable thud of a battering ram against the cabin door. One hit, two hits, three—the door began to bend under the assault. With a final, thunderous crash, the door flew off its hinges and slammed to the floor.

Pedrito blinked against the sudden influx of light, his heart pounding so hard he thought it might burst from his chest.

In the doorway stood a group of armed men in uniform, flanked by what appeared to be medical personnel in white coats. All wore masks over their faces, their eyes darting around the room as they took in the scene. Yet the masks did nothing to reduce the stench of the room, as the group at the door made vocal sounds of disgust, waving their hands in front of their faces.

One soldier, his rifle held at the ready, barked out an order in Spanish. "Everybody, come out into the hallway."

The cabin's occupants remained frozen, fear and confusion paralyzing them. Pedrito, realizing he was the only one who understood, quickly translated. "He says we need to go out to the hallway," he explained, his voice hoarse from disuse.

Slowly, hesitantly, the men began to rise and shamble toward the door, their movements stiff and uncertain after days of confinement.

In the hallway, medical personnel moved efficiently down the line of young men, checking vital signs and assessing their conditions. Pedrito strained to hear their comments, picking up snippets of their rapid-fire Spanish. Medics with stretchers arrived and all were loaded aboard.

Pedrito continually translated the discussions for the others, feeling a glimmer of hope for the first time in days. They were being rescued, not attacked. They were going to receive medical care. Then he saw Alex, his supervisor, being handcuffed by the soldiers. He yelled, "Alex, why have I been imprisoned? What's going on?"

But Alex ignored him and stared at the ground.

*****

Tad was grateful to be outside again. The ambulance personnel placed him back into the ambulance while Michele, her father and others stood by and watched with concern. Where could he be heading now? It had to be better than where he'd just been.

The ambulance took off again, but this time the road was a little smoother. In minutes, he was removed and then whirled down a long hallway, but the smooth floors, pristine walls and soft yet efficient lighting were a far cry from the dingy, crumbling corridors of the previous hospital. Yet, despite the pleasant surroundings, his chest and back still felt like they were being caught in a vice and his head felt like it would explode.

He arrived in an examining room, in which a swirl of activity surrounded him. Somebody put a blood pressure cuff on his arm, while another inserted an I.V, another checked his pulse, and another listened to his chest and back. All wore masks, and they'd put a new one on him as well.

He still struggled to maintain consciousness. He felt jittery. He decided that was the result of fear, and not the illness. If this was that virus they'd just started talking about days ago, how in the hell did he get it and how could it have made him so sick so fast?

Michele rose again to the top of his mind. Then he remembered he'd seen her. He closed his eyes and imagined Michele being by his side.

Thursday, March 19, 2020

Chapter 13

Elena's eyes darted nervously around the bustling Miami International Airport. She leaned in close to Jude and Roosevelt, her voice barely above a whisper. "Let's get some *pastelitos de guayaba*. And ... don't look, but we've got company."

Jude's eyebrows shot up. "Company?"

Elena nodded subtly toward some serious-looking men scattered throughout the waiting area. "Non-Latinos. They look like you, Jude, but they're ... different. I think they're cops."

Roosevelt's grip tightened on his carry-on. "Following us? How could they have known we're going to Cuba?"

"I don't know," Elena murmured, "But they keep looking at us, talking to each other while almost not moving their lips. It's unsettling."

Sometime later, boarding the plane and heading toward her seat, Elena noticed that the suspicious clusters of mysterious men were seated separately, and one was right across the aisle from her.

Roosevelt watched the tiny square dwellings shrinking below as the jet went wheels up and sped easterly toward the office buildings along Biscayne Bay. Nearing the cruise ship docks, he shuddered to think how Tad must have felt as the yacht he was aboard headed out to sea a couple of days prior. Over the ocean, the jet banked to the right, veering to the south over water of varying hues.

Jude was seated in a middle seat, making it difficult to view the dark-blue waters of the ocean and Biscayne Bay and the light turquoise waters kissing the sands on the shores of Key Biscayne. The plane cruised southward over ever-shifting shades of water, to the southeast of the Florida Keys before veering off to the left above the Florida Straits and toward Havana.

Elena gazed down at the deep blue water, reminiscing of Pedrito in his youth and the young man he had become. And poor Elenita, without her father.

The plane veered south-westerly over the Florida Keys and then over open waters. Minutes later, the shores far to the west of Havana, near Mariel, came into view. The jet cruised southerly over bare land, spotted with some farming activities and, after some minutes on that route, banked and veered to the left toward the José Martí airport, south-west of the city of Havana, where it gracefully touched down minutes later.

******

Kim's eyelids fluttered open as fingers touched her arm. She groaned from the discomfort and squinted to avoid bright light. She'd been dreaming, it seemed. Something with her mom and dad years ago, when they were still married. Although she still ached, she realized that the hard, unforgiving cot had been replaced by a soft, almost luxurious bed. Cool oxygen flowed into her nostrils. She blinked, taking in her surroundings. Sheer curtains danced in the morning breeze, sunlight filtering through and casting dappled shadows across the room. A small fan hummed softly, stirring the warm air.

A dark-skinned woman dressed in a crisp white uniform stood beside her, rubbing her arm. A green surgical mask obscured most of the nurse's face, but her eyes sparkled with warmth.

"*Buenos días,*" the nurse said softly. "*¿Cómo te sientes?*"

Kim tried to formulate a response in Spanish. Frustration bubbled up as the words eluded her. Instead, she pointed to her chest, hoping to convey her discomfort.

The nurse nodded sympathetically, her movements gentle as she took Kim's temperature and listened to her chest. Kim watched as she scribbled notes, then prepared an injection.

Fear gripped her. "Wait," she croaked, "What is that? Do you speak English?"

The nurse held her fingers to indicate she could speak some English and said, "A little. I inject Interferon, to reduce the symptoms and help you recover more quickly."

Kim was surprised that Cuba was using Interferon, which she remembered her father taking in a failed attempt to eliminate Hepatitis C back in the 90's. She remembered him sometimes just lying on the ground, saying how bad he felt. She glanced at the nurse and said, "Really? I didn't know that drug was used for anything anymore."

The nurse smiled and nodded as she walked to the window and slid the curtain to the side. "It appears some people you know are outside."

Kim startled and glanced down, checking to see if she was properly covered. She found that she was dressed in a light robe, with a bed sheet covering up to her waist. She wondered who had undressed and dressed her. Michele was grinning at her through the glass of the window.

She gasped. "Michele, you're all right." She wasn't sure if Michele had heard her, yet Michele nodded, her eyes glistening. Then Kim remembered that she was unsure about Michele's getting her into this mess and whether she should trust her.

Michele asked, "How do you feel, Kim?"

Kim held her chest as she croaked, "Like I've been run over by a steamroller."

But as the initial joy of seeing a familiar face faded, questions began to surface. Michele looked normal. Clean clothes, well-rested. Nothing like someone who had just endured the same ordeal.

"Michele," Kim's voice hardened slightly, "How'd you get off the boat? And how'd your dad get here so fast?"

Michele's smile faltered. "I'll tell you later."

Kim felt a knot in her stomach. Had Michele somehow avoided everything, including getting sick? The anger and suspicion she'd felt before their capture came rushing back.

Franklin piped up. "Kim, your dad will be here soon. We'll bring him back to the window. Get some rest."

"My dad?" Tears rolled down her cheeks.

As the trio outside nodded and waved goodbye, Kim managed a weak smile in return. But inside, her emotions were in turmoil.

Kim stewed as she sank back onto her pillows. How had Michele escaped unscathed? Could she trust anyone ever again?

******

Tad lay facing the ceiling, thinking that this was the worse he'd ever felt. But at least he was off that hellish yacht. And he'd seen Michele and that she was Okay.

GIGA TROUBLE

A nurse dressed in white, with her mouth and nose covered, entered and took his vitals. She said something a few times, but he didn't understand Spanish. As she talked and smiled, he supposed it didn't matter that he couldn't communicate. Finally, she said with a strong accent, "You be all right. Soon. In some more days."

The shrill ring of the phone made Tad wince. The nurse answered, her eyes never leaving his face. As she hung up, she beamed. "Visitors," and drew the window curtains open.

Tad gulped at the site. Michele, her dad and a woman stood at the window all smiling. He also tried to smile, but closed his eyes, unsure what his face showed.

"Tad," Michele's voice was muffled through the glass, but to him, it was the sweetest sound in the world. "I hope you are feeling a little better. I can imagine it's been quite awful."

He managed a weak nod.

Michele's dad stepped closer. "Your dad will be here this morning, Tad. You're not alone."

Tad sighed with relief. He almost couldn't believe it. He guessed he was safe now.

As the visitors seemed about to leave, Tad said, "Wait, Michele. Somebody needs to leave all the computers on the yacht turned on but disconnect them from the internet so they can't be erased."

Michele nodded. "We'll arrange that right away."

After the group had departed, Tad sank back into his pillows, exhausted but oddly at peace.

******

Elena, Jude and Roosevelt exited the plane's cabin and padded up the ramp, past various workers in the jetway. They entered the hallway outside the glassed departure area, glancing in at departing passengers looking out. After a couple of turns down hallways, they passed the elevator that rarely operated, walked down the escalator, which, as usual did not function, and arrived in the immigration area. Only a few passengers stood in line ahead of them.

They each stood at a line marked on the floor in front of a different booth. As usual, since their flight was the first arriving for the day, the immigration officials stood in a group to the right, and then entered their respective booths, turned on the old computers and set up their desk areas. The computers seemed to take some time to boot up.

Roosevelt said, "The possible cops have spread out completely. Uh-oh, Cuban police recognize a fellow cop when they see one."

Officials took two of the Caucasian men from the flight into rooms.

Having been cleared, Elena and the two fathers exited immigration and joined lines at the inspection area, which was much like security when boarding a plane. They removed items from their pockets, belts, phones and other items, placed their carry-ons on the belt, and passed through without incident.

They turned right and approached three tables with personnel dressed in white medical garb and masks, who asked where they were coming from, whether they had traveled to any other countries in recent weeks, and whether they had been ill with the new coronavirus or had been around anyone who was.

They arrived at the belt where baggage would appear. Since they all frequently traveled to Cuba, they were prepared for the wait, knowing that all luggage was x-rayed before placement on the belt.

Elena turned on her Cuba phone, with its Cubacel SIM card, and rang Franklin on the number he had given.

Franklin came on. "*Bienvenidos.* Luz should be waiting for you when you exit. Officials have been removing ill workers from the boat first, but we haven't seen Pedrito yet. Tell Jude and Roosevelt that Kim and Tad have coronavirus but appear to be recovering fine."

A couple of the suspicious characters entered the bag pick-up area and lingered. The last of the trio's baggage came out and they headed for the door. An official examined the tags, looking for notes from the inspectors about weight or items to inspect. Exiting the area, they found Luz standing in the crowd waving and smiling.

A thrill ran through Jude when he realized that Luz had come to pick them up. As Roosevelt and Elena greeted Luz with mutual cheek kisses, Jude hung back and gazed at Luz. Seeing her shy smile when she turned to him, he tried to act nonchalant so others wouldn't notice what he believed was their connection. He hadn't seen her in quite a few months, and they'd never engaged in anything, but he was certain she wanted it too. They exchanged greeting kisses like the others had, but he felt a flush burning his face and saw it on Luz's too.

Luz introduced two men, who took bags from the arriving passengers. The group exited, ignoring all the men hawking official or unofficial taxis, and crossed the street to the parking area.

******

Michele grabbed two *cafecitos* and water from the hospital food area and took a seat with her father and Luz. "We need to develop a procedure for interviewing and investigating. Luz, would you handle the initial interviews, and match the workers with the investigators?"

Luz reached across the table, squeezing Michele's hand. "Of course. I'll take care of it."

Michele looked at her dad and said, "We're all set with housing for the others, right?"

Franklin nodded. "We're placing the workers at Hotel Palco, which is connected to the conference center, El Palacio."

Michele looked back at Luz. "Do we know how many they've removed from the boat?"

Luz's eyes darted between them. "They're removing all the kidnapped workers now, by bus. They found the two young Cuban girls, locked in a room on the boat with ... with video cameras."

The color drained from Michele's face. "Oh God," she breathed. "Were they...?"

Luz shook her head quickly. "No. Thankfully the raid occurred before there was a chance."

After a silence, Michele said, "Good. What a relief." She took another sip of her coffee. "We can start interviewing those who aren't sick today, correct? And as soon as the sick ones feel well enough, we can interview them from outside the windows of their hospital rooms."

Michele downed the rest of the tiny cup of coffee and gulped some water. "Luz, can we connect with my brother and my mom via WhatsApp on your cell? They're in the office expecting us to call."

Franklin was the first to speak, explaining that Jude, Roosevelt and Elena had arrived and were enroute to the hotel and that Tad and Kim were recovering in a hospital. "Of course," he said, "Elena is still extremely concerned about Pedrito because we do not know where he is yet."

After a pause, he continued. "I'm going to let Michele explain some ideas she's developed, which I strongly support."

Michele said, "As I think you know, Dad's having brought cash and having the others bring more really saved the day. We've been able to fund medical care and lodging for all the workers."

Diana nodded. "Thank goodness."

Michele said, "But *abuelo* would roll in his grave if we just blew the money he'd set aside to help Cuban people. We need to find a way for it to be reimbursed. So, I'm suggesting a reimbursement plan."

Diana and Miguel smiled and nodded their heads.

Michele paced the floor, sometimes traipsing out of the video camera view, her words tumbling out faster now. "We're proposing to organize the logistics of lodging the international investigators and media who are on their way here, as well as employing and helping all of the now-jobless former employees of Giga-BATS. We intend to charge fees to countries that want to be involved, which would reimburse the Foundation, help Cuba cover its costs, and support the workers … both now and for as long as we are involved, while here and after we return to the States. We have long-term plans to keep this going, ensuring continuous employment for the workers."

Miguel said, "Will the Cuban government go along with that?"

"I think so. They should … they need organizational support too. We've started talking to representatives of countries who are coming here. So far, countries seem on board to pay reasonable fees because they need help."

A slow smile spread across her mother's face. "My God, Michele. That's … that's brilliant. I'm so proud of you."

Franklin said, "That's what I thought too."

Miguel said, "Excellent, Michele and Dad. We'll start working on the office setup."

Franklin said, "Miguel, I'm sending you an email about creating a company to handle this effort, and I intend to allocate at least two currently vacant floors in the Morales and Morales building to carry on these goals afterwards. If we can help long-term, the parties that benefit will continue to pay fees."

Michele said, "Many of the workers probably want to go home, but that's not going to be so easy. It would have to be an arranged transport with advance agreement by U.S. immigration because of their probably having no passports with them. Many probably have never even been issued passports. Some international workers may have visa problems too. And a few illegal immigrants apparently were working for the company. Two are even from Cuba. We hope we can convince U.S. government to offer immigration benefits for helping despite their immigration issues."

At the end of the call, all participants seemed upbeat, with new goals to work toward.

Chapter 14

Roosevelt, Jude, Elena, and Luz piled into the ancient Willys jeep, which rumbled to life, its engine coughing and sputtering like an old man waking from a deep sleep.

In the backseat, Jude found himself pressed against Luz, her warmth and the faint scent of her perfume a welcome distraction from the knot of anxiety in his stomach. As they pulled out of the parking lot and climbed the ramp to a highway that led to Vedado and Playa, he realized they weren't taking the usual route toward Havana Vieja.

"Where are we going, Raul?" he asked the driver.

Suddenly, Raul muttered, "We've got a tail," as he stared into the rearview mirror. "Hang on." He swerved onto an exit ramp. At the bottom of the exit ramp, he glanced at the mirror again. "They exited too. I'm doing a U-turn and heading back toward the airport to see if they follow." He turned left and headed under the overpass and up the opposite ramp. He glanced back again, and said, "*Mierda*, there they are."

At the next exit enroute to the airport, Raul pulled off again, then turned toward the city again, following the same surreal dance on and off the highway like characters in an old spy movie.

Roosevelt couldn't help but chuckle at the absurdity of it all, even though he was anxious to get to his son.

Finally, Raul pulled a bold move, stopping abruptly under an overpass. The pursuing car came down the ramp and skidded to a halt, its driver and occupants clearly caught off guard.

Elena gasped. "They are definitely part of those who were watching us on the flight."

Once their pursuers had retreated, the visitors quietly gazed out the windows as Raul cruised toward their destination.

******

Tad's eyes followed the graceful movements of a luscious, milk-chocolate-skinned nurse as she checked his vitals. He knew he shouldn't think of any woman in the way he was. But she seemed to him to be acting a bit flirtatious too. Was he just imagining that she was interested? Thoughts of Michele flitted through his mind. Should he feel guilty? After all, he and Michele weren't anything. Not yet anyway.

"I have a question, if you don't mind," Keily said.

He again imagined being with this beautiful woman. "Of course I don't mind. Can you understand me through this annoying thing?" He gestured to his own mask.

Keily nodded. "Are you sure you feel well enough to talk?"

Tad smiled, wanting to say something flirtatious, but simply answering, "My throat feels better. … I can talk a bit."

Keily smiled. "This is my question. I've always been confused about … what words do people in your country use to describe people with skin like ours. I mean, how would I be identified or described?"

Tad hesitated, wondering how he could answer.

"Uh … beautiful," Tad answered, grinning.

She giggled. "Tad. I'm asking a serious question."

He tried to put on a serious face. "In current times, you would be called … Black. Shade or tone is irrelevant."

She looked perplexed. "But Black in Spanish is *negro* or *negra*. I've heard that people in your country use those words too."

Tad nodded. "Note the difference in pronunciation. You say it like 'nāgro', and we say it like 'neegro'. Many years ago, our people were often called 'negro' in the United States. They did not use the word *negra* because they were speaking English, not Spanish. We don't distinguish masculine or feminine in words. Our ancestors were insulted by the word 'negro'."

She nodded and crinkled her brow.

He continued. "And some very negative white people morphed that word into a very offensive and hateful word which I will not say."

He continued. "Nowadays it's even more confusing because many young black singers, like in hip hop, use that offensive word or a variation in songs. They often call each other that. Older generation Blacks don't like the use of that word at all."

His chest was starting to feel like it was full of lead again. But he managed to continue. "There was another word that was quite common in the past: 'Colored.' Maybe white people thought Blacks wouldn't be as offended by that word because some of us, like you and I, have different shades of brown skin. Still, many white people used it in a rather hateful way. And our people did not believe it was respectful."

Tad found himself struggling to articulate concepts he'd never fully examined before. Again, he tried to breathe normally.

"Are you feeling all right," she asked.

He nodded.

"Okay, then, back to my original question. ... What would I be called in your country?"

"A gorgeous black woman."

It was hard to see a blush with only the tops of her cheeks showing, but he was sure he saw one.

A knock sounded on the window. She walked over and pulled the curtain aside. "A man who looks like you is standing there."

"My father."

"Thank you for the lesson, Mr. Tad Harris," she said as she slipped out.

******

As Michele, Franklin, Luz and Mario sat in a room off the reception area in La Pradera comparing intended procedures, Elena ran into the room, panting and trying to catch her breath. "The car is outside … the one that followed us with the men from the plane."

Luz gasped. "Are you sure? How in the world did they follow us again?"

"I don't know, but the car is parked behind a clump of bushes around the corner. And the men are inside it."

Michele said, "Luz, alert security. Tell them to lock all entrance doors, and secure at least Kim's and Roosevelt's doors. Mario, do you have any officers with you, and can you get more? Their dads must be outside already. We need to get them inside. Dad, let's go."

Michele and Franklin sprinted out the front door and around the side of the building. The two fathers were already standing at their children's windows, with chairs by their sides. As Franklin and Michele passed by, they yelled through the window telling Tad and Kim to have nursing staff lock their doors and told the dads to follow them inside. They couldn't hear any response from the patients inside but both dads asked to know what was going on.

Michele yelled back, "Some men seem to be preparing to infiltrate and are probably from Giga-BATS. Run."

******

Within minutes, Mario and security announced that four men were walking across the grass toward the building. If they remained spread out, the goal would be to capture each separately. Mario said, "I couldn't get any other officers here on such short notice. They're going to surround the complex from the street and await instructions."

Mario and Franklin monitored the front door, while the three security officers monitored other doors. Michele, Luz and Elena were stationed at windows on the side of the building. The procedure was to watch and listen, but not to be seen and not to speak loudly enough for those outside to hear.

Michele watched one man creep toward the exterior door on the side of the building. She saw him try to open the door, but since it was locked, he moved toward the rear of the building, which was the direction that one of the others was also heading.

Mario and Franklin saw the first one walk toward the automatic sliding-glass door at the front of the building. Mario disconnected the lock on the door, removed his badge, gun and other equipment that would reveal his position, stood and wandered around the reception area, telling Franklin to remain hidden and that they'd tackle the man when he was inside.

The man came close to the door and monitored the situation inside. Mario ignored him and walked around. The man walked casually back and forth as he continued looking in. Mario pretended to ignore the man. Eventually, the man turned and walked in, but again Mario was facing the other way and apparently ignoring him.

The man approached the empty reception window, and finally, Mario turned around and said, in Spanish, "Good afternoon, what can I do for you?"

The man answered in rather odd Spanish, "I'm here to see a friend."

Although Mario was somewhat taken aback by the man's answering in Spanish, he said, "What's your friend's name?"

The man hesitated, and then again spoke in his strange Spanish, "He has a lot of names, so I don't know which one he's using. He's here with the new disease."

Mario invited him toward the window to look at the book of patients, but as he approached, Franklin leapt up, and he and Mario grabbed the guy and tried to push him to the ground.

Franklin was shocked at the strength of the man, who seemed completely unmovable. He spun and slung Mario and Franklin loose, causing them to fall to the ground. Then he began walking into the corridor leading toward patients' rooms.

Franklin scrambled up and pushed the master alarm so the security personnel would be aware of entry and take action while Mario grabbed his radio and called for backup. "Officers come in the front door. Intruder inside. Three more are outside but may be let in."

Moments later three police cars arrived along with a military truck full of soldiers. They fanned out outside the building and inside, racing through corridors. All exterior doors were now open, but none of the men could be found.

Franklin and Mario ran to Kim's and Tad's rooms and yelled through the doors, relieved that both replied that they were alone and fine.

Finally, all the troops were gathered together to state what they had seen. Two soldiers announced that four large men ran like wild animals across the grass and out of view.

Troops were stationed around and inside La Pradera to protect from further attacks.

Michele said, "Dad and Luz, let's go to the apartment and get the rest of our things and bring them here."

******

Within the hour, Luz, Michele and Franklin stood, mouths agape, at the door of the company apartment where they'd come to collect their belongings. It had been ransacked. Suitcases had been emptied all over the living room floor. Furniture had been moved. Couch cushions had been pulled up.

Luz's voice trembled as she spoke. "Who could have done this? And why?"

Franklin clenched his jaws as he scanned the room. "We know who did this," he growled.

Michele's breath caught in her throat as she noticed something on the floor. "Dad, look," she said, pointing to dark spots staining the tile floor. "Is that blood?"

Luz's face paled. "Yamilé," she gasped. "The manager. They must have forced her to let them enter."

Without another word, Luz bolted down the hallway, Michele and Franklin hot on her heels. She knocked on the wall outside Yamilé's apartment and called, "Yamilé, are you there? *Estás bien?*"

They heard a light banging. Exchanging a worried glance, Luz and Michele pushed the door open. Michele lurched when she saw Yamilé lying on the bed, her body shaking with silent sobs, her wrists and ankles bound, a facecloth jammed in her mouth. Dried blood caked her forehead, and angry bruises bloomed around her eyes.

Michele and Luz untied her hands and removed the gag, as Luz said in Spanish, "Who did this?"

Yamilé's voice was hoarse, barely above a whisper. "Two men ... Very odd. Spoke English, but the way they spoke was like something I've never heard." Looking at Franklin and Michele, she said, "They asked for the two of you by name."

Michele said, "What do you mean about the way they spoke? Did they have accents?"

Yamilé shook her head. "They talked like they were machines."

Franklin grimaced. "Hmm. I don't know what to make of that. We need to get out of here. Let's go."

Luz, said, "Yamilé, we need to take you for a medical examination."

They hastily packed, grabbed their belongings and left, taking the injured manager to La Pradera. Michele glanced around the apartment, looking for cameras or recorders. Giga-BATS was not giving up.

Chapter 15

Michele, Franklin and Luz met with Mario, who had brought with him an imposing figure—a tall man with deep, richly dark skin, dressed in a uniform adorned with a tapestry of medals. Mario made formal introductions in Spanish. "Colonel Freyre, these are the people I spoke of. Franklin and Michele also speak Spanish quite well, so that would be the best method of communication."

Mario asked Michele to explain her proposal to Colonel Freyre.

"Colonel," Michele began, speaking steadily despite her nerves, "We are pleased to meet you and appreciate your taking the time to allow us to speak. We have a proposal that could benefit everyone involved. As I'm sure you know, many countries around the world are suffering the effects of crimes committed on the Giga Blue, and want to come here, to be involved, to learn what is happening to protect their people. Their involvement is important but so is protecting the workers who were kidnapped and have lost their jobs. The workers' knowledge and ability to access what occurred that is on their computers is all important."

The Colonel nodded his head and watched her intently.

She breathed and continued. "My family contributed financial support for the innocent workers' medical care and housing initially, but much more is needed, and we need reimbursement. We wish to offer our services to help organize investigations and help Cuba with its expenses. And we need to provide financial support for the Giga-BATS' former workers. We are willing to organize and collect money from other countries that are sending investigators. Many of the countries are already on board and we believe all countries that will benefit from what we learn will pay fees for such participation."

As she continued outlining their plan, she could see the Colonel's expression shift from skepticism to interest.

"Cuba has done so much already," Michele concluded, her eyes locked on the Colonel's. "Will you allow us to assist further?"

Mario and the Colonel exchanged a look that seemed to reflect a long history and trust between them, as the group waited in silence.

"We will work together," the Colonel said finally, his voice gruff but not unkind.

Before Michele could feel full relief at the positive outcome, Mario said, "The U.S. Consul is here. Shall we bring him in?"

The U.S. Consul strode in and shook everybody's hands. He nodded to Michele and Franklin and said, "We are aware of and appreciate your involvement."

The Consul looked at the Colonel and said, "As you know, Giga Blue left from the United States carrying only U.S. citizens or residents. Thus, the United States had and has jurisdiction over the vessel and the people."

The Cuban Colonel smiled in a manner that did not reflect pleasantness. "Hmm. I am sure Cuba is outside the U.S. Contiguous Zone of twenty-four miles. And I'm sure your country's powers under the U.S. Exclusive Economic Zone are quite limited. And once the activity is within our jurisdiction, your prior claims become ... how do you say? Moot."

Michele bit her lip, fighting back a laugh at the verbal sparring match unfolding before her.

The Consul for the United States said, "Cuba has no right to detain officers of a U.S. federal agency that have come here to investigate a crime that began in the United States."

The Colonel said, "Your country did not seek permission to bring U.S. federal agents into our country. Instead, they flew on a U.S. airline with tourist visas issued by the airline. We are not required to allow anybody to enter the country, especially when those trying to enter are not reporting honestly their purpose for visiting, which may mean they represent a threat to our sovereignty. Your government agencies have a long shadow of historical conflicts with our government."

The Consul said, "There was no time to obtain permission."

The Colonel simply glared at him.

Michele kept her eyes fixed on the table as the chess game continued.

The Consul said, "Why is the Cuban government being so difficult?"

The Colonel smiled. "Our reason is simple. Your country's treatment of Cuba is illegal, immoral and contrary to international law. You do not allow any products to benefit our people. You call your illegal rule that forbids selling products to Cuba an embargo, but we call it what it really is, a blockade, or *bloqueo* in Spanish. Why should we cooperate with your government and its long, long history of attempts to overthrow our government and kill our former Maximum Leader, Fidel Castro?"

The U.S. Consul's face turned crimson red. Michele wondered whether the U.S. Consul even realized that the Colonel was referring to the CIA. Michele saw that her father also showed zero expression.

The Colonel said, "All countries that wish to be involved are required to pay fees to cover what this situation is costing our government and other necessary expenses."

The U.S. Consul grimaced, saying that it was against international law to require payment to investigate a crime.

The Cuban Colonel said, "You may be surprised to know that the parties who have suggested fees and who are taking charge of the financial aspects are your citizens, Franklin and Michele Morales."

The Colonel continued. "All agents from the United States shall be transported on U.S. Coast Guard boats, which can have no weapons. Our Border Patrol boats will search yours before entry. The individuals may not carry arms, must sleep onboard Giga Blue or other vessels and may not enter our soil without explicit authority to do so."

The Consul looked dismayed, but nodded approval. The tension seemed to lessen a bit as negotiations continued.

Michele asked whether a stronger internet could be available since the hotel's own coverage probably would not be sufficient for multiple video calls at once.

The colonel nodded without saying anything.

Franklin said, "We also are affiliated with an association that assists private restaurants in Havana, which can prepare meals for the numerous events."

Mario grimaced. "All the hotels have food establishments. We do not need or want outsiders taking that business."

Franklin argued that it would be more feasible for off-site restaurants to deliver meals to the yacht and the convention center while workers and international visitors were working in those locations.

The Colonel gave a stern look but finally agreed.

Just as it seemed they'd reached an accord, the door burst open. A police officer whispered frantically to Mario.

After the man left, Mario announced, "Three foreign men have attempted to infiltrate this facility. Two entered here in the convention center ... one through the hotel. We've detained one, but the others escaped. The captured man argued strongly that he was the father of one of the kidnap victims, but of course that was a lie."

Security personnel rushed in and out. Michele said, "Mario, we've had these weird descriptions of men who have intruded in the apartment and La Pradera, including from you and Franklin. Were the intruders who entered here like humans of normal strength and speaking like people?"

Mario shook his head as he answered, "I'll inquire, but I didn't sense anything weird from what I was told."

"Well," Michele said, "... if they are like robots or machines, I can't imagine how they could have gotten on a plane or gotten through immigration here. Can you?"

Mario shrugged his shoulders. "No, I can't."

*****

Roosevelt and Jude huddled around an old-fashioned land-line phone as they dialed the Roasted Oak office. When Gloria answered, Roosevelt said, "Hi, Gloria. Tad and Kim have been found. They're in the hospital. COVID-19."

"Oh God," Gloria whispered. "Are they ... will they be okay?"

Jude's hand tightened on the receiver. "They're recovering. It's tough, but they're fighters."

"Give them our love," Gloria said, her voice cracking slightly. "Things are changing here too. DeSantis just closed all the bars and nightclubs. For a month."

Mark announced that he was in the room too. "Other states are imposing restrictions. We're preparing for limited capacity, ramping up takeout and delivery. It's a whole new world out there, guys."

Gloria said, "A ship with British citizens onboard was allowed to dock there in Havana after the Bahamas rejected it. Do you know about it?"

Jude answered. "The few sick cruise-ship passengers are hospitalized in Havana, but we don't know where. Perhaps where those guys from Italy are. Tad, Kim and others from the yacht are in a different hospital."

As they exchanged updates about cruise ships stranded at sea, Disney World shuttering its gates and other shutdowns, reality of the global shift taking place became evident.

"One of those first Italian cases here ... he died ... from the virus," Roosevelt said quietly.

After a short silence, Gloria said, "Oh my God. You said there were only a few cases there, right?"

Roosevelt nodded, forgetting for a moment that she couldn't see him on an audio call. "Sixteen as of this morning. But Kim, Tad and others from the yacht ... they're not even in that count yet."

Mark said, "Also, news agencies are reporting massive internet-based crimes all over the world ... scam e-mails, ransom-ware attacks, theft, hacking of government and military sites, thefts from financial institutions. Media is trying to link the crimes and the kidnapping, but our government agencies are mum."

Jude said, "I'm sure the crimes and the kidnapping are going to be tied together."

"I'm just glad we know where our kids are," Gloria said finally. "... and that you're with them. That they're safe ... relatively speaking."

Jude spoke up. "Are you managing Okay without the internet? What has happened about that?"

Mark answered. "We have made contact with one of the companies that says they've had success in paying the ransom at a great discount. They're negotiating."

Roosevelt shook his head. "I don't know about that. Did Miguel, Franklin's son, contact you? Does he suggest that?"

Gloria said, "No, he wanted to contact the FBI, and the insurance company. Mark convinced him to wait one day to see what happens with the negotiations."

Roosevelt hesitated but finally spoke. "All right, but really, be prepared to abandon the negotiations and get moving on the other front quickly. Are you able to communicate and take action without the website and e-mail?"

"We're doing the best we can," Mark answered.

******

Michele, feeling beyond nervous, stood at the side of the auditorium stage with the others who would join her at the dais. She'd never spoken to a large crowd in her life, especially to a television audience. But it was necessary. The workers and their families deserved and needed assurance. She said a silent prayer, trying to calm her breathing, hoping she could relay what was needed. "Ready. Take your places," the cameraman called out.

Michele's legs felt as heavy as lead as she approached the podium, her father's reassuring hand on her shoulder. The others formed a semicircular wall of support around her. As the red light on the camera blinked to life, Michele took a deep breath.

"Hello, my name is Michele Morales, speaking from Havana, Cuba," she began, her voice steadier than she felt. "I have news about the Giga-BATS employees."

As she delivered the update—that everyone was alive, a few battling COVID but recovering—Michele hoped her words gave the right amount of positivity without giving the impression that she didn't care. She said that workers would have their phones and be able to communicate soon. "But," she added, "It seems that Giga-BATS installed spyware on workers' phones so we need to evaluate and cleanse them before they can call. We warn families and friends of workers that your phones may have the spyware also. She turned to the topics of allowing workers to go home but explained that employees needed to be interviewed and possibly would need to enter their work computers before they could leave.

Michele concluded with, "We are arranging for workers to be employed and paid for their services. We will be giving the workers this same information in a few minutes."

The moment the broadcast ended, a sea of co-workers flooded into the auditorium, whispering and looking around nervously. Michele steeled herself for the next challenge.

"Some of you may know me," she began, her voice carrying across the room. "I was on that boat with you. But I jumped. ... I jumped because

I feared if no one escaped, the world would never know what happened to us."

A man yelled from the back of the room. "Traitor!"

The word hit Michele like a physical blow. She felt the sting of tears threatening to fall but forced them back. "I'm sorry if you feel that way," she managed, her voice wavering slightly. "But if I hadn't escaped, if I hadn't reported what was happening ... the location of the ship and the workers would likely still be unknown."

"Now she's a hero," another man hollered.

Michele's composure was crumbling, but she pressed on, outlining their plans for communication, employment, and interviews. The more she tried to explain, the more her nerves threatened to derail her.

"No shit, man. You're not continuing the wrongs and holding us hostage," someone shouted, eliciting laughter from a small group.

As Michele opened the floor for questions, the atmosphere grew increasingly hostile. She fielded each query as well as she could, but doubt wouldn't leave her. Had she failed them? Was she prepared for this kind of leadership?

Just when it seemed the crowd might turn completely, a voice called out, "Thank you!" Applause rippled around the room, but it was quickly followed by a bitter, "Yeah, thanks for nothing."

Michele felt her face flush.

As the crowd filtered out, chatting and grumbling, Michele felt her father's arm wrap around her shoulders. "I'm so proud of you, Michele," he said softly. "Great job."

She choked back a sob. "I'm not so proud of myself."

He kissed the top of her head. "Don't feel that way. You were outstanding. Remember, there's at least one asshole in every crowd."

Michele managed a weak smile, but inside, her emotions were a storm. She had faced her former colleagues, offered them hope and a path forward. But received a scathing rebuke.

Yet, she fought to feel positive about what she'd done and finally felt a little stronger as she worried about what would be next.

******

Tad's body still ached, but the fog of illness was finally lifting. He watched his father through the window, pacing outside like a sentinel. The negative COVID test results from that morning had injected a new energy into him—he was ready to get back in the game.

When Michele appeared with her father and the Cuban woman, Tad couldn't help but smile. "I guess y'all have been busy," he said, his voice still slightly raspy.

As they filled him in on the plans, Tad felt a spark of excitement. "Great, Michele," he said, locking eyes with her. "I'll stay too, as long as you're here ... and I'm employed." He winked, hoping his father wouldn't notice the flush creeping up Michele's cheeks.

They gave him the run-down of activities and how a number of workers would stay to assist, at least for a while. She suggested that Tad be interviewed in the morning and then go to the yacht to begin research of the computer data along with the international representatives.

She said, "Listen, Tad, I located my phone on the yacht this morning. I talked to two guys you worked with, Tim Goodrich and Zeke Hill. Tim seems to be a guru on iPhones and Zeke is a master with Androids. Tim found spyware called Pegasus on my phone. I'd never heard of it, but you probably have."

Tad nodded grimly. "Oh yeah, it's bad news. There's been a lot of international chatter about it."

Michele said, "Miguel had his and dad's and mom's phones checked. Dad's and Miguel's had Pegasus, but my mom's was clean. We need to have all employees' phones checked and cleared before they can use them. In fact, the criminals surely have enough information that will provide a GPS connection, so they know the phones have been moved from the yacht to the convention center. Maybe that's how they keep finding and attacking us."

Tad's dad explained that Roasted Oak's web site had been attacked with ransomware and that it was still unusable.

Tad looked crestfallen as he said, "I'm sorry, Dad. It's my fault. I logged in from the ship's computers to try to communicate with you. What a mistake."

As the group at the window started wandering away, Michele lingered for a moment. Her smile was soft, private. Tad felt his heart clench as he waved goodbye.

Once alone, Tad sank back into his pillows, his mind whirling. The spyware, the hacking, the international implications—it was all coming together. And brave, brilliant Michele was the one who risked her life and was organizing everything. He closed his eyes, picturing her smile.

Tomorrow, Tad would be back at it. And he couldn't wait.

******

The cough that had plagued Kim for days seemed to be finally subsiding. She saw her father dozing awkwardly in his chair outside the window and wanted to tell him he didn't need to stay there any longer. She worried about whether she had caused everything by pushing Michele to arrange the meeting.

A flicker of movement caught her eye. Her father was smiling at someone out of view, his expression softening in a way that made Kim's stomach tighten.

Sure enough, Michele appeared, flanked by her father and the Cuban woman. But it was that woman who drew Kim's attention–the way she sauntered straight to Kim's father, rested her hand on his shoulder, and smiled too warmly, too familiarly.

"Hi, Kim," Michele's voice cut through her rising indignation. "Are you feeling any better?"

Kim felt a war of emotions raging inside her. Anger at Michele for her role in this mess. Confusion and a hint of betrayal at whatever might be sizzling between her dad and the Cuban lady. She settled for a noncommittal shrug and a glare that she hoped conveyed the depth of her dissatisfaction.

Michele said, "We need to interview you, Kim. After that, you can go home to your family."

The words "go home" should have brought relief, but Kim's thoughts were fixated on the Cuban woman's lingering touch on her father's shoulder, the knowing looks they exchanged. She felt her face contort in disgust.

As Michele led the group away, Kim watched her father's gaze follow the Cuban woman, which made her stomach turn. She stared at the ceiling, her mind a tumult of conflicting thoughts.

Friday, March 20, 2020

Chapter 16

During a video phone call among Michele and Franklin in Havana, and Miguel, Agent Banks, and Carlos Martin in the United States, Carlos said, "A Coast Guard cutter is prepped and ready. Cuba's given the green light for it to dock right next to Giga Blue."

Michele leaned forward, concerned. "And the supplies for the workers?"

"On board," Carlos confirmed. "The workers' families and friends delivered troves of personal belongings, including clothing, personal items and passports for those who have them."

Agent Banks said, "We've secured clearance for seven tech specialists, especially in combating ransomware, to join the mission."

Miguel said, "The media will be descending on Havana. The Associated Press and numerous international outlets."

Agent Banks glanced at the screen. "You have your work cut out for you Michele. Besides the rabid media's normal bloodhound attitude, they're going to be very critical. The international criminal activities and false attacks by countries against other countries are more rampant than we thought. The White House is breathing down our necks. Congress is in an uproar. There's talk of... well, of a potential World War Three."

Michele shook her head. "Does it all relate to the actions of Giga-BATS?"

"That's what we believe," Banks confirmed. "Every threat, every hack seems to stem from whoever is behind that company and its subcompanies."

Miguel voiced the question that had been nagging at him. "What about COVID-19? All this panic about a pandemic ... could that be part of their game too? Could they even have created the illness? Or could they have created the media reaction?"

The line went silent for a moment. Finally, Agent Banks spoke again. "We don't know. Our own government is at odds with WHO and CDC. Even the President and Dr. Fauci are butting heads. Plenty of people are saying it's a ploy, a conspiracy, but they don't say by whom."

After the call ended, Michele and Franklin sat in silence.

Finally, unable to sit still, Michele rose. "Let's go. We've got to get this investigation underway quickly."

******

In the convention center, now a hive of frenzied activity, Michele darted around, shouting instructions to workmen over the rumbling and clattering of equipment rolling down truck ramps and across the concrete floors.

"Satellite connections, that room!" she called out, pointing to a space crammed with cables.

Her eyes met those of the Colonel, who was engaged in a heated exchange with a Cuban official.

"You can't let the Empire connect through our internet, and you can't connect us to a military satellite from the empire," the man hissed. "It's a trap ... a Trojan horse!"

GIGA TROUBLE

The Colonel's patience was visibly fraying. "There's no other choice," he growled. "We won't be connecting Cuba's protected sites."

Michele knew that the Cuban government often called the United States the Empire as an insult. But there was no time to worry about the unstable relationship between the two countries as former Giga-BATS employees streamed into the hall, searching for their phones. She moved to the front and spoke. "You may pick up phones that you think are yours, but please, don't turn them on!" she pleaded. "They're compromised with spyware … GPS tracking, complete access to everything. Now that the phones have just arrived here from the boat, it's very likely that Giga-BATS knows where they are and where we are. The Cuban Air Force is flying above us to provide protection. We don't need more attacks."

She continued. "Four workers are standing in the room. The ones who specialize in iPhones are those two," she said pointing, "… and the ones who are experts in Android phones are those two. If you think you've found your phone, hand it to one of them, and they will back up your data and cleanse your phone."

She felt jittery. Too much caffeine to make up for a lack of sleep, as she and her dad had worked non-stop on organization. But she couldn't stop.

"Then, you will go to the room over there, and you will be helped to log into a United States satellite system."

The connection room gradually filled with workers, laughing, sobbing and chatting with friends and loved ones.

Michele picked up her own phone and connected by video with her mom, whose eyes gleamed. "Oh, Michele," her mom said, her voice quavering. "I saw you on TV. I'm so proud."

Michele was shocked and proud that her mother would say that, but there was no time for emotion now. "Thanks, Mom. It's great to see you. Can you connect the other moms please?" Her mom disconnected, and momentarily a video call came in. She clicked on and found all three women, smiling, though hesitantly.

Michele said, "Tad and Kim are almost fully recovered and ready to leave the hospital. They should have their phones back shortly, and there is a decent internet connection. I'll update my mom so she can tell both of you when to expect the video call." After chatting just a little longer, she said, "Sorry, but I need to get back to work. All will be well ... soon."

******

On disconnecting, Michele and Luz went to the hotel that housed foreign tech experts, where Michele outlined the plan to access the yacht's computers.

Then they went to the hotel in which international press members were lodged and found the atmosphere hostile. The moment Michele stood at the lectern, a voice came from the back. "Exactly who appointed you press secretary for the world, Miss Morales?"

Michele glanced around, trying to pinpoint the negative person. She found a man, sneering at her in mockery. He continued. "What gives you the right to restrict our access?"

Michele gulped, her stomach rumbling like she'd vomit. She hadn't asked for this role, hadn't been appointed by anyone. She was just trying to help. "I have no authority," she admitted. "I was not appointed by anyone. Somebody needed to move forward. I'll be happy to step aside."

GIGA TROUBLE

Just as she fought to maintain her composure and not to cry, a young woman who introduced herself as a journalist from Europe stood up and yelled, as loudly as the unpleasant man who'd berated her, "Miss Morales, your work is appreciated. Thank you for organizing this complicated effort."

As applause rippled through the room, Michele allowed herself a small smile. But the reprieve was short-lived as questions about worldwide internet crimes and attacks began flying.

"I'm not an expert," Michele deflected, her unstable composure about to crack again. "That's what the specialists are here to determine."

She walked off the stage, again wondering how she'd gotten herself into this line of fire. She told herself that she needed to keep marching forward. The job she had undertaken was crucial. She could take it. Somebody had to.

*****

Michele entered a room to meet with the non-computer expert employees, most of whom were younger women. Kim, with a mask covering her nose and mouth, and her father appeared in the doorway. Catching sight of Michele, Kim stopped abruptly, her body language radiating tension.

"Kim," Michele breathed, rushing forward for an embrace. But Kim remained rigid, her arms at her sides like she was a statue.

Michele stepped back, feeling hurt. "Listen, Kim," she began. "If you can be interviewed soon, you can go home Monday. We'd love your help with the yacht's computers too, but...."

Kim's dad stood nearby, looking chagrined.

A cacophony of shouts and pounding footsteps intruded. Michele's head whipped toward the door, her pulse quickening. Police and soldiers streamed past with weapons drawn. "What the hell?" Michele thought as she crept to the door and looked down the hall. A group of terrified young women burst into the room, almost knocking Michele to the ground, and scrambled toward the rear of the room.

"Some guy grabbed Janet!" one of them gasped. "An older white guy … American, I think. He's using her as a shield!"

Michele shuddered. She turned to find Kim huddled in a corner, tears streaming down her face. Without thinking, Michele knelt next to Kim and wrapped her arms around her.

Kim started bawling and hugged her back. "It's not worry for me. It's for my darling little girl, the light of my life."

Michele held on, squeezing tightly. "I know Kim. I know." She kissed Kim on her tear-stained cheek. A gunshot rang out, followed by screams. Michele felt Kim stiffen in her arms.

A thin, dark-skinned girl appeared in the doorway, her eyes scanning the room frantically. Then, she sprinted toward where Michele was holding Kim.

"Honesti!" Kim cried, her voice a mix of disbelief and joy.

Michele slipped to the side to avoid being caught in the collision. Honesti banged into Kim and clung to her, a tangle of limbs. But their moment of comfort ended with the sound of another gunshot.

Michele crept to the door again and peeked out. Officers surrounded a man on the ground and dragged him away. Then she saw the trembling young woman curled up on the floor. She rushed down the hall, leaned down, helped the woman to her feet and brought her to the room where the others were. As soon as they entered the room, the women already in the room surrounded and hugged Janet.

Michele moved to the front of the room to give a pep talk. "Although most of you were not working on computers for Giga-BATS, we need to inquire as to what you know before we can send you home," she announced. "The interviews will be brief. If anyone hurt you, or did anything inappropriate to you, please tell the interviewers. A Coast Guard boat is coming soon to take you home. We will have positions for you in Miami, if you wish."

She paused, looking at the sea of young, scared faces. "Be strong," Michele said. "We are one."

She and Kim rushed out, heading to the next crisis.

******

At mid-day, Tad was released from La Pradera, instructed to wear a mask, and transported to the yacht in an old car with no air-conditioning and steaming air flowing through the open window. Tad gasped at the memories of his captivity as the vehicle rounded the corner and he saw the Giga Blue.

Tad's father said, "You okay, son?"

Tad's hands trembled as he gripped the car door. "Just ... just give me a minute, Pops. It's not the COVID. It's ... everything else." He closed his eyes, drawing in slow, deliberate breaths. Michele's face flashed in his mind, giving him some hope. "Alright," he said finally, his voice steadier than he felt. "I'm ready."

His father put an arm around his shoulder and coaxed him into the building at the beginning of the pier. As they mounted the ramp to the yacht, a familiar face greeted them with a warm smile—the woman who'd been with Michele during his hospital visits. "Good morning, Tad. It's good to see you outside."

Tad managed a weak smile in return as he scanned the deck searching for Michele.

Inside the yacht, each step down the familiar corridors sent a chill down Tad's spine. The tiny cabins that had been their prisons now with doors open or knocked off their hinges, somehow more menacing in their emptiness.

In the main work area, Tad was introduced to a team of international investigators. As he led them to the server room, his palms grew slick with sweat. "Alright," he said. "Let's see what we can find."

The moment he checked the Wi-Fi connection he was relieved to see that it was new. When he connected, a pop-up appeared: 'Good afternoon. This message is from the server. If you can read it, please reply.'

He shivered. "Oh my. I got chills again," he said. "This is eerie." He typed, 'I can read it.'

What followed was a whirlwind of digital exploration. Tad's hands flew across the keyboard, his eyes darting back and forth. The investigators watched in awe as he navigated through a labyrinth of government sites, financial institutions, and shadowy corners of the web.

"My God," the Russian investigator choked out as Tad revealed connections to his country's systems.

Tad was in a trance, his hacker brain fully engaged. Pages flashed by in a blur of code. He was no longer just a recovering kidnap victim. He was a digital bloodhound, tracking the scent of a conspiracy that spanned the globe.

"You'll note," Tad said, "that this server has historical references the others might not. Every PC and server here could have different data."

He revealed blackmail threats, ransomware attacks, and infiltrations into military systems. The Cuban and Russian investigators exchanged shocked glances as Tad exposed manipulations of their governments' websites.

"If you'll please excuse me for a moment, I need to try to stop a ransomware on my dad's company's site, which I inadvertently caused." He posted some words and searched portions of the URL of Roasted Oak. Then, he found a route to what he hoped would get him into the site from which the ransomware was emanating. His dad and Jude stood behind him, struggling to follow the quick work. "Dead end," said Tad. "Hold on. Let me try another route." He continued struggling and backtracking. "I'm sorry. I've found pieces, but at the moment, I'm stuck." But then he had one more idea.

He clicked another route and found something shocking. He backtracked, hunted for another way to get what he was looking for and found a folder, which he clicked on. He clicked further and gasped.

His dad said, "What is it, Tad?"

Tad shook his head. "You're not going to believe this. This folder contains memos and communications about the Roasted Oak ransom attack. It seems the company that is offering to negotiate is part of the Giga-BATS family of businesses. I've heard that this ploy has become commonplace. You need to tell Mark to cease talking to them and move on with the insurance company, or law enforcement."

Jude and Roosevelt ran out of the room to contact Mark and Gloria, so Tad moved on.

Moments later, when Tad uncovered evidence of a scheme to exploit COVID relief loans, an investigator from the United States looked shocked. He then said, "Is our government even offering loans?"

Tad shook his head. "They're not. But Giga-BATS is ready to steal it all the moment they do."

The Russian investigator held up a hand, overwhelmed. "Can we stop a minute? Or at least slow down? This is too much to grasp. We need a plan."

Tad's fingers stilled on the keyboard. He looked at the Russian man and said, "For every second we wait, another million people, businesses, and governments are compromised."

Somebody said, "Keep going, as fast as you can."

But as Tad started again, a pop-up appeared, stopping him in his tracks.

******

The sterile hospital room felt suffocating as Pedrito waited for the doctor's verdict. His mother, Elena, sat nearby, concentrating on her son's face.

"Your condition is much improved, young man," the doctor said, smiling. "The drugs are out of your system. You've recovered from the anemia and malnourishment. I'd say you're ready to be discharged."

"Were there others in the same condition?" Pedrito asked.

The doctor nodded. "Seven others. All in better shape now, like you."

Just as Pedrito began to relax, the door swung open. Three stern-faced men walked in. One said, in Spanish, "Pedro Rosales, we are from the FBI, Cuban police and Interpol. We're here to talk about your role on the ship."

Pedrito's eyes darted between them as his mother appeared concerned. Then, he answered, "I had no role, I was imprisoned! If you acknowledge I wasn't working as a guard, I'll cooperate," Pedrito said, trying to keep his voice steady. "But if you accuse me...."

The FBI agent's eyes narrowed. "You're not in charge here, young man. You'll answer our questions, period."

Elena leaned forward, her protective instincts flaring. "My son was a security officer, yes, but he was immediately imprisoned when he boarded on Monday morning. He wasn't involved in anything on that boat!"

The Interpol agent glared at her and responded in a cool tone. "Ma'am, we need to ask about events for some time prior to this week. And we can't have you here for that."

Pedrito knew he had to cooperate, but he was terrified. What if they knew about Doolittle? He turned to the doctor. "Doctor, please," he pleaded. "Tell them about my condition when I arrived."

The doctor nodded and described the state in which Pedrito and the others had arrived–drugged, malnourished, victims of confinement. Pedrito felt a small measure of relief, but he was still petrified. *They can't know about Doolittle*, he thought desperately. *They can't.*

Chapter 17

Tad perched atop a table, facing the expectant faces of international investigators, hungry for answers about what had been uncovered so far and anticipating much more.

"We've learned a lot," Tad explained. "But there is likely so much more." He didn't want to reveal the message he'd received, which stated that he was playing a dangerous game and that the yacht's computers themselves were in charge. He realized that at any moment, he could be blocked or manipulated. The computer system seemed to have a plan, without a human leading it.

Tad's head whipped around at the sound of Michele's voice as she and Kim raced toward him with Kim's father trailing behind. Kim wore a mask over her mouth and nose, just as Tad did.

Tad leapt from the table and enveloped the three in a group hug. "I'm so glad to see you guys."

Michele glanced at Kim, and said, "Do you think you could try to access the data on the PC you worked at?"

Kim hesitated but then nodded. As she approached her old workstation, all those present silently gazed at her screen. She took a deep breath, closed her eyes for a moment, then began to type, tickling the keyboard with her fingers, which brought up the screen. When she saw that she was already logged in, she checked the internet connection and typed a few letters into the browser.

She tried to remember the beginning of a link she'd used—it was something that reminded her of her grandmother's first name. *What was it? What was it? Ah.* She typed a few letters. The rest showed up, and she entered. The screen exploded with information—dark, ominous pages giving way to a flurry of white text on black backgrounds. Kim's eyes widened as she recognized a familiar thread.

She glanced at Tad. "The data is still here. All of it."

Lines of code scrolled rapidly across her screen.

Beside her, Tad leaned in, wondering how long it would take for the computers that were against him to reveal themselves.

Kim said, "Tad, can you decrypt this stuff?"

Shortly after he took control, the screen filled with data—names, dates, financial transactions. Then the warning popped up. "You'd better stop this before it's too late. All the data you seek will disappear very shortly."

Tad tried copying and downloading, but data kept sliding away. He pulled out his phone and handed it to Kim to take photos as he skipped through pages. Sweat was on his forehead and upper lip as he tried to backtrack what was being eliminated. He was fighting a battle against an unknown and unseen force. He jousted and it jousted back. Every time he progressed, he also lost. When he was finally thrown out of every space he tried to enter, he felt exhausted and defeated.

But Kim put a hand on his shoulder and said, "Don't worry. I got a lot of shots that should help."

******

Pedrito's head throbbed as he slumped in the hard plastic chair. The convention center's fluorescent lights seemed to bore into his skull after hours of relentless questioning. He rubbed his temples, trying to focus on the latest interrogator—a stern-faced woman with a crisp Spanish accent.

"Tell me again about your relationship with Braxton Doolittle," she demanded, her pen poised over a notepad.

Pedrito's stomach churned. *How much could they know?*

His palms grew clammy. "I ... I've already explained," he stammered. "Mr. Doolittle contacted me after leaving my grandfather's firm. Said he had a new business ... said he thought I'd be a good fit."

The FBI man narrowed his eyes with suspicion. "You swear that you never discussed your uncle or the law firm?"

Pedrito swallowed hard, praying his face didn't betray him. "Never," he lied, trembling inside.

The Cuban woman leaned forward, her gaze piercing. "I don't believe ..."

A deafening roar cut through the air, drowning out her words. The building shook as a screeching alarm blared. Tension crackled like electricity.

"*¡Atención! ¡Atención!*" A male voice boomed over the loudspeaker in rapid Spanish. "We have received warning of a possible air attack. Everyone must evacuate to the basement immediately!"

Chairs toppled as people scrambled for the exits. Pedrito's exhaustion evaporated, replaced by a surge of adrenaline. He spotted his mother in the hallway, her eyes wide with fear.

"¡Mamá!" he called, grabbing her hand. "This way!"

They hurried down the stairs, the thunderous sound of military jets growing louder. In the musty basement, a security guard's words cut through the panicked murmurs: "Of course the United States is attacking."

Elena bristled. "Not possible," she snapped. "It's not the United States."

The guard sneered. "You people always deny what your country does."

Elena said, "Cuba is my country too. I never lost my country just because I left."

The man sneered. "*Mierda*", he said.

Pedrito felt his mother tense, ready for a fight. He squeezed her hand, silently willing her to stay calm. The basement fell eerily quiet as the building again vibrated with another jet roaring overhead.

*****

Michele stood at a podium on the yacht, summarizing the presentations and explaining what was to happen next. Her voice faltered mid-sentence as a bone-rattling roar shook the yacht's auditorium. The stage vibrated beneath her. A hush fell over the crowd, broken only by the ominous rumble of roaring engines above.

The loudspeaker crackled to life. "*¡Abandonen el barco! ¡Abandonen el barco!* Abandon ship. Go to shore!"

The crowd pushed and shoved toward the exits in an explosion of panic. Michele found herself swept along in the tide of humanity stumbling out and onto the deck. The harbor, usually a picture of tranquility, had transformed into a war zone.

Three planes screamed across the sky, locked in a deadly dance. Two Cuban fighters swooped this way and that like in an acrobatic contest, trying to block the other plane as it dove toward the yacht. Michele's breath caught in her throat as she watched the aerial ballet, unable to tear her eyes away.

BANG! BANG! BANG!

Machine gun fire erupted from the Cuban jets. Michele flinched at each report, her heart pounding in time with the staccato bursts. Boats sped through the harbor, adding to the cacophony as they fired skyward.

A sickening screech of metal on metal pierced the air as one of the Cuban planes clipped the wing of the attacker. Michele's stomach lurched as the enemy jet spiraled out of control, tumbling end over end toward the iconic El Morro fortress.

"Oh God," she whispered, transfixed by the impending disaster.

One of the military boats rushed out of the path of the enemy jet, now completely out of control. Finally, it slammed into the concrete walls of El Morro, sending a fireball of shrapnel and flames cascading through the air before it splashed into the water. The ghastly odor of burning fuel filled the air.

A piece of flying metal seemed to flip faster until it slid along the concrete wall protecting the fort and beneath the statue of Christ Jesus, which stood peacefully farther inland of the fort, gracing Havana with his solemn look and hands beseeching the world for peace.

Finally, the Cuban jet hit the smooth harbor water, seeming almost to lose control but then sliding across the water like a water skier. The military boats chased after it. As it came to a stop, the pilot lifted the glass cover over the cabin, disconnected, and stood.

Michele ran toward safety. Then, she was chilled by the site of another air attack to the west. Could it possibly be as far as the convention center?

The traumatized crowd silently streamed along the docks and into the building next to El Malecón.

******

The basement of the convention center trembled, dust raining down from the ceiling. Pedrito instinctively pulled his mother close, shielding her as best he could.

"Jesus Christ," a man nearby muttered with a trembling voice. "It's like an earthquake. If a plane came down, it must be right on top of us. What if it explodes?"

Pedrito gazed around the room, taking in the pale faces and trembling hands of those around him. The investigators who had been grilling him earlier huddled in a corner, urgently whispering into their phones.

Another rumble shook the building. Bits of plaster rained down, coating Pedrito's dark hair with a fine, white powder. When he saw that his mother was trembling, he took her hand and said, "It's okay, Mamá. We're safe down here."

After a few minutes, they got the all-clear. Pedrito saw no sign of the investigators, so he led his mother up the stairs. The smell of smoke hit him like a wall as he and Elena reached the main level and then walked through the glass walkway to Hotel Palco, seeing a surreal view of the chaos outside.

Through the glass, they could see orange flames licking at the sky, stark against billowing black smoke. The wail of sirens filled the air, punctuated by the staccato pop of what could only be gunfire.

"*Dios mío,*" Elena gasped as she tightly gripped Pedrito's arm.

A group of journalists rushed past, cameras at the ready.

Suddenly, a convoy of military trucks roared down the street. Soldiers in olive-green uniforms stood rigid in the truck beds. One truck screeched to a halt at a nearby intersection. Three soldiers leapt out, immediately moving to block both vehicles and pedestrians. "*¡Atrás! ¡Atrás!,*" they shouted, pushing back the crowd of onlookers and reporters.

Pedrito watched as the journalists flashed credentials, arguing loudly with the soldiers. But the military men stood firm, shaking their heads.

"We need to get out of here," Elena urged, tugging at Pedrito's sleeve.

He nodded, but found himself rooted to the spot, eyes fixed on the hellish scene before them and hearing the whump-whump-whump of approaching helicopters.

His stomach churned with a mix of fear and guilt. Had Doolittle manipulated him into helping create this disaster? And where had that damn Doolittle disappeared to?

******

The acrid smoke stung Michele's nostrils as she approached Hotel Palco. People scrambled in every direction.

"Stop here," she instructed the driver, spotting El Palacio ahead. As she rushed into the building, a man intercepted her, his eyes gleaming with barely contained excitement.

"Miss Morales!" he called out, brandishing a press badge. "Can we interview you? We're with…."

"I can't give any official statements," Michele answered, trying to cut him off as she pushed past.

The reporter's hand shot out, gently blocking her path. "Please," he pleaded, "We can't find anyone official to speak with us. You seem to be the only one who knows what's going on." Michele hesitated, weighing her options. *What harm could it do?* With a sigh, she nodded.

Before she knew it, she was whisked into a makeshift studio. A flurry of activity surrounded her—makeup brushes dusting her face, a microphone being clipped to her blouse, wires snaking behind her back.

A woman's face appeared on a video screen, with an expression of professional calm. "Good morning, Miss Morales. Can you tell us what has occurred in Havana today?"

Michele took a deep breath, choosing her words carefully. "We've been conducting interviews and analyzing data from the ship's computers as part of the international investigation. About an hour ago, unidentified fighter planes attacked two areas of the city … the ship and this building. Both intruders were shot down, but one of them also took down a Cuban military jet. As far as we know, there were no casualties on the ground, but the situation is still unclear."

The reporter leaned forward, her eyes intense. "Is progress being made in finding the criminals?"

Before Michele could respond, the door burst open. Two men in crisp white shirts and ties stormed in.

"Stop this interview immediately," one of them demanded. "This young lady has no authority to speak for the United States government."

The reporter responded indignantly, "Sirs, it appears she was only commenting on personal knowledge."

"Doesn't matter," the man snapped. He made a slashing motion across his throat, then lunged for Michele's microphone.

Time seemed to slow as his hand connected with her blouse, nearly ripping off a button. Michele's palm connected with his wrist in a sharp slap. "That's assault!" she shouted, her voice ringing through the studio.

The man's face contorted with rage. "Get out of the chair. Now."

Michele held her ground. "No. You haven't even identified yourself or your agency."

The reporter's voice echoed through the room. "Sirs, you're making a grave mistake. We are live on U.S. national television."

Suddenly, Michele felt a vise-like grip on her arm. The man yanked her from the chair, the force of his pull tearing the back of her blouse as the microphone wire snagged.

"You're under arrest," he growled, shoving her toward the door.

Michele's elbow connected with his ribs. "You've touched me inappropriately and ripped my clothing, asshole!"

The second man grabbed his partner's arm. "John, this is a bad move. Let's go."

But the man was beyond reason. He shoved Michele hard, sending her stumbling over a tangle of cables. She felt a sharp pain as her head connected with the edge of a table, and then the world went black. The man who was trying to halt the action said, "Dear God. I'm out of here. Not part of this shit."

When she came to, Michele was vaguely aware of voices arguing above her. She blinked, trying to focus through the haze of pain. A new authoritative voice stated, "Place this man under arrest for assault, using false identification to enter Cuba, suspicion of being a spy from los Estados Unidos, and ... well, that's enough for now."

Michele's vision cleared enough to see Colonel Freyre kneeling beside her. "Are you all right, Miss Morales?"

She tried to nod but closed her eyes again.

******

Jude burst into the computer room on the yacht and raced toward Franklin, who was hunched behind a worker in front of a computer terminal. "Franklin," he whispered frantically in his ear, "Michele's been injured."

Franklin looked back, aghast, as he stood. "What do you mean?"

Jude shook his head, helpless. "I don't know. We need to go. Now."

As they rushed out, Jude paused by Kim's workstation. "Michele's been hurt," he murmured. "We're going to check on her."

Kim's fingers froze over her keyboard, her eyes widening with concern. She lost her concentration for a moment, realizing that the Cuban woman was with her dad. She glared at him as she said, "Let me know how Michele is."

Outside, Franklin, Jude and Luz piled into a police vehicle with a swirling blue light perched on top.

"Please hurry," Franklin urged the driver as he gripped the seat.

As the car sped through Havana's chaotic streets, Jude became acutely aware of Luz's presence beside him. Her touch sent electricity coursing through his body.

Luz intertwined her fingers with Jude's, as they gazed into each other's eyes.

When the car screeched to a halt in front of El Palacio, the three leapt out and rushed inside. They ran into the room where medical personnel were evaluating the wound to Michele's forehead.

Her dad grabbed her hand. "Michele, who did this?"

She shook her head. "Some idiot from one of our government agencies."

A medical person said, in Spanish, "I think we need to suture. It can't heal unless we close the flap. An ambulance is on the way."

Michele said, "I don't need an ambulance just to get a couple of stitches."

They wouldn't let her rise, so she and her dad waited, and when a stretcher arrived, she climbed aboard, annoyed.

The ambulance stopped in front of a public hospital. Franklin said, "Oh, no. Not again." He tried to explain that they should take her to La Pradera where they already had others under care, but the men rolled her inside the hospital despite his protests. A warm trickle of blood slid down her forehead and over her eyelid.

An older man in a wrinkled white coat bustled into the bare examination room, muttering under his breath in rapid Spanish. Michele watched, her anxiety growing, as he yanked open drawers and cabinets, clearly frustrated. No new equipment, no sterile needles and surely no anesthesia.

GIGA TROUBLE

The doctor finally approached, but Michele couldn't help but recoil. His fingers were stained yellow with tobacco, and she could smell the lingering scent of cigarettes.

She looked at her father, shaking her head. Her father said, "That's it. No. We're leaving." Her father helped her stand up, and they marched out of the building and took a taxi to La Pradera.

Saturday, March 21, 2020

Chapter 18

On Saturday morning, Franklin, Michele and Luz entered a room at police headquarters, where Colonel Freyre and Mario sat together across the table from the U.S. Consul. Guards entered pushing the two angry and haggard FBI agents, still dressed in the same clothing they wore previously, although the shirts were now quite wrinkled. The one who had injured Michele was handcuffed.

Colonel Freyre narrowed his eyes as he addressed the U.S. Consul. "We are here to set forth the rules of your country's involvement." His voice was sharp, cutting through the tense silence. "These two agents are expelled from our country."

The U.S. Consul's jaw tightened, but he remained silent, his gaze fixed on the Colonel.

The Colonel said to the Cuban police officers, "Take these two men to the Giga Blue. They may not touch Cuban soil again. They will leave on the first Coast Guard vessel that departs."

As the agents were led out, their eyes burned with barely contained fury. The air in the room seemed to crackle with hostility.

The Colonel's attention snapped back to the Consul. "I understand your government has obtained permission for other investigators to enter our country," he said. "But I've seen nothing to confirm this."

The Consul pulled a stack of documents out of his briefcase.

Colonel Freyre's eyes scanned the pages. "What are these agencies?"

The U.S. Consul shuffled through the documents and pointed to what was printed on various pages. "The agencies are listed at the top of each page ... Homeland Security Investigations, Department of Justice, FBI and Internal Revenue Service.

The Colonel asked, "Is any person part of your CIA?"

"No," responded the Consul.

The Colonel said, "You mention FBI. Are not the two that we just expelled FBI?"

The Consul nodded and said, "Yes, they are."

Colonel Freyre huffed. "Your people had better behave."

The U.S. Consul rolled his eyes, resulting in a steady glare by the Colonel, who said, "I'm not allowing any of your investigators to leave the boat. They will work and sleep there."

The Consul shook his head, but did not respond.

The Colonel continued. "Besides my concern for your agents' behavior, I am also concerned about visitors from your country bringing the virus to Cuba. I understand that Florida now has one thousand cases of the coronavirus, and your government is not taking significant action. We have only twenty-one cases. Your president is saying ridiculous things and not listening to your experts, and your Florida governor seems to be following that national rhetoric. We are not going to take chances. Cuba is closing all entry on Tuesday. Your Coast Guard will be able to come and go even after the shutdown, but no occupant will be permitted to touch Cuban soil without prior approval."

*****

Tad again sat at a computer in front of investigators. He said, "For those of you who are not aware yet, Giga-BATS operates its own ISP, using its own satellite or satellites. It has millions of customers that directly or indirectly connect to the internet through its services, including its own e-mail provider, social media provider, password saving system, and cyber-protection company.

I've encountered some resistance and counteractive issues the last couple of times I entered their servers. I'm getting threats from the computer, which says it's operating on its own, without human contact."

He handed his cell phone to one of the observers and said, "The moment I say start shooting, just photograph the screen constantly so we don't lose the data. Maybe it won't happen. We'll see how far we get without them trying to hinder me. If and when it happens, you'll probably notice me having to play a weird chess game with whatever or whoever it is. We're going to attempt to follow URLs we've already gathered to their sources."

Tad's cursor hovered over a string of code. "Do you see this pattern?" he asked, leaning forward. "This could be our way in."

The investigators' faces were illuminated by the glow of the screen as they leaned close. One of them, a young woman with dark-rimmed glasses, pointed at the monitor. "There," she said. "That sequence of numbers ... it's not random, is it?"

Tad's eyes lit up. He focused on the digits and nodded. "Excellent catch. Now, let's see where this rabbit hole leads us."

He tapped and clicked into various sites, copying source codes into the browser as he went.

"We're getting further in. It appears there's another source of criminal activities. On or near an island in the area of the Bahamas. A similar set-up of PCs and servers as are here on Giga-Blue. They are still in operation. Perhaps the parties performing the work were also taken against their will."

Tad continued tunnelling as more and more locations were found. He finally had something to show to law enforcement. But then, just as he started to feel relieved, his digital opponent posted a typical note and started shutting down links that he'd already found. "Keep clicking the photos ... as quickly as you can," he ordered.

******

In the evening, Jude and Luz gave each other a customary Cuban kiss on the cheek as they met at the door of a tiny, quiet restaurant where they'd agreed to meet for dinner. When seated, they silently glanced through the menu and ordered.

Jude sighed and shook his head, not meeting Luz's eyes. "Kim is going home, so I need to as well. I have no excuse to remain, although...."

Luz said, "I understand."

Jude reached across the table and grasped her hand. "Our connection has come about so naturally," he said, finally looking into her eyes. "I've never known anybody like you."

"I knew you were special when I first laid eyes on you as well," Luz said, her eyes meeting his.

The waiter appeared with their food, oblivious to the weight of the moment. As he set down their plates, Luz and Jude both stared at their meals, neither making a move to eat. Little by little they nibbled and managed to get a little down, while occasionally catching each other's eyes.

After eating about half of their meals, he said, "Do you want dessert?"

Luz shook her head. "No. Let's go someplace."

Jude quickly paid the bill in Cuban convertible pesos. As they walked out, Luz said, "Let's go to the company apartment to talk a bit."

They walked along dirty, dog-poop-dotted streets. He imagined and hoped that lovemaking was ahead.

After quite a few more blocks, she stopped, stuck a key in the door, grasped his fingers and pulled him into the vestibule. She said, "Either the elevator is broken, or the electricity is off," as she dragged him up the completely dark inner stairway, using the light on her phone to guide them. After stomping up several floors, he was breathing deeply and perspiring. He wasn't sure if the climb, the view of her luscious body, or the thought of what may be to come was making him feel dizzy, but decided it was probably a combination.

She finally stopped at a floor and fumbled to locate the correct key, and then to insert it into the lock. As soon as the door closed, they were immediately intwined, kissing and grasping at each other. Within moments, they were naked and in bed, anxiously engaged in a romping interchange. Afterwards, they lay quietly, both lost in thought.

******

Michele had called a meeting with Tad, Franklin, Luz and Kim. When all were present, she leaned forward, her palms flat on the table. "We need to talk about some urgent matters." The three looked at her, so she continued. "Luz has interviewed all workers and determined which specialists should meet with which innocent Giga-BATS employees. We have engaged twenty countries to be involved, and thus they are all paying fees. We determined the amount each country would have to pay based on the country's gross national product. We need to be sure the funds do not quickly fizzle. We strongly believe that even though we are finding locations where crimes are committed and arresting superiors, the crimes will not immediately disappear or even diminish.

The question is, how long will we be able to be involved ... how long will the countries think we are important ... what can we do long term to help reduce or eliminate the crimes? We certainly do not want to just make business for ourselves that is not needed and helpful. But we want to help the victims, including the workers who lost their jobs and have much information to offer."

The others in the room appeared to be giving her rapt attention.

Michele turned her intense eyes to Tad. "Can you think of any way to improve the internet itself? To prevent these crimes at their source?"

Tad grinned. "Michele, you've read my mind. I've been thinking about this very thing. We need a renaissance, a new internet."

Franklin's eyebrows shot up. "A new internet? Is that even possible?"

Kim nodded slowly, considering. "It sounds ambitious, but if anyone can do it, it's Tad. And it would give us a long-term goal, something to work toward."

Tad said, "I also think that when we get to that phase, we should invite companies that have businesses of protecting people from the internet in various ways instead of only having governments involved."

Michele smiled, feeling a surge of hope. "Exactly. This could be our chance to make a real difference."

"And Kim," Michele said, "This is what you will also be working on in the offices being created for us in Miami until we get there. We need you to organize what you can. We'll meet by video call as soon as possible to plan."

As the meeting concluded, the group stood and formed a circle, their arms linking in a moment of unity. Michele was confident that they were on a new positive course.

Monday, March 23, 2020

Chapter 19

Tad met with the newly arrived U.S. agents from Homeland Security Investigations, Department of Justice, the IRS investigative arm, and the FBI, as well as several non-agents with special skills in countering crimes.

Tad said, "I'm sorry that you've missed some of what we've been doing, but you aren't the only newcomers. Several investigators from other countries have just arrived as well. Come on into the auditorium."

Tad faced the assembled group of investigators inside the auditorium. "We've learned more every single day and are now prepared to share it all, so you, investigators, can take it from here. Basically, we went through the PCs to the servers. Every computer had its historic data showing the chains leading to sources. We kept going upstream and finding servers in other locations from where instructions were being given. We found numerous communications in the archives about businesses, owners of businesses, and activities. We had URLs of customers and the companies themselves, and thus IP addresses which led to various sources.

Yet, we've also discovered that somebody or something still has accessed at least some of the computers. Often when I'm progressing through the systems, a rogue program, possibly or possibly not managed by humans, counters what I'm doing, erases data and reroutes me. We have still obtained much, but not all we need."

He pointed to the massive screen behind him. "I'm going to show you the evidence I have managed to keep, often by photographing screenshots with my phone, which we'll also give you digitally and in notebooks. You know how eager the press corps is to learn of this, but we do not intend to disclose anything without mutual agreement from the group."

"We've uncovered a web of criminal activity so vast that it's almost beyond comprehension. Giga-BATS isn't just a company ... it's a hydra, with tentacles reaching into every dark corner of the cyber underworld."

He displayed slide after slide of damning evidence. Murmurs of disbelief and sharp intakes of breath resonated throughout the room as the true scope of the conspiracy unfolded.

"Ransomware, data theft, arms dealing, drug trafficking ... you name it ... every type of major scam and crime we've ever heard of is being performed by Giga-BATS and its related entities and organizations, including some countries themselves. But here's the kicker: they're not just perpetrating these crimes. They're profiting from both sides of the equation. They're selling protection against the very threats they create. Insurance, cybersecurity, even companies that claim to negotiate with ransomware attackers."

As Tad delved deeper into the intricate network of Giga-BATS' shell companies, cryptocurrency exchanges, and international connections, the atmosphere in the room grew continually more intense.

"We've also identified multiple locations worldwide, including a yacht in the Bahamas that mirrors our setup here."

He pulled up a final slide—a map dotted with potential targets and hideouts. "We have addresses, phone numbers, data trails. But we need to move fast. This organization has its fingers in so many pies, they could disappear in an instant if they catch wind of our knowledge. And as I mentioned earlier, they know what we are doing and what we are finding in our searches of their systems."

"We've also tracked down Mr. Braxton Doolittle on an isolated island not far from the ship I mentioned in the Bahamas, as well as other principals in Berlin, Moscow, London and China."

Michele stepped up to the podium. "Now, you know everything we know," she said. "The next steps are in your hands. We're counting on you to bring these criminals to justice and dismantle this network."

But just as she finished her statement, a sound screeched through Tad's telephone. He yanked it out of his pocket and stared at the screen. His eyes bulging, he said, "Michele, I need to read this aloud."

She stood aside, as he read, "This is all in capital letters. 'MR. TAD HARRIS. IT'S RATHER HUMOROUS THAT YOU MAKE ALL THESE STATEMENTS ABOUT YOUR SUCCESSES WHILE YOU SHOULD REALIZE WE'VE JUST LET YOU INCLUDE US WITH YOUR EXPLANATIONS. WE KNOW EXACTLY WHERE EVERYBODY IS ... WHERE EVERY PIECE OF DATA IS ... WHAT YOU ARE DOING. YOUR PHONE WILL NOW BE ERASED ALONG WITH THE PHOTOS YOU JUST DISPLAYED. IF YOU DOWNLOADED IT, DON'T WORRY, WE WILL FIND THAT TOO.'"

Tad shook his head sorrowfully. "You are still dismissed to spread what you have learned. Hopefully some of you took your own shots of what we displayed, and we still have good parts of the data. Hopefully we can keep it. Decide right now what you will deliver to the Press."

Investigators yanked phones from their pockets and urgently spoke to home offices as they filed out of the room.

******

The small cabin on the yacht felt cramped as Kim, Tad, Michele, Franklin and Roosevelt gathered to plan the next stage since three of the five were going to depart. Tad said, "I've removed the memory chips from a few computers, and also loaded a disk with data. Kim, when you get started in the office, I'm hoping you or somebody you engage can study and organize this data and prepare for more."

Franklin said, "The new non-profit company has been filed with the state using the name you chose, 'Safe and Secure Cyber Computing, Incorporated' or 'S-A-S-C-C-I' for short. I was told you intend to pronounce it 'Saschy'. It will work with a coalition including numerous international government agencies and committees. As you know, it is already a viable company being paid for its work, and the Foundation that was involved initially has been reimbursed. Most of the financial aspects and employment procedures are ready to go."

Michele nodded. "Dad, Cuba's starting to worry about the virus. They need masks and hand sanitizer. Can you see if the Coast Guard can bring some?"

Franklin looked unsure. "I'll do what I can."

Michele wrapped her arms around her father in a tight embrace.

"Be safe, Dad," she whispered.

Tad hugged his father. "We'll finish what we started here, Dad."

As Franklin prepared to leave for Marina Hemingway to retrieve M&M, Michele turned to Kim. "Alright, let's get the rest of the team ready to go. We need to brief them on their roles back in the States."

******

Franklin stood at the helm as he piloted M&M into the large commercial harbor and approached the Coast Guard vessel, which was still floating next to the Giga Blue.

Kim stepped aboard the Coast Guard boat and went inside. The Coast Guard vessel's engines rumbled to life and hummed as its crew untied the lines and hopped aboard. Franklin backed off as the larger vessel eased into the channel.

Jude stood next to Franklin on the M&M, glancing back at Giga Blue as Luz slowly approached the railing. Luz and Jude shared a silent farewell, hands pressed to hearts.

*****

Michele and Tad climbed into a Lada driven by a police officer and headed toward the yacht for the Convention Center to inform the media that they'd handed over crucial information to international law enforcement. The old Lada limped along the Malecón, the sea breeze carrying the salt-tinged air through the open windows. Michele and Tad sat in silence, both lost in thought as they approached the convention center. "Ready for this?" Tad asked, his hand finding Michele's and giving it a reassuring squeeze.

She nodded and took in a breath. "I'm so tired of having to tell them we have nothing for them."

As they crossed into Playa, Michele noticed the driver's eyes darting nervously to the rearview mirror. She leaned forward and said, "What's the matter?"

Before the driver could respond, a violent jolt rocked the car. Michele's head snapped back, pain lancing through her neck. She twisted in her seat, her eyes widening as she saw an old American car bearing down on them again, its chrome grille gleaming menacingly in the bright sunlight. The metal bumpers of both cars screeched as the American car crashed into the Lada again.

Tad's arm instinctively wrapped around her shoulders. "Are you alright?" he asked, his fingers gently massaging her neck.

The Lada driver's fearful eyes kept darting forward and into the mirror. The next time the American car hit and backed off, the Lada driver zoomed to the left, entering a side street. The American car lost some traction from the slow-down but soon was closing in again.

The pursuit turned into a frantic chase through Havana's narrow streets. The Lada's tires squealed in protest as its driver swerved and dodged, the larger American car threateningly racing behind.

The Lada swerved onto the sidewalk to avoid hitting two elderly women crossing a street. As it veered back onto the street, the American car slammed into its rear fender, sending it careening. Time seemed to slow as the Lada rolled onto its roof with a sickening crunch of metal and slid along the asphalt.

Stars exploded behind Michele's eyes as her already injured forehead smacked against the dashboard. Then, she tumbled, disoriented, coming to rest with her head cushioned against Tad's midsection. Blood trickled into her eye as she reached out, touching Tad's face. "Are you alright?" she cried, panic rising in her throat as he remained unresponsive. She struggled to decide what she should do. Should she run or wait for help?

The sound of car doors opening jolted her into action. Just like when she'd escaped the yacht, the fight or flight instinct kicked in. With one last agonized look at Tad's still form, she climbed over the driver's blood-stained body and slithered out of the window, her heart pounding a frantic rhythm.

Then, like a mouse escaping a cat, she crawled behind an ancient American car, her breath coming in short, painful gasps. Hearing footsteps approaching, she made a break for a nearby alley, every muscle aching.

Hearing a man yell, "There she goes," she ran, hoping to draw the pursuers away from Tad. Reaching a tiny yard, behind a two-story home, she spotted a partially destroyed concrete stairwell leading to the second floor. She pulled herself to the top of a wall bordering the adjoining property and then leapt to the bottom concrete step that remained and scrambled up, using every ounce of strength to pull herself to safety. As she lay on the cold concrete outside the second-floor door, behind planters and mop buckets, the sounds of her pursuers grew fainter.

******

Consciousness returned to Tad slowly. Every inch of his body ached, and his head throbbed. He became aware of hands trying to pull him from the wreckage, the metal of the car groaning in protest.

"Ah, dammit man. Stop!" he cried out as his shoulder caught on a jagged piece of metal.

Hope returned somewhat when he heard sirens. Somebody spoke to him in rapid Spanish.

"I don't speak Spanish," he managed to croak out.

As more rescuers arrived, Tad hoped that Michele had escaped.

Suddenly, three men and a woman were on their knees outside the car looking at him. The woman said in English, "Hello, are you injured?"

Tad almost laughed at the absurdity of the question. "Those idiots who caused the wreck tried to pull me out and caught my shoulder on a piece of metal. Please don't let these guys pull me." He paused, swallowing hard. "I feel like I'm going to vomit."

She held fingers up in front of him and asked him how many. He answered twice, but finally, he said, "No more, please."

A man lay on his back examining him. The man said something to the woman in Spanish and she reported to Tad, "Your shoulder is impaled with a piece of metal from the roof of the car. We will need to cut the metal or widen the cut of your shoulder to free you."

"Oh, God," Tad said. "It hurts like hell." He cringed at the thought of them trying to cut him free without anesthesia.

She said, "What's your name? Where is your home? Why are you here in Cuba?"

"Tad Harris. In the car with me was a friend named Michele Morales. I think she escaped. I heard the bad guys chasing her. Please try to find her. If you can find a police chief named Mario, he knows who we are and what's going on."

A couple of metal boxes were slid into the upside-down vehicle. A man slithered in on the other side of Tad and measured his blood pressure and heartbeat. He heard the sound of metal sawing metal and felt excruciating pain in his shoulder. He shut his eyes and silently prayed for Michele's safety, clinging to the memory of her touch, her smile, hoping he could escape the pain.

******

Michele huddled in her precarious hiding spot at the top of the stairs as the continual wail of sirens pierced the air. She strained to hear any sign of the men following her. Only minutes before, she'd seen two of the large men silently moving through backyard below. She couldn't help but think that they seemed very odd, lumbering along like bears in pursuit of prey.

The sirens stopped nearby. Men's and women's voices repeatedly called her name in Spanish. But were they the police or her pursuers? She was sure they were not the weird voices of the men who had tailed her. She remained silent and still, afraid to answer, continuing to gaze, looking for somebody in uniform.

She tried to hear action near where the car and Tad should be. She hoped that medical personnel were taking care of him. Finally, she decided she couldn't stay hidden forever. Taking a deep breath, listening and searching for enemies, she cautiously inched her way down the stairs. *Hold on, Tad*, she thought as she crept back toward the scene of the crash.

******

The gentle rocking of the Coast Guard boat failed to soothe Kim's turbulent emotions. She lay in her bunk, one arm over her eyes, confused by the mix of anticipation and dread that kept churning within her.

She wanted so much to enfold her daughter in her arms, to breathe in the sweet scent of her hair, to feel the warmth of her small body against her chest. But her feelings about Denver were uncertain. He'd been so nasty the last time they'd talked, seeming to blame her for the issues at her work.

But, then again, although she could question Denver's temperament, she resented her mother making accusations. She bristled at her mother saying, *"You know I've always thought that Denver was too bossy with you...."* But she couldn't deny her mother's negative observations. Yet she dreamed that she could prove her mother wrong, and she could salvage what she and Denver had built together.

The loudspeaker crackled to life, jolting Kim from her thoughts. "A military-style aircraft appears to be heading our way from the east...."

******

The vibration of whatever tool they were using to free Tad from the metal shard holding his shoulder sent waves of agony through his entire body. He gritted his teeth, fighting against the urge to cry out.

In a desperate attempt to distract himself, he forced himself to focus on the success in finding the criminal actions of Giga-BATS. He walked through the steps in his head, reconstructing the path through firewalls and security protocols.

A particularly vicious jolt of pain tore through him. He tried to hold back a cry, but tears trickled from the corners of his eyes.

Through the haze of pain, he became aware of raised voices around him. His hope frayed as he realized the frustrated rescuers were arguing about how to free him.

******

As the M&M trailed the Coast Guard boat, Roosevelt smiled and said, "Damn, Jude. You look like you've lost your best friend."

Jude silently glared at him.

Franklin gestured toward the horizon. "That plane doesn't look friendly. I've asked Cuban and U.S. officials, and both deny it's theirs."

Gazing at the sky, Jude worried about Kim on the Coast Guard vessel.

Roosevelt said, "I don't see any defensive activity on the Coast Guard boat. Why aren't they doing anything?"

Franklin shook his head. "Cuba forbade the Coast Guard vessel from bringing weapons."

"What do you mean there are no weapons?" Jude demanded. "You're telling me that my daughter is on a quasi-military boat with no weaponry?"

Franklin said, "Well, hopefully it at least has a bulletproof hull … which is more than we have …. But we DO have a rifle."

Roosevelt said, "That's it? One rifle to counter a military style plane?"

Franklin said, "One of you take the wheel. Let me go below to get armed."

Jude said, "Are you a good shot, Franklin?"

"Reckon I can hit an airplane."

"But can you hit a vital part, like a gunner or a fuel line?"

Franklin shrugged his shoulders. "We'll see."

When he returned with the rifle, he peered at the plane through the binoculars. It approached rapidly, with a gunner hanging below in a protected ball turret. The gunner strafed the deck of the cutter, throwing shattered wood into the air, and then turned and headed toward M&M. Franklin stood in the cabin, and lifted the rifle as it approached, firing at its fuselage as rapidly as possible for a single shot weapon.

As the plane veered off, an enemy boat headed their way with a machine gunner on the bow. The gunner shot at M&M, splintering pieces of the bow and the top of the cabin. Franklin fired at the attacking boat's bridge, cracking its windshield.

The attacking boat continued straight at M&M's bow, so Franklin grabbed the wheel from Roosevelt and veered to the right, aiming its bow at the attacking boat, which then veered to the right. Franklin fired, hitting the captain and then the other man on the bridge. The wounded pilot fell, pulling the wheel down with him, which caused the attacking boat to veer sharply back to the left and into a tight circle. Franklin veered away and sped up, now realizing that the plane was circling back.

Jude said, "A fighter jet is coming from the north. I hope it's ours."

But the attacking plane was on track to arrive first. Franklin swung the wheel and swerved left and right across the waves of the Coast Guard vessel. The Coast Guard boat started swerving back and forth also in a silly dance routine, causing the oncoming plane to swerve too.

Turning the wheel back over to Roosevelt, Franklin posted up. "Come on, man, get overhead and I'll shoot your ass." But the enemy aircraft realized that a U.S. jet fighter was attacking and veered away.

The U.S. jet fighter shot a missile at the escaping plane and blew it up, throwing flames and huge metal chunks hurling through the air and then racing across the water.

"Jesus Christ," Jude said. "Please radio and see if Kim is all right."

Franklin did so, and Jude crossed his heart as he heard, "One casualty ... a crew member ... one injury ... a passenger ... shrapnel that entered the berth ... in the arm, but not critical it seems."

Jude said, "Please, ask if I can board."

Franklin announced on the radio, "One of our crew is the father of one of your passengers, and he wishes to come aboard."

"Granted. Slowing down. Approach the stern."

Jude was pulled up on the transom of the Coast Guard vessel by two Coast Guardsmen and rushed inside.

*****

Tad was a mass of sweat, about to pass out again. A piercing pain dug into his shoulder. *Oh my god, are they cutting into me?* He moaned. He heard another vehicle stop and the dull, empty sound of doors on an old American car creaking open and closing.

The sudden appearance of a news video camera felt like the final insult. "Please stop," Tad pleaded, trying to turn away from the intrusive lens.

And then Michele crawled into the wreckage, her face streaked with dirt and dried blood, her hand finding his, her touch relaxing him a bit.

"Tad," she whispered.

He managed a weak smile.

Reporters spoke in Spanish as the rescuers worked to free him. Tad focused solely on Michele, on the warmth of her hand in his and the concern in her eyes.

Tuesday, March 24, 2020

Chapter 20

At approximately two in the morning on Tuesday, the Miami Coast Guard base hummed with anticipation as the Coast Guard cutter and M&M veered into the calm water, lit by floodlights, and slid alongside the dock. The crowd clapped and yelled as passengers began emerging onto the deck.

Jude and Kim were the first to climb onto the dock from the cutter, blinking in the harsh light of camera flashes. At the same moment, Franklin and Roosevelt exited the M&M, and for a moment, the four stood frozen, gazing at each other. Then, as if a spell had been broken, they rushed together in a tangle of arms and relieved laughter.

Kim's eyes scanned the crowd, her heart sinking at not seeing Denver and Neveah. But then she decided that it wouldn't be reasonable for her husband to bring Neveah at this time of night. Catching a glimpse of her mother, Kim ran toward her.

"Oh, sweetheart," her mother breathed, enveloping Kim in a tight hug. "Thank God you're safe. I heard about the attack. I was so scared."

Franklin and Roosevelt saw Miguel, Diana and Gloria running toward them, pursued by a swarm of reporters. As cameras clicked and microphones were thrust forward, Diana yelled, "Franklin, Roosevelt, Michele and Tad have been attacked! They're in the hospital!"

Roosevelt's voice quavered as he embraced Gloria. "What happened? Are they Okay?"

"They'll be Okay," Miguel said. "Michele's just a little banged up. Tad's in surgery to remove a piece of metal from his shoulder. Neither will need to be admitted."

Franklin shook his head. "What an ordeal," he murmured. "It just won't end."

*****

Kim's mom silently drove to Kim's apartment. As her mom turned into the parking lot, Kim's stomach churned with a mixture of anticipation and dread.

"Do you want me to come up with you?" her mother asked softly.

Kim shook her head. "No, I ... I need to do this on my own."

A knowing look in her eyes, her mom said, "You two need your time together. Call me in the morning."

Kim felt a rush of gratitude. "Thanks, Mom. I love you."

Taking a deep breath, she made her way to the apartment door. After hesitating for a few long seconds, she pressed the doorbell and stood anxiously.

Eventually, she heard movement inside. Then, Denver's voice, muffled through the door ... "Jesus Lord. She's home."

The door flew open, and Denver enveloped her in his arms, his familiar scent welcoming her. "I was afraid you'd never come back, Kim, so afraid."

Kim was struck by how familiar and yet how strange it felt as he ushered her inside. As the door closed behind them, she realized that this reunion would determine the course of their future—together—or apart.

******

Tad's arm was in a cloth sling when he was released from the hospital and driven by a police officer to a small open-air breakfast place in Havana Vieja to meet with Michele. Her face lit up as she stood and embraced him. He pulled her in with his good arm.

As they settled onto wooden benches, cats swirled around their legs. Michele waved flies away with one hand and placed the other on Tad's. A spark of electricity seemed to pass between them as their eyes locked.

Michele said, "The cop makes me nervous. Why's he hanging around?"

Tad said, "Somebody decided that you and I need some protection."

She smiled. "I guess so. But what I can't understand, Tad, is how our enemies keep tracking us. We removed Pegasus from the phones. What else could it be?"

He shook his head. "Well, maybe some of their people on the ground are placing devices in vehicles they know we travel in. The boat must be full of ways to track. More likely though, it's the phones. Even though they don't have Pegasus anymore, there could be a tracker in the phone itself, and it could even work when the phone is off."

Michele nodded. "And how did they find and attack the boats on their way to Florida?"

"Well, they had phones too. But also, they had the brains we removed from some computers, and they had separate memory disks with their data on them. Maybe there was a tracker in the data. There are a lot of possibilities."

Michele said, "It's just so complicated. Why are they trying so damn hard?"

"Money," he said. "Lots and lots and lots of money."

As the waiter scribbled on a small pad, they each ordered a *cortado*, bottled water, fresh juice, toast with honey, freshly cut pineapple and eggs. It was only when their tiny cups of espresso with a dash of milk arrived that they let go of each other's hands. As he sipped the coffee, he said, "I'm really getting to love this coffee. So rich."

The waiter then brought fresh juice. "Oh, wow," he said. "I'm so tired of bottles of tasteless juice." He sipped. "Amazing. What is it?"

"*Fruta bomba.*"

"What?"

"That's what they call papaya here."

As they savored their meal, stolen glances and soft smiles punctuated the comfortable silence. Tad placed his good hand on Michele's. "This feels like an important day. I feel at peace, but it's an exciting peace. And I feel ... connected to you."

Michele smiled. "I feel it too," she whispered, leaning in to brush a soft kiss against his lips.

"Mmmmm. Thank you for that," he said. "I wanted to do the same, but I remember the last time I tried to kiss you."

She said, "That was a different situation. Now is now, and I'm ready to become closer to you ... if you want."

He grinned. "I want."

The kiss on the street as they left the diner was different–passionate, urgent, full of promise. When they finally broke apart, both were breathless.

"We have work to do," Michele panted, her eyes dancing with mischief. "Need to save the rest of this for tonight."

Tad's eyes lit up. "What's happening tonight?" he asked.

Michele's answering smile was enigmatic. "We'll see," she teased, taking his hand as they walked toward Giga Blue.

*****

In the afternoon, Michele limped across the stage at the Convention Center, followed by Luz, Mario, Colonel Freyre and investigators from U.S. Homeland Security, Interpol, and two European countries.

Panels had been moved, thus joining the two separate conference rooms so that tech, law enforcement and media personnel were all together.

"I know you've all been eager for answers," Michele said. "I'm pleased to introduce you to the investigative team, who will be sharing some remarkable breakthroughs in the investigations."

As Tad and the investigators took turns presenting their findings, the atmosphere in the room grew electric. News of arrests, of criminal networks dismantled, of victims rescued sent ripples of excitement through the audience.

The final investigator stood to speak. "We are making arrests, but there will be many more. We are shutting down locations, but we expect to find more. We have learned the locations of other workers like those found here in Havana and will be freeing them soon."

When the presentation concluded, reporters raced to be the first to break the story.

GIGA TROUBLE

******

Franklin juggled meetings with attorneys, accountants, and staff members to finalize countless details in the creation of the new non-profit company that Michele had suggested.

He'd just hung up the office phone from a call with Agent Banks, in which Banks had presented an amazing surprise—the United States government had confiscated Giga Blue and dedicated it for the investigators' use for the next mission.

But Banks also pointed out certain restrictions and expectations. "Franklin, investigators that the group intends take to the Bahamas must be approved," Banks had said, his tone leaving no room for argument. "We can't permit countries that have committed cybercrime to be involved, even if they managed to get invited to Havana."

As Franklin hung up the phone, wondering whether Michele would like the offer or not, he received a call from the receptionist telling him that Kim had arrived. He headed straight down to the floor on which SASCCI would operate, where he found Kim holding her young child. He gave Kim a light hug and then asked, "What's your daughter's name?"

"Nevaeh."

"How does one spell Nevaeh?"

She spelled it for him, "N-e-v-a-e-h. It's Heaven spelled backwards."

Franklin touched Nevaeh's toes and said her name. She giggled and stuck a tongue between her lips. "I'll take you to the child-care area," he said. They went into the elevator and down to the third floor.

After Franklin rang a bell, a middle-aged woman opened the door and smiled at Nevaeh. "Well, hello. What a little angel," she said.

Franklin introduced them, after which the woman said, "That name has become quite common. A little heaven. That's what she is."

Back on the floor where SASCCI would operate, Franklin couldn't help but feel a sense of pride that he had empty space for the operation that could make a real difference.

He introduced Kim to two of his employees who could help with whatever she needed.

Franklin turned to walk out, saying, "Michele will be giving you the real details of what you will do. Just buzz us if you need anything or have a question."

Kim smiled brightly, full of excitement and determination. "Thank you, Mr. Morales. I'm ready for this challenge."

Wednesday, March 25, 2020

Chapter 21

Roosevelt and Jude arrived at the Daytona Beach principal offices of Roasted Oak promptly at noon on Wednesday. With the help of Miguel Morales, the insurance company and Agent Banks, the company's web site and domain were back in operation.

Mark had created booklets for each and reviewed the details. "Governor DeSantis may not be following federal guidelines," he explained, "but pressure's mounting. We anticipate a shut-down of restaurants soon. But people need to eat and to purchase food, so one way or the other we will be busy, probably busier than we ever have been if we are properly prepared."

The receptionist announced that Franklin Morales was on the phone, and Jude punched a button to connect on speaker phone. "Hey, Franklin."

"Turn on CNN, now!"

As soon as they tuned in, images of Braxton Doolittle, once a respected lawyer, now a handcuffed criminal, his face full of dread, flashed across the screen.

The announcer said, "A senior executive of Giga-BATS named Braxton Doolittle, of Miami, Florida, who is alleged to be one of the ringleaders of the criminal enterprise, is seen here in the custody of Bahamian authorities."

"That's your former law partner?" Roosevelt asked, his eyebrows raised in disbelief.

Franklin nodded.

Newscasters spoke as videos revealed arrests across the globe and the discovery of another yacht near the location where Doolittle was found in the Bahamas, packed with kidnapped workers performing the same kinds of criminal acts as what occurred on Giga Blue.

"Damn, man," said Jude. "The dragnet operation is underway. Have the cyber-attacks diminished?"

Franklin said, "It's too soon to tell, but when the operations aboard Giga Blue were shut down, the crime did not diminish one iota."

After a long morning of intense work at Roasted Oak's office, Jude fixed up his hydration drink, changed into exercise attire and headed down to the beach. He'd sure missed this daily pleasure and exercise. He was surprised to see signs at the beach ramps that the beaches were closed to vehicles because of COVID. He also saw signs indicating that social distancing was necessary. Well, they couldn't very well mark the sand with where people should stand. He enjoyed the quiet, the lapping of waves, the seagulls and pigeons battling for food, especially considering that there was less possibility of getting fast food from people at the beach.

He found Irene sitting outside the Starbucks, which seemed to be open as usual. Irene looked up. "Where you been?"

"Away on business, Irene. How are you?" He fished out a five-dollar bill and handed it to her.

She said, "I'm fine. Thank you, Sir."

He kept moving, thinking of Luz, looking at his watch and noting seventeen and a half minute miles, unhappy that he'd lost almost a minute per mile of speed since he'd gone to Cuba. He'd probably gained a bit of weight. He needed to increase his time and get healthy again.

******

Michele and Luz met on the yacht to interview prior crewmembers. "Luz, you have been an active part of this process from the beginning. Would you be interested in joining our organization?"

A faint blush colored Luz's cheeks. "Yes, I would, very much."

"All right. Well, then, before we interview the crew, I'm proud to make you our first hire after Tad, Kim and me. I just can't discuss the salary yet."

Luz stood, hugged Michele, and said, "I'm sure it will be more than what I get paid working in Cuba, which has a value of approximately thirty-two U.S. dollars per month."

Michele said, "I assure you, the pay will be much, much better. I hope you have a passport."

Luz smiled again, "We Cubans were only allowed to apply for passports in recent years. Most of us applied immediately, so we would always be ready."

"All right. Let's get to work," said Michele. "Let's start the crew interview process with the captain and then go to lower levels."

The attempt to interview the captain did not go well. Glaring at Michele and Luz, he said, in his gravelly voice, "I'm sick of this place. I've been accused of all kinds of things. I'm not talking to anybody. I just want to get back to the U.S. of A."

Michele tried again to encourage him. "We're looking for people who operated as crew on Giga Blue. We were here to present you an opportunity. We are not the police, not the government, and not the old company. But if you don't want to discuss it, fine."

He scowled, arms crossed.

Finally, Michele said, "Thank you. You may go." She walked from the tiny office into the waiting room, where the entire prior crew waited, probably wondering why they'd been brought to the meeting.

She said to the crowd, "Giga Blue has been confiscated by the U.S. government. We will be operating the yacht and need a crew to take us and the yacht to another venue and then to Miami. Tell me, who was the next senior officer below the captain?"

People yelled out answers and pointed to a bald man with a perpetually smiling face.

Michele said, "Sir, you appear to be next. Follow me please."

In the interview room, she asked the man's name, and he answered, "Charles Leatherwood. I go by Chuck." When asked about his prior position, and whether he answered directly to the captain, he simply responded, "Yes."

Michele said, "Are you interested in being the captain of this boat?"

The man said, "I've never been the actual captain of a ship, but I have captained from time to time in my position. Kind of like the vice president of a country or company. There is excellent equipment on board. I would be very proud to take this position."

"Very well, I cannot tell you the salary yet, but I assure you it will be as close to the prior captain's salary as possible, and anyway, it is an immediate paid job. Will you accept?"

"Yes, yes. Thank you."

"And Chuck, we'd now like to ask you to help us choose others. Starting with the positions below captain, can you please suggest people for each level."

The man said, "I can't promise that all will have positive attitudes. I'll give you names of people who are the best."

He began reciting levels and designees as Luz wrote the names on a list.

Michele said, "Thank you, Captain. We'll keep interviewing. We may be leaving quite quickly."

"That title has a nice ring to it," he beamed.

Michele and Luz smiled as he departed.

******

The familiar chime of a WhatsApp video call broke the evening quiet of Jude's office. Luz's lovely face filled his screen.

"I'm so happy to hear you've joined SASCCI, Love," he said, unable to tame his smile. "We'll be able to see each other soon and often, I hope."

Her face lit up. "Yes, Jude. I'm so happy about that."

"I'd love to be able to take the supplies and set up the food operation on the yacht, which I understand is going to the Bahamas, but I'm sure I'd get a lot of flak."

Luz responded, "Of course, your daughter would have a fit. Where are you now?"

"In my office." He stood and walked around. "Here's my desk, worktable, television, computer setup. I have a shower because I go out for exercise during the workday. This window overlooks the beach, but it's too dark to see out now. Oh, wait." He opened the door and walked out onto the balcony. "It's dark, but you can see here what we call the Boardwalk, which is not made of wood but of concrete, the Bandshell, where musical events are still held, just like when it was originally built in 1937. And farther away, the clock tower. These and other structures were built under a program created by President Franklin Roosevelt using coquina rock from a beach in the next county north. That over there on the water," he said, pointing, "is the pier. The building on it has been there for many years. It used to be a dancing and party area and now is a restaurant, with live music on the rooftop."

"I'd love to walk there with you someday," Luz said softly, her eyes drinking in the unfamiliar landscape.

After chatting for a while longer, they silently gazed at each other for what seemed to Jude like an eternity. He didn't really know how to express himself.

Jude said, "Goodnight. Sweet dreams, darling."

Luz whispered, "Sweet dreams," and blew him a kiss.

******

In the evening, Michele and Tad arrived on Giga Blue carrying all their belongings, as they would not return to Havana.

As they trekked down the dock and boarded the yacht, Michele said, hesitantly, "I have chosen our cabins next to each other, at the end of a hall, so that we can be closer."

Tad smiled. But he was not sure exactly what to say, wanting to express his hope and desire, but knowing that if he pushed his expectations of love and sex, she'd turn off. He snuck glances at her as they walked, drinking in the sight of her—the sway of her hair, her luscious smile.

As they reached their cabins, Michele lingered, her hand on the doorknob. "Goodnight, Tad."

"Goodnight, Michele," Tad replied, wanting to say something more but unsure.

After a couple of light pecks on the lips, they entered their separate rooms, both were keenly aware of the thin wall between them, and wondered if something would occur.

Thursday, March 26, 2020

Chapter 22

Michele and Tad sipped warm cups of espresso and munched breakfast goodies in the wheelhouse as Captain Chuck Leatherwood reviewed charts. Captain Leatherwood brought the engines to life and instructed the crew to cast off. He lithely moved the yacht away from the dock, gently pushed the gear into forward, headed toward the statue of Jesus, and then veered to port and the open sea.

A Cuban border patrol boat led the way to the mouth of the inlet while another posted to the starboard stern. Michele walked out onto the deck and gazed to the east where the initial rays of the sun peaked over the Jesus statue, La Cabaña, and the upcoming El Morro lighthouse. A few small, colorful fishing boats puttered toward the sea, while others remained anchored and bobbed in the water.

Michele and Tad walked back through the wheelhouse and stood gazing at the waking city of Havana, hearing roosters crow from the rooftops of inner-city buildings and the hum and roar of buses, trucks and 40's and 50's U.S. cars.

Tad stood close to her. "I like this interesting and unique city," he said.

She nodded with a wistful smile. "Yes, I've always loved it, and the people."

GIGA TROUBLE

The yacht slipped out of the harbor, met the smooth, round swells of the sea, and headed northeasterly toward the Florida Keys, flanked by the protecting vessels fore and aft.

As they stood at the stern, watching Cuba recede into the distance, Michele's hand found Tad's on the railing. He smiled and silently squeezed her hand.

******

In less than two hours, they approached a bay, where a yacht, which showed the name, "GB II" on the stern, and two U.S. Navy ships, were docked. Ahead, light blue water lapped a sandy shore; beyond the beach, the ground of a tiny island rose steeply upward, past heavy stands of trees. Slightly below the peak stood a building that seemed to be built into a natural cave. Uniformed military personnel were walking outside the building while others roamed the decks of GB II, and the navy ships.

Moments after docking, Michele and Tad stood before a large, silent crowd in an auditorium. The group of investigators who had come on the new step of the investigation also stood on the side of the stage. The Russian investigator had not been allowed to join them because of suspicion about his country's involvement in cyberattacks. The few press and television media personnel who'd remained with the group stood in the aisles. Michele rather nervously walked to the podium, although she did feel she was getting somewhat accustomed to making such presentations. The crowd seemed nervous too, but nobody was speaking out negatively—at least not yet.

Finally, she began by introducing herself and Tad, explaining that they'd been employees of Giga-BATS also and that they'd experienced the same situation that those on GB II had. She explained how Tad and the international investigators standing to the side had found evidence of this ship and were sent to look for information on this yacht's computers. Then she explained the creation of a company that would hire workers if they wished to work in solving the crimes. Finally, she said that they wanted everybody to gain access to their computers and allow investigators to peruse their systems, even if they did not wish to perform the work long-term.

Tad's technical explanations were met with keen interest, the gathered workers eager to understand their role in unraveling the complex web of criminal activities.

She dismissed the silent crowd to have a meal, relax and contact their homes.

The tasty food had been set out buffet style, including chicken, steak, rice and beans, yuca, all cooked Cuban style, with onions, garlic and seasoning. Michele and Tad sat at nearby but separate tables and were peppered with questions.

******

After the meal and the break, workers, who seemed to be more at ease, streamed into the conference room again and were instructed to access their computers using a new internet connection. Workers and investigators dove into the GB II's computer systems in the afternoon. Tad had again given warnings about counteractive computer attacks and explained how they had to grab and retain the data.

Michele moved through the room, offering encouragement and guidance where needed. The progress was noticeably faster than their initial investigation on Giga Blue due to their growing experience and refined methods.

******

In the evening, the team unwound over dinner and drinks. Tad engaged in conversation with the younger employees. He slowly munched on the magnificent food and sipped a smooth, cold, reddish *Bucanero* beer. He smiled at the fact that the U.S. had restrictions on returning to the U.S. with Cuban alcohol or cigars but figured it would all be gone by the time they returned home.

He chatted with a young guy who sat next to him about what had been found. The kid said, "Man, I was so scared when I saw all these foreign languages and words like bomb and war. Most of the time I didn't understand."

"I know exactly what you mean," Tad assured the young man. "I experienced the same."

Michele stood and walked toward the exit, still chatting with a small crowd. On the deck, Tad nonchalantly moved nearby. She briefly caught his eye and made it clear that he was next on the agenda.

A pretty, young woman suddenly appeared in front of Tad, and said, "Hi."

He nervously glanced toward Michele, and then said, "Hi."

"It seems you have great computer skills," she said.

"Well, I wasn't the only one," he said. "I learned what I learned right there on the boat." He glanced at Michele, hoping she wouldn't be jealous. After an awkward silence, he finally said, "What kind of work did you do for the company?"

"I created apps, worked on all kinds of social media technology, hacked, stuff like that."

Tad saw Michele breaking away from the group and looking his way, with what might be a stern face.

He glanced back at the young woman, "I'm sorry but I must go. It was nice to meet you … uh … what was your name?"

"Irie."

"Irie. Is that Jamaican?"

She nodded.

"Well, it was nice meeting you, Irie. Bye."

He walked briskly to where Michele stood, facing the sea. As he arrived, he slid his hand down her forearm. "I'd like to hug and kiss you. Can't wait till we aren't the subject of constant review."

She glanced at him, looking a little concerned, a little flirtatious. "Who was the hot young woman?"

"Hot? She wasn't exactly hot."

Michele laughed. "Oh."

Tad turned to her, his hand sliding on hers. What could he say? What should he say? "Michele. I love you. I mean it."

He felt her shudder. She didn't respond. *Oh, no.* He'd blown it. He started pulling his hand away. But she topped it with her other hand. He glanced at her face, saw tears rolling down her cheeks, and said, "I'm sorry. Don't be mad at me again."

She shook her head. "I love you, Tad. Let's go someplace." She turned and walked, not touching him.

He walked behind her, admiring her lithe figure, vibrating with anticipation and hoping they were heading to one of their cabins. Could it be about to happen? *Calm down,* he told himself. *Remember, if you act fast and she thinks you just want sex, she'll shut you down. Be a gentleman—a loving gentleman.*

When they'd crossed the bridge that joined the Giga Blue, she stopped suddenly, wrapped her hands around his head and pulled him in for a long, tongue entwining kiss.

Oh, man. He thought he might faint. Their bodies were so close. He backed his pelvis away so she wouldn't realize he was already excited. Maybe she was having such thoughts this time. She sure acted that way. He started thinking how complicated it was, always trying to act interested enough, passionate enough, but not to the point that she would think it was only physical.

She slid her hands to his shoulders, and then around his back, down, down, down. Well, if she could do that, he could and should follow suit. So, he wound his arms around her thin body, began sliding his hands along her back and then, ran his thumbs up and down the canals on each side of her spine. She moaned. Mmmm. He'd found a spot. Her body reacted against him.

They continued long, luscious, stroking kisses with tongues darting in and out. He wanted to say, 'Let's go to the cabin,' but again was afraid to act too insistent. She had to want this.

Suddenly, she said, "Let's go." And she let go and started walking.

He stood still a moment, trying to stop thinking, trying to soften. She looked back. "What's wrong?"

He pointed to his crotch. "Please, wait a second. I can't be seen like this."

She grinned and walked away. He followed, trying to think of anything other than what might be about to happen.

She had her key out before they reached her cabin, smoothly unlocked and opened the door. Within seconds, while kissing deeply, they'd crazily removed each other's clothes and wrestled all over the bed.

Friday, March 27, 2020

Chapter 23

At dawn, Michele remembered the night and the peaceful sleep, wondered whether she'd made a mistake and decided no, she hadn't. Maybe he really did love her. He'd better, dammit. She didn't just give herself to some horny guy. She didn't know how she'd fallen for him so suddenly. She'd failed to say she loved him last night. If it hadn't been for this bizarre fiasco caused by their employers, this never would have happened.

She sat above him, skimming her fingers across his face, and then his chest. His face looked so angelic. He stretched, moved his head from side to side, and suddenly opened his eyes, looking her up and down, and sat up, looking surprised. She said, "Do you remember anything?"

He smiled. "Everything."

"Go on to your cabin and get ready. We need to get breakfast. You can go through the door there if it's unlocked on your side. It's locked on mine." She smiled.

He grinned. "Certainly, I did NOT lock it on my side."

"Bad boy, hoping I'd sneak into your room and climb into bed with you."

"Well, it was wishful thinking, Michele."

She hugged him again. "I'm heading out in about fifteen minutes, Tad. Let's arrive separately. We can glance at each other all day, but romance waits for tonight."

"Okay." He hugged her and kissed the top of her head. "Have a good day. I loved last night."

"I did too, Tad."

Not long thereafter, they were seated, nibbling breakfast and sipping juice and coffee, talking with tablemates.

During breakfast, Michele delivered a brief speech about the importance of secrecy in their ongoing investigation, as Tad had suggested. The gravity of their mission settled over the group as they prepared to dive back into their work.

******

Kim arrived in the Miami office earlier than usual to tackle a day full of meetings. As she reviewed the meticulously organized documents prepared by Honesti, a knock at the door surprised her. It was her father, there to collect memory disks for his trip to the yachts.

Jude put his arms around her and kissed her on the head. "Wow, this place is like Fort Knox. Snipers on the roof, and helicopters landing up there. There wasn't all this security just a few weeks ago. And all the construction activity. I guess they've converted part of this floor to sleeping quarters. They have on Roasted Oak's floor too."

Kim hadn't realized that the restaurant chain of her father and Tad's father had moved its Miami food prep operation into the Morales and Morales building. "Well, Dad, the criminals have been trying and trying to end the investigations. What do you need, Dad?"

He gave her an odd look and stammered a bit as he said. "I'm going on a ship this morning to deliver food and supplies to Giga Blue and the new boat. I understand you have some memory disks I am supposed to take."

She was instantly pissed. How had he maneuvered to go to the yacht to meet up with that Cuban lady? What the hell was her name? Oh, yeah, Luz. He certainly got himself on the trip just to spend time with that whore. "Why are you going, Dad? Isn't there anybody else who could have gone?"

"Well ... uh ... I have to be sure the food gets there properly ... and ... uh ... that somebody knows how to prepare and serve it."

She glared at him but decided not to say more. "The drives are over there in that box."

He meandered to the table, grabbed the box, said, "Thank you. See you soon ...," and left.

Honesti looked at her. "Is something the matter?"

Kim looked at her. "He's such an ass. He's got the hots for a woman younger than I am."

Honesti stood silently, trying to think of what to say. Finally, she said nothing.

In each meeting of the morning, Kim explained which organizations, people and agencies were joining a coalition and reminded the participants that each country, company or organization had to pay for its involvement.

For the most part, the participants in the video calls were friendly and supportive, and treated Kim with respect. A few did question whether SASCCI was supporting the U.S. more than the international community, and a couple questioned the high cost. Kim answered such inquiries and insisted that the U.S. was paying the same as other countries, and even more, and there was no special consideration to its interests.

The stress of the morning was offset by a pleasant lunch and playtime with her daughter, Nevaeh, providing a much-needed moment of normalcy.

******

Aboard the Coast Guard vessel, Jude stood on the bridge, watching the crystal-clear waters of the Caribbean pass beneath them. His mind was filled with thoughts of Luz and their burgeoning relationship, tempered by the knowledge of Kim's disapproval. He shouldn't feel guilty, having been divorced for years and never having had a serious relationship since he'd left Joyce.

His connection with Luz was just undeniable. It had been brewing since the first time they'd met several years ago. He hadn't known that she felt the same way. Light teasing in the past hadn't resulted in anything. That night before he left Havana had been magic.

A seagull landed on a railing, its feathers ruffled by the strong wind. A couple of smaller white birds flying alongside were rocked from side to side by the breeze.

The captain pointed ahead. "See those two large yachts next to that island. That's the destination."

Jude had the jitters. He and the small crew needed to get everything on board and organized in time for lunch. He hoped he'd have time to be with Luz before the Coast Guard boat departed for Miami. He said to the captain, "We're carrying great food from the company I work for ... a restaurant company ... Roasted Oak. You and the crew are invited to lunch too."

GIGA TROUBLE

The captain said, "Great. That'll be a nice treat," while the wheelhouse crew smiled.

As they approached the two yachts anchored near the mysterious island, Jude felt a mix of excitement and nervousness.

In minutes, he deboarded and was directed to the galley, where he introduced himself, asked questions, and explained the meals they had brought. Before long, the workers and Jude began filling the serving pans with food and taking the pans to steam tables in the dining room.

Soon, the crowd came in, grabbed their meals and spread out. The din of conversations grew louder. It seemed some women from the yacht were a bit entranced by the young, handsome men of the Coast Guard crew.

When Michele and Tad entered, he moved toward them, anticipating Luz's entrance. It would be perfect and natural to greet Michele and Tad first anyway. Michele hugged him. "I wasn't expecting to see you. Did you bring the food?"

"Of course," he answered, smiling. Then he hugged Tad.

Jude said, "We'll catch up later. Let me greet Luz. She just came in."

Luz's face lit up as he approached, and he knew his did too. He arrived in front of her, hugged her with one arm, and kissed her on the cheek, like friends would in Cuba, and she responded in the same manner. Her smile and the fine laugh lines around her eyes captivated him.

She looked around. "Let's eat together. There's a table in the galley."

After choosing tiny portions of food, they pulled the small galley table onto the deck in a shady area. As they sat, Jude said, "I missed you so much, Luz. I've been planning for days on how to see you. Franklin wasn't very happy about my coming and seemed quite suspicious. My daughter wanted to kill me."

"I can imagine, Jude. I'm so glad you made it here. I've missed you terribly too."

He said, "I hope you'll be in Florida, and that you'll stay there."

"I hope that too, Jude."

They munched on the food rather quickly. When they'd finished, she said, "Would you like to see my cabin?"

His heart pounded. "I'd love to."

She stood. "Leave the plates here. Let's go." She yanked him from his chair, pulled him by the fingers along the deck, across the bridge to Giga Blue, through a door, down a hallway, and suddenly she was fumbling with her key. She managed to get the door open and dragged him inside. They embraced frantically, kissed deeply, hastily removed each other's clothes and were wrestling in the bed in seconds.

"Slow down," she said. "I want to enjoy this. We've got time."

******

Michele had trouble talking with her tablemates since having a dessert of Tad kept pushing itself to the forefront of her mind. They should have time to have some fun right after lunch if they could escape quickly. She stood, placed her plate, glass and silverware on the tray and walked to the table where he was sitting. She leaned down and said quietly. "Do you think we have time to review that work we started last night before recommencing?"

He looked at her, surprised. But it seemed he got it and was trying to look nonchalant. "Uh, sure, Michele, I'll meet you there in the same office on the Giga Blue." She nodded and walked away. He tried to think of something other than what was going to happen. A young woman asked him a question about his research.

"I need to go take care of something. Can we talk a little later?" His tablemates eyed him quizzically as he rose and walked away.

He almost ran to Michele's room, tapped on the door with a finger, and was dragged into the room. In seconds they were entwined.

Tad stopped for a moment as they were both breathing hard. "I hear a noise just like the noises we are making. Somebody else is doing it."

She looked at him. "Oh my God. That's from Luz's room. She and Kim's dad must be there."

Tad gave a shocked look, while smiling. "Good for them."

They lay together, spent, holding each other, giving each other little kisses, listening to the romp that was still going on next door. "Damn, man, how old is Kim's dad?"

"Over sixty-five, I imagine," Michele responded.

They both smiled. Michele said, "I'm glad Kim's not on board. She'd be so pissed."

Shortly, they got cleaned up and dressed. While in the bathroom they heard water running and voices from Luz's room.

They listened at the door. She said, "Do you think they've left?"

Tad said, "I don't hear anything."

"OK, Tad. Let's walk out, but when we're nearing the deck, I'll back off and you walk out first so the workers don't catch on."

He nodded and opened the door. They crept out and walked quietly down the hall. But just as they neared Luz's cabin, Jude and Luz walked out. The four froze, looking at each other. Finally, Tad shrugged, smiling. The others smiled, all making similar 'you caught me, but it was worth it' looks.

Tad said, "Let's go single file. Michele and Luz, you walk out together, talking like it's about work. Then we will do likewise."

They nodded. But Luz turned back to Jude, hugged him and kissed him on the mouth. "I'm glad you came, Jude. I hope to see you soon in Florida."

He responded with a kiss and hug. "I do too, Luz."

Weekend, March 28 and 29, 2020

Chapter 24

Roasting in the early morning sun, Tad and Michele crossed the bridge to GB II where they, along with agents from U.S. and international agencies and uniformed U.S. military personnel, would board tenders to cross the small sliver of water between GB II and the island to begin the trek uphill on the island.

Within moments, they arrived at a concrete embankment and disembarked. Military personnel wrapped thick belts with radios, ammunition and similar items around their waists, slung rifles over their shoulders and hefted backpacks. Many investigators and non-military men also lugged heavy bags with laptops and other equipment.

The group trudged up the severe incline like a line of working ants, all leaning into the incline as the baking heat rose from the cracked asphalt, through which dried weeds struggled to survive.

Tad wanted to grab Michele's hand but thought better of it. He could daydream about tonight though. He knew he really loved her. He'd never experienced this level of true love before.

Passing by semi-round areas of concrete block were turrets containing fixed anti-aircraft weaponry facing the sky, the group slowed and looked upward at ominous, buzzing aircraft. One of the military men radioed somebody. Tad couldn't make out the scratchy response. But the military man pointed to one of the turrets, shouting, "Incoming. Take cover!!"

Military personnel slid weapons off their backs and took positions while the group scrambled for the nearest concrete turret. Michele's hand found Tad's, her grip tight with fear.

Bullets ripped by and struck all around, shredding leaves, skimming off asphalt and concrete and spraying dust into the sky.

A soldier was hit in the arm and rolled to the ground as blood spewed forth like from a geyser. A medic crawled to him and struggled valiantly to staunch the flow with a tourniquet. Michele wept as the blood continued to soak the tourniquet and the soldier's face turned pale.

An American fighter jet streaked into view and pursued the enemy plane until it disappeared over the horizon. The rumble of an explosion echoed from the cave above.

Shaken but determined, the group pressed on, seeming to have a new energy. When they finally reached the cave entrance, they gazed into the dark space. The leader of the military patrol said that the soldiers would keep watch at the entrance while the group would be inside the cave. A soldier with blonde curls flowing out from under her helmet, walked toward them, flanked by two four-legged robots with heads shaped like dogs'. She announced herself as "Sergeant Gordon" and explained that she was in charge of the post.

Michele said, "Thank you for having us. Who created the robots?"

The sergeant said, "The prior group that operated here created them. There are twenty. They are very helpful."

Michele and Tad looked at each other. Michele said, "Excuse us for a moment please." She and Tad walked back outside and approached the leader of the military outfit.

"Sir, may I ask, do you know this Sergeant Gordon? Is she legit? She's acting odd and she says the robots were from the prior group. The prior group is the enemy, isn't it? Did somebody investigate this and approve these robots being involved?"

The officer shook his head. "This is our first time here too. We hear there was some contingent here, but we have no details. I don't even know whom to ask. If you ask her which division she's in and who oversees it, I can investigate."

Suddenly, the officer looked up, and Michele heard the sound of the clicking robot feet. She and Tad turned to find the Sergeant standing there. The robots tilted their heads like dogs would. They had two eyes but no ears. Michele had seen prototypes of four-legged robots before, but those that had heads had one large 'eye' in the middle.

The Sergeant said, "Who among you sought entrance to this facility?" The robots looked at her inquisitive as she continued. "Somebody contacted my leader and asked me to greet you. Now, suddenly, you aren't sure you want to be here?"

Michele said, "Sergeant, please inform us of your division and its chief officer, or the parties that told you to meet us here."

The woman said, "I'm going to turn around and go inside. This is foolishness. You came here wanting to research something, and now you apparently don't want to."

Michele and Tad looked at each other again. Michele whispered, "Tad, we need to go in." He nodded.

Michele said, "We apologize for questioning your authority. Obviously, you know who we are and why we're here. Please take us inside."

"Follow these Bots" she ordered, so they walked behind the robots while the sergeant stayed behind. Quite a few more robot dogs wandered about as they were led into the heart of the enemy's digital lair. Within a few minutes, they arrived at a large space with about twenty PCs at separate desks.

Tad sat down and quickly evaluated the system and data. "Looks like the others," he said as he clicked. First, let me see if I can find the routes this computer outside this facility and then I'll see if we can just take the memory chip with us. He assigned a few others to do the same research, including Tim and Zeke, the phone experts.

A person stood behind each person in front of a computer and took photos with their phones of the data they turned up. After a while, Tad announced, "All right, now we'll see if we can remove the memory chips. Is everybody ready? Does everybody have the necessary tools?" The other specialists nodded and withdrew screwdrivers. Tad started removing screws just as the others did. Then they started working on the parts of the motherboard that sat about the memory chips and then, finally, they were at the memory chips.

The robot dogs started moving toward the exit. Michele noticed and said, "Tad, why do you think they're leaving?"

Tad looked up, surprised, but finally just shrugged his shoulders. "Okay, let's begin removing the memory." As each techie started unscrewing the supports, a loud click sounded in the computer Tad was working on, and then the same click could be heard from all of them. Tad yelled, "I hear a countdown. Shit, I think they're going to blow. RUN!!!!" Everybody leapt from their seats and raced toward the front of the cave, but at the same moment more than twenty small, black drones, each with scissoring blades, came toward them from the front.

"Oh my God," Michele said, "Duck, crawl, roll, whatever." But the drones were quick, zooming this way and that.

Zeke screamed as a drone attacked his face, and he went down in a thud, still screaming. Several others were hit, causing blood to spray from their heads and faces. The groans and screams were horrifying. Those who hadn't been hit continued to flee. As they rounded the last turn and approached the cave's entrance, they found that all the robot dogs, lined up two high, blocked their exit.

Michele yelled, "Keep running, to dive over them, or under them. We need to get past." A drone dug into the throat of an international researcher, and he went down without a sound.

Then, a heavy rumble began somewhere behind them. Michele again yelled, "It's gonna blow. Don't stop." As they reached the dogs, she dropped and tried to slither underneath one. But was kicked in the ribs by one of the robot's legs, while another leg from another direction held her in place. Hoping the robots were too heavy, she pushed to her knees and stood up, toppling the robots on top of her.

And then she saw Tad and some others leaping over the wall of robots, falling and rolling on the other side. The soldiers who had accompanied them up to the cave rushed toward the crowd, realized their plight and began shooting at the robots. The rumbling sound grew louder and louder until the unmistakable sound of an explosion echoed through the passageways along with billows of smoke and finally blew all the robots and humans out of the exit and flattened the soldiers outside, causing some to tumble down the hill. The mouth of the cave collapsed, causing more screams and groans.

******

After an afternoon of hearing the rumble of medical airboats, helicopters and jeeps running up and down the side of the hill, everybody seemed to be in a trance of suffering. As dinner was about to be served, Michele stood in front of the somber crowd, tried not to choke up, and said, "We never thought our last day together would bring such a tragic end. The number of people who were killed and injured is just unimaginable. One of our members would like to say a prayer for the fallen and injured, as well as for all of you."

A woman who'd worked at Giga-BATS stood beside Michele. "Please bow your heads," she ordered, and then prayed for the people lost and injured, their families, co-workers and loved ones. The crowd remained shocked and silent.

Finally, Michele took over again. "As you know," she began, the plan for tomorrow was to enter Braxton Doolittle's home and perform the same kind of searches we've done before. But now, that is just too dangerous. Tad, Tim and some others, along with the U.S. military will travel there on Giga Blue as the rest of us travel to Miami on GB II. One of the navy vessels that has arrived this afternoon has brought a number of EOD robots, which I am told stands for explosive ordnance disposal, meaning they can locate and dispose of bombs. Although investigators will still go to Doolittle's home, nobody will enter the dwelling, at least until the EOD robots have declared the place safe, and probably not even then. It seems our research has come to an end. That is also really sad because we know there are more kidnapped workers in multiple places around the world. So, the military will continue raiding those locations, but there is no sense for us to attempt to obtain more data, and there is too much danger for our people to keep trying to do so."

Michele continued. "We are ready to turn all further communications with media, your governments and the world over to law enforcement and the military. Tad will provide the details."

Tad rose, paused and then spoke. "I think we all realize that the multiple types of crimes committed by Giga-BATS and related companies and organizations has likely surpassed any criminal enterprise ever. We feel certain that even with all the arrests and shutting down of computers and facilities where these attacks have been generated, these illegal activities will likely continue."

"We are moving to our next stage ... to attempt to rewrite the rules," Tad explained. "... to create an internet that will not permit such actions to ever happen again."

As he spoke, Michele watched the faces of the assembled agents but couldn't gauge whether the overall view was positive or negative.

Tad continued. "I believe we should, in effect, eliminate the hodge-podge of numerous pieces of the internet and clean it up ... tighten down all the different ways that criminals can misuse it.

I have had phone calls this week with two large international companies, one a software company and one a company that seeks to protect against malware and similar means of attack. I asked whether they would be interested in joining a group of all such companies as well as international computer crime specialists in trying to do something new with the internet, and they said yes. Then I asked whether they would be willing to contribute funds for the ability to work with us, including paying for our employees and costs, and they said yes. So, now, I am mentioning it to you all, for you to consider and talk to your countries, as to whether you would be interested in participating."

Attendees glanced around the room, and many nodded. Tad said, "All right. I will not ask you more now, but all representatives will be on the list to discuss willingness of your countries to participate. I will talk to more companies and will give more details, including what we need financially to continue. But I will tell you now that we of SASCCI intend to move forward with this idea so long as we have enough support."

Tuesday, March 31, 2020

Chapter 25

Michele awoke to the sound of her iPhone alarm at seven on Tuesday morning. She turned and snuggled with Tad, who'd arrived just a few hours before. "Good morning, Sunshine," she said, kissing him on the cheek. "I know you're exhausted. I need to get going but you can sleep more if you need to."

Tad yawned and stretched. "I surely am exhausted honey, but I need to get going too."

Michele said, "Florida finally implemented a stay-at-home order. The whole country is in turmoil and disagreement about what, if anything, should be done. About seventy percent of the staff will be here in the newly constructed sleeping quarters. Some workers went home for a day but will be here this morning. And some of the international investigators will be lodging here too. We made a hybrid rule here. Even though the Russian man wasn't allowed on the boat, he flew here from Cuba and will also be on-site. Russia has agreed to pay to be a part of the new procedure. Here in the building, masks are encouraged but not required. They'll be suggested more strongly of outsiders coming in and for us when outsiders are here. There's a box of them on the dresser." She kissed him again and stood up, as he dragged himself through the adjoining door to his own room.

*****

Michele, Tad, Kim, and Luz stood in the front of the Zoom Room, as they'd begun referring to the huge conference room surrounded by large and small screens, including for group Zoom conferences. The room began to fill with those who were present in person as faces began popping up on the Zoom screen, one after the other.

Michele introduced herself and those standing near her, then steeled herself to speak clearly and calmly. "We welcome everybody to the first official meeting of the members of the Cyber Renaissance Coalition, which we are calling CRC for short, consisting of approximately one hundred people, all specialists of some sort in computer and internet technology ... representing companies and agencies of the United States and other countries. Because so many are involved, rather than introducing or having members introduce themselves, we have sent via email a list of people and the entities they represent, with photos. The list also indicates who are present on site and who will be attending from afar. As we progress in research and work, all departments and groups will perform in rooms with constant live video for those off-site to be involved. I now turn it over to Mr. Tad Harris."

Tad began, "The Giga-BATS criminal enterprise's tentacles have infiltrated every aspect of the internet; thus, it is likely impossible to prevent future intrusions or to remove viruses and malware already in systems or stolen personal and company data that is already on the dark web. A small part of our group that helped in finding the criminals has been planning the development of a new internet project and that is what CRC is all about. We invited commercial interests to join the teams, including all legitimate businesses that offer virus-protection and other types of protection, password generation and saving, memory storage, software creators, email providers ... basically every type of industry that has an interest in the success and safety of the internet. All such legitimate businesses will benefit from being involved at the outset.

We've also added a great number of international governments and agencies of governments, most recently including U.S agencies, 'NTIA', the acronym for the 'National Telecommunications and Information Administration', 'Trusted Internet Connections', a cybersecurity initiative that issues permissions for broadband use, and we have also involved an non-profit international organization called the 'Internet Corporation for Assigned Names and Numbers', or 'ICANN,' which has responsibility for internet protocol, address allocation and a number of other aspects. Also, another U.S. agency 'FINCEN', which stands for Financial Crimes Enforcement Network, that operates under corporate transparency laws to make it harder for criminals, terrorists and money launderers to hide behind ghost companies. We think it is important to tighten issuance of access to the internet as a whole and monitor such access. Other countries may have similar agencies and they will be welcome to join as well.

We'd considered trying to create a means for obtaining data on individuals that owned or had interests in companies, but it was too broad, especially considering that entities are created worldwide, with no connection or correlation among countries as to procedure. We will not monitor or check to see if a person is really connected to a company, but a party with authority in the company would have to vouch for any new person. We also will not monitor what a company does or sells or anything else beyond who is logging in on behalf of a company. But governments are likely to require certain other protections, and of course we will comply with such edicts."

Tad cleared his throat and sipped some water, glancing around the room and at the others standing around him. He continued. "We have developed several components of the proposed replacement of the internet and will have different teams involved in each.

We will not be forcing any person, company, agency or country to adopt the new internet. Some may replace it. Some may utilize both. Some governments are likely not want to use it at all. But with the safety mechanisms that we plan to build in, we believe many companies and governments will accept it, eventually, as the only means of access.

Companies that currently offer virus protection can continue to provide that for the old internet, or not. The whole point of the new internet is to replace the old hodgepodge of connections that has existed forever with one that has built-in safeguards to reduce the possibility it can be tampered with. Of course, after it exists, some will try to attack, but we don't believe it will be nearly as easy as it has been. And with all of us continually involved, we will together be able to staunch attacks. Service companies should still have services to offer and can alter their prior services as they deem appropriate.

The other aspects of the new internet include a simple way to prove to the user that he or she is in the new internet. A symbol or some identifying feature that cannot be cloned or recreated would always be evident.

All data that may exist on the Web or in a computer or other device will have to be cleansed before it can be added to the new internet. Any time that data is accessed, downloaded, uploaded, amended, etcetera, it will automatically require a new cleansing to be verified clean in the cloud.

A huge additional feature is that no party can share data, sell a product or service, or receive any benefit from anything without an

GIGA TROUBLE

individual person being vetted. To log into the new internet at all requires digital verification, such as facial, eye, fingerprint or similar verification of the person. No company or business can access the new internet without an identified person logging in. To log into a business' internet connection, the person must be verified. Then when logging into the bank account, the person was already vetted by the new internet itself but is still also verified there. No shadow entities will have a presence on the new internet.

Finally, we've decided not to call it the new internet, but instead, we have come up with a name for it, as well as new, fresh names for everything about the internet, including the cloud, domain names, and other features. As for other languages, countries or their agencies can suggest alternate names for foreign languages."

He then introduced Luz and Honesti to explain the proposed new internet identifiers. Honesti took the podium first and explained that the goal was to make the name of the internet and terms more easily understandable and memorable to laypersons. She continued. "The name for the new internet is "Interstellar". We settled on this name partly for the idea of outer space, but also because it seemed simple, and it starts with the same base as the word 'internet'. Although it was decided some years ago that the word 'internet' was generic and thus one should not capitalize the first letter of the word, the name 'Interstellar' and a logo are being registered as a Tradename so that it cannot be used as a noun generically. And we'll also introduce a simple abbreviation, being 'IS', which will also be registered. 'IS' will be pronounced as the letters I and S."

Then she explained other easy-to-remember terms to replace common terms. "'Cloud' will be known as 'IS Cloud' ... logins will be known as 'IS Accounts', domain names will be 'IS Codes', and various other names have been adopted and will be implemented."

Luz stepped behind the podium and said, "We are also working on controlling applications for phones and other devices because the same protections must be there. Applications for phones will become IS App. Like everything else, old ones can remain as long as the original vendor wants to continue to use them but won't be able to connect through Interstellar without altering the terms and being approved."

Luz then explained changes to the suffixes to email addresses. "We intend to replace the very generic suffix, '.com', but would retain the suffixes, '.gov' and '.org'. The code to be used as a suffix for any address that is not a not-for-profit organization or a government entity would be '.pers' for purely personal, '.biz' as the first part of a business, with a second suffix. One second suffix would add 'pers' or '.bizpers' for a business of any kind operated by one person, and '.bizent' for a business operated by any company, corporation or other type of entity with more than one owner operating a business of any kind, and '.gen' for anything else, whether operated by a person or an entity. A '.gen' site could read but not promote anything although it could communicate with other members of social media as long as it did not promote or offer any item for sale or otherwise receive payment for any product or service.

As Tad explained, to create any type of business page, one would have to identify at least one responsible person, and any time one wished to add additional personnel they could do so after the new person met the identification standards."

Tad closed the meeting with an announcement that as many as were available should remain for another Zoom meeting to begin within minutes, involving an interview of the group by a sub-committee of the United States Congress.

GIGA TROUBLE

******

Almost everybody stayed in place for the Zoom meeting with members of a sub-committee of the House of Representatives.

Before the House sub-committee had joined, a young woman with blonde hair, dressed in a pant suit, entered the Zoom Room, followed by a young woman with a still camera, who focused on the Zoom panels and the room in general.

Kim said, "Hello, Ms. Ellenwood. You may sit over there," as she pointed to the location.

When the House sub-committee members appeared in the Zoom panels, Kim said, "I thank you for having an interest in the vital matters at hand. Ms. Melinda Ellenwood is attending on behalf of the Associated Press. All others in the room and on the Zoom call are members of what we have now named the Cyber Renaissance Coalition ... or CRC. Members of the congressional sub-committee may introduce themselves, to be followed by Agent Banks of the United States FBI."

After the introductions, Agent Banks summarized the different types of data that had been obtained in the criminal investigations and explained why he believed that SASCCI representatives were correct in saying there was no way to eliminate the crime without a new internet. He said that the three heads of SASCCI had accomplished numerous important goals including finding locations and masterminds involved in Giga-BATS' activities. He ended with, "I personally believe that the members that have joined CRC are perfectly qualified for this next step in thwarting internet crime."

Then Tad explained further how deep the infiltration by the criminal actors had been and why a new internet was now proposed as the only reasonable means of eliminating viruses, malware and other methods used by criminals to infiltrate computers. He concluded by saying, "The new Internet needs to be able to block use of anything that is in or has come from the Dark Web."

One of the congressional sub-committee members, a chubby, balding man with half glasses perched on the tip of his nose, introduced himself as C. Cornwall Foxworthy. He said, "I must interrupt you here. I think you all are completely crazy ... nuttier than fruitcakes. How in the hell can you think you're going to eliminate and rebuild the internet? The world was getting along just fine other than a little white-collar crime once in a while until you people suddenly popped up and decided you'd take over and change the world. Where did you come from anyway?"

He glared into the camera. A couple of other sub-committee members, who'd seemed suspicious previously, nodded and looked proudly at their compatriot. Others seemed a bit embarrassed.

Michele braced herself and began. "Thank you for your input, Sir. Where we came from is truly nowhere."

But as she started trying to explain, the man said, "Listen, we all know your little sob story. What happened on that boat sounds like a Patty Hearst story to me. What I don't get is how you went from being victims of a ruse to creating your company and huge group of nuts, getting certain factions of our government to support you, spending hard-earned taxpayer funds on whatever, and now wanting to get Congress' authorization."

"Sir," Michele stated, "... the United States government did nothing at all to try to free the kidnapped workers, or to find the data we found or to help the world work on solutions. If we hadn't done it, nobody would have. We invited the international tech community to Havana. We helped create this ...", she put quote signs in the air with her fingers, "'group of nuts'", to which many members of the group of nuts smiled or laughed ..., "which until very recently the U.S. has shown no interest in, and we have created helpful procedures to move forward. Fortunately, now, some agencies of the U.S. government have joined this ... ", she made quote signs again, "'group of nuts'."

"Listen, ma'am. You got yourself to commie country where the United States was not invited and did all this stuff with those commies."

"Sir," she rebounded, "We were involved in many ways with the U.S. government. Agent Banks, would you like to confirm U.S. involvement?"

Agent Banks said, "Mr. Committee Member, Sir. You are truly off base in your accusations. What Ms. Morales has stated about how it all came to pass is accurate. We of the FBI and others were in constant contact with Ms. Morales and her group and obtained very much support and information from them. They asked us to help get U.S. agencies involved, which they now are."

The man said, "So the FBI was involved in this insanity of replacing the internet and this guy ... ", he pointed to Tad, " ... trying to tell us that the China virus or kung-flu, or whatever you want to call it, and a computer glitch are the same? This guy is the Fauci of computers."

Agent Banks shook his head. "Sir, as we just said, SASCCI has asked our government from the beginning to appoint agencies or individuals. No agency of the United States government was interested in joining the discussions, until now, at the behest of the FBI rather than an agency that should have stepped in."

Foxworthy said, "How exactly were the agencies appointed? Who had the power to do so? Why was Congress not involved? Will one of the agency representatives please help us to understand?"

A middle-aged, dark haired man reported which agency he represented and said, "Sir, every agency of the United States government has rules and regulations and procedures. Their workers answer to levels above them. I do not know how the United States Congress or even the executive branch would be involved in such decisions."

Another sub-committee member who'd seemed on the negative side spoke up. "What I would like to know is exactly what your group has made application for. Are you seeking money? Why are you wishing to speak to Congress?"

Michele said, "We have not made any application for anything, Sir. We are not seeking money. We did not ask to appear in front of this sub-committee of the U.S. Congress. We were invited, or should I say instructed, to appear in front of the full Congressional Committee soon. What we really wanted was for the United States to appoint somebody to join CRC and be part of the decision-making process. We now have that."

Congressman Foxworthy again scolded the SASCCI representatives. "You people need to be better prepared for the hearing."

Michele responded. "Sir, again, we'd be happy to have the hearing canceled. We do not want anything and do not need authorization for anything. And you have no authority to force us to attend."

Foxworthy huffed. "You people and your group of nuts are the ones who have no authority without our blessing."

Michele shook her head.

Tad spoke up. "Sir, please allow me to show you a sample of something that was posted through the Giga-BATS' connections. This is a feed that attacked both Republicans and Democrats with the same arguments, twisted somewhat. It is a communication inside a site that is what you in Congress believe is private, but it was infiltrated."

GIGA TROUBLE

He slowly displayed screen shots of what should be a private page, including the email addresses of Congresspersons, although he had redacted portions of the addresses. Tad pointed to a post in which Congressman Foxworthy touted the U.S. presidency's cooperation with Russia. Tad said, "It is very clear that Giga-BATS had been paid by a third party to create the false emails."

Congressman Foxworthy floundered in trying to find words.

Tad said, "We know it is false, Sir. But the recipients of the string do not know that. I believe we should not display this at the Congressional Committee hearing, because a larger group of reporters will be present and may reveal it to the public. But I suggest that you take this into account if you continue to bash us."

Foxworthy said, "Watch what you say, young man."

Tad smiled, as did the other SASCCI executives, and the video feed was disconnected, leaving a heavy silence in the room.

"Well," Tad said, hoping to break the tension, "I think that went about as well as we could have hoped." Many in the audience smiled or snickered.

******

In the evening, the three executives met in the conference room to watch television news and read newspapers. A photo of the group sitting at the table in front of the screen appeared on the front page of the Miami Herald. The article had been authored by the AP reporter. Photographs showed Michele and Tad with their mouths open and hands raised. Then a screen showed Congressman Foxworthy pointing with his finger with a stern look on his face and with his mouth open so wide it appeared he was yelling.

"Wow," Michele said. "I can't believe this article has been posted so quickly."

The article's headline said, "Group Tackles Internet Attacks." It began with a summary of SASCCI's work to locate the figureheads of Giga-BATS and various locations from which they operated, its intentions and the international coalition that had been created.

The article stated,

> *Certain factions of the House sub-committee challenged the reasonableness of this vast expectation. One member referred to them as crazy and irrational and accused them of improperly taking money and other benefits from the United States government, which of course the executives vehemently denied.*
>
> *The executives of the Company, Michele Morales, Kim Armstrong and Tad Harris, stood their ground in fiery denials of the accusations. All three very cogently explained their positions and beliefs in spite of the attacks. Members of the Cyber Renaissance Coalition also spoke out with explanations of the problems that had occurred and the necessity of rebuilding the internet.*

Tad said, "YES!!!," giving a thumbs up. "The reporter got it all. She understood. What a great article!"

The article continued, "It does not appear that the Cyber Renaissance Coalition is jumping toward proposed action without great study or without collaboration of international computer and internet service companies, together with the collaboration of the governments of the United States and other countries. As Ms. Morales stated, 'We have been disappointed in the United States' failure to become involved, but we finally have some agencies involved as of now.'"

The article continued. "It also appears that SASCCI and CRC are working on procedures to obtain identification of people who wish to log into the new internet it will call 'Interstellar' and monitor entities that receive access to domain names, QR Codes and hyperlink possibilities."

"This is great," said Kim. "I'm happy. She paid attention and was supportive of us."

"True," said Michele. "But it won't be that way in the future. As other media representatives that support certain political parties or politicians or ideas get involved, we will be attacked by some and supported by others. This one was not that way. I am certain that we will be attacked based on privacy concerns because Interstellar will require identification of all who enter it. Get ready."

"I'm ready," said Tad.

"Ditto," said Kim.

******

Later that evening, Michele entered Tad's room for a private dinner that he'd arranged with Roasted Oak, enamored by the view and aroma of steak, asparagus, salad and roasted potatoes.

Tad popped open a bottle of champagne and poured it into two glasses.

"Oh my God, Tad. How special!"

"Special food and champagne for a special lady."

Michele giggled like a little girl. "I love you, Tad." She gave him a sensual kiss.

"Mmmmm." Tad said. "Well, we should eat the food while it's hot."

She said, "I'm kind of hot."

So, they had a romantic, sensual interlude before dinner, followed by the delicious dinner and the champagne.

Afterwards, as they snuggled, he said, "How do you feel about our progress and our future?"

"Are you asking about our personal future or the future of the business?"

"Uh … well … Michele … I guess both."

She smiled. "I'm delighted with both."

They kissed.

"Let's take a bath," she said.

As they settled in and she added some aromatic soap, he said, "It's really nice. How'd you manage to get a bathtub and shower in an office? And why don't I have one?"

"Well," she answered, "I said to Kim that if the executives were going to have to sleep here, we needed and deserved some luxury. There wasn't enough room in yours for anything larger than a shower, and anyway, I knew you'd be here. And Kim knew too. Is that all right?"

He smiled. "Sure, as long as I'm invited over."

"Tad," she said softly, "do you ever wonder if we're in over our heads?"

He pulled her closer. "Every day. But then I remember what we've already accomplished, and I know we can do this."

Finally, they drifted off to sleep, wrapped in each other's arms.

Monday, April 20, 2020

Chapter 26

Michele stuffed enough masks for all to use into her backpack as she prepared for the trip to the United States Congress.

Tad rose from Michele's bed and walked to the door to answer a knock. Kim walked in, as Tad asked, "Do you really think we'll need them?" He traipsed around the floor. "Especially this many?"

Michele sighed. "I don't know. Better safe than sorry, right? It's unclear what they'll require on government aircraft or in Congress."

Kim chimed in. "The confusion about what should be done is ridiculous. The World Health Organization says we should wear masks in public, but some people are acting like it's a violation of their rights."

"I understand why you wear them," Michele muttered, zipping up the bag. "I don't think it's a violation of my rights or anything. I'm just so tired of putting them on all the time, but we have to be prepared for rules that we don't expect."

Surrounded by military weaponry and troops on the roof of the Morales and Morales building, Michele and the other SASCCI executives watched their colleagues board a helicopter for the short ride to the Miami airport. As the helicopter rose, Michele fought to stabilize her stance and shield her eyes from her hair being whipped by the downdraft of its roaring blades.

The wait for the third and last transport felt interminable. Finally, their helicopter arrived, descending onto the roof with a flurry of wind and noise. They leaned down and headed for the entry door. As the helicopter rose and turned toward the airport, Michele gazed out over Biscayne Bay into the gleaming early-morning sunlight, and then downtown where lights were still twinkling as the city was waking.

Kim said, "What if the congressional committee members attack us like the preliminary sub-committee people did?"

Michele shrugged her shoulders. "We stand our ground. We're prepared. We know our stuff."

Tad grabbed hands with the other two and said, "Yes. We're in this together."

After the helicopter landed near the commercial hangars, the passengers marched across the tarmac and boarded the plane, joining the others who were already seated.

In moments, the plane took off, heading east. Michele had a view of the Morales building and Biscayne Bay. As the plane passed downtown and then the beaches, it veered toward the north, sped up and rose.

Michele nervously continued trying to picture how things would go. Would they be able to present in the order they had planned? Could they argue sufficiently? Would the new members of CSC properly present their case? She hoped so. She again clasped hands with Tad, who was sitting next to her, and Kim, who was across the aisle. "God, I'm nervous," she said. Tad and Kim nodded and squeezed her hand.

*****

Jude paced in his room wondering if Kim and all the others had really left the building for Washington, D.C. Finally, he messaged Luz on WhatsApp. 'I'm in my office in the building. Can you get away?'

The response came almost immediately. 'Of course. I've been waiting with urgency.'

Jude's tapped his fingers rapidly on the phone screen. 'Take the stairs down to Floor 2. I'll meet you at the exit door.'

'I'll be there immediately, my love.'

Jude opened the door into the fire escape stairwell and heard her rapid footsteps pounding on the stairs. She slammed into Jude at the door, their lips meeting in a passionate kiss.

He grabbed her hand and pulled her rapidly toward a back door of the office that led into the bedroom. In seconds, they were inside, and he was pulling her to the bed. They slowed down enough not to tear each other's clothes but immediately were naked and entangled.

As they lay together later, Luz sighed contentedly. "I should probably get back to work."

Jude tightened his arms around her. "Will they notice if you're not at dinner? And if you sleep away?"

Luz shook her head, a small smile playing on her lips. "I doubt it."

"OK. I'll have a special meal prepared for us to enjoy here. Buzz me when you're ready to come down after work."

After sharing one last passionate kiss goodbye, Jude felt alone, counting the hours till dinnertime.

******

Michele nervously watched the huge crowd in the hearing room. Congressmen and congresswomen milled around, chatting. As usual, Kim wore her mask and so did one of the CRC members. The congressional committee members, only two of whom wore masks, began to take their places. The CRC group took seats at or near the table facing the interrogators. Reporters and T.V. camera persons stood in the aisles. The familiar face of Congressman Foxworthy made Michele's stomach churn.

"Oh no," Michele muttered.

Kim leaned in. "What is it?"

"I hope he's not in charge," Michele whispered back, nodding toward Congressman Foxworthy.

Kim's face fell.

Soon the gavel banged, and the meeting was called to order.

After some other business, which Michele paid no attention to because she was trying to remember the first sentence she intended to say, the higherups called on exactly whom she hoped would not be in charge, Congressman Foxworthy, who began his rambling opening remarks, with a southern drawl.

"Ms. Morales," he said in a condescending tone, "… what are you seeking by speaking to this committee of the United States Congress?"

Michele felt her temper rise. "Sir, just as I told you in our prior conversations, we were summoned here. We did not ask to be put on your agenda. We have never asked the United States government for money to support our program, other than the fees charged to least thirty other countries, which have engaged us to investigate the cybercrimes committed by Giga-BATS and its related entities and now the next step in our work."

Ignoring her answer, the Congressman drawled, "How is it that you and your team got to spend a week on a luxury yacht that the United States now owns? Who did you convince to grant you that perk?"

Michele forced herself to remain calm. "Again, Sir, you are accusing our company of taking actions that are not true. We were not aware of the yacht being seized or that we would travel to the Bahamas on it until shortly before we boarded it for the investigation in the Bahamas. Believe me, it was no luxury cruise. Many were killed or seriously injured in that horrendous attack."

She could see Agent Banks fidgeting in his seat, clearly itching to jump in. Michele caught his eye, giving a subtle shake of her head.

The vicious Congressman spoke again. "Ms. Morales, how did you manage to get military protection at your offices? That must cost a fortune."

She shook her head. "It was in place when we arrived in Miami. We did not request it."

"Ms. Morales. How did you get the FBI on your side?"

Exhausted, she glanced at Agent Banks and responded. "I presume it was because we communicated with Agent Banks and provided data we had obtained. But you could ask Agent Banks, who is here to speak."

But Foxworthy ignored the offer and continued. "Who came up with the hair-brained idea to replace the internet? Was it your compatriot, Tad Harris?"

She smiled. "We will be happy to explain if we are ever allowed to speak."

As Foxworthy continued his barrage of accusations, Michele felt her patience wearing thin. Finally, she stood up, her voice ringing out clear and strong. "Sir, you are wasting time so there will be no time for us to present. Your attitude and intentions to derail us are ridiculous. All we have asked for was for the United States to involve some members of its investigative agencies, which has finally occurred. I am completely embarrassed that we brought CRC members from other countries to watch this fiasco of our government. We do not need Congress's approval. We did not ask for anything. If the procedure here is not turned around to allow us to make our presentation, we are done. We will walk out right now."

A hush fell over the room as Michele sat down, her heart pounding in her ears. For a moment, she feared she had gone too far. Then, a slow clap began, building to a crescendo of applause and cheers. She wasn't sure who was applauding, thinking that the only people besides her team, the Congressional members and media were present.

Finally, a woman who appeared to oversee the assembly crashed a gavel on the wooden block and said sternly, "No applause or other outbursts are permitted in this committee meeting." When it had died down, the woman said, "Ms. Morales, please, introduce your team and make the presentation." A couple of claps started, but immediately stopped as the woman gave the audience a stern look. The media snapped multiple photos and videos and scurried frantically around.

Kim removed her mask as she stood. "Thank you," she began, "… for inviting us to discuss the goals, procedures and progress already made by the Cyber Renaissance Coalition in stopping the international cybercrime, creating a new internet world that will make it virtually impossible for this to occur ever again, and helping the world to be safeguarded from any type of intrusion. As Michele Morales stated, several CRC members are here to present the components of the plan."

Part of the audience seemed receptive but also remembered not to react. Agent Banks stepped up. After giving some history of what had occurred and what was learned, he said, "It was I, because of what this group was doing to benefit United States law enforcement, who suggested the group's utilization of the yacht and of providing the military protection at the office building. My team and related law enforcement agencies have been in communication with this group almost daily since the very beginning and completely support the work of SASCCI and the CRC." He sat. The part of the crowd that had previously applauded looked like they wanted to do so again, but they knew better.

A man said, "Why was the FBI involved since the crimes committed were international?"

Agent Banks answered, "The FBI was contacted by Miami police because of police reports filed about criminal activities, which led to a common thread. We realized early on the connection of the crimes to Giga-BATS and that Braxton Doolittle was a founder and senior executive of Giga-BATS. The international reach of the criminal enterprise was not immediately known."

When Michele called on Tad, he fought off nerves, cleared his throat and began. "Good day. I am pleased to have been invited today. As Ms. Morales stated in response to the attacks made on her by the Congressman, we faced the same negativity with Congressman Foxworthy during the sub-committee meeting. I hope and expect that this time I will be able to speak." He noticed the chairperson glaring at Foxworthy as he sat still, eyes lowered.

Tad explained the history of the research to locate the criminals and the determination that the best way to resolve the issues for the future was to build a new internet; then, he gave some details about the intended procedure.

A few hands were raised. Kim pointed to a woman sitting two rows back.

The Congresswoman said, "I understand that CRC has members from some countries that have hacked U.S. government and state government internet sites and have even interfered with the free elections of United States government officials. Is that true?"

Tad said, "We have not discriminated or restricted who may be involved in the investigative aspect. Now that we are in the mode of creating a new internet, we have a smaller group of countries, and the only ones involved are those that intend to utilize it. We believe that with so many countries and businesses involved, and with the safety features having been created by all, no individual member will be able to perform bad acts, but if any does, we will know immediately and remove them. No person, business or government is required to use Interstellar, as we are going to call the new internet. But many businesses will likely require it. One could have the old internet, Interstellar, or both. There is no conflict. Data will always be cleansed before entering Interstellar. We will be happy to consider issues raised by a government agency that is part of CRC."

Michele also explained the new terms that would be used to describe everything related to the existing internet, and the new suffixes on what used to be referred to as Domain Names, but now was called IS Codes.

Kim introduced the primary speaker of CRC. He stood, stroked his long, gray beard, and spoke in a German accent tinged with British English tones. "Good day. Thank you for allowing us to present to this august government body of the United States of America. It is our sincere goal to have every major country of the world involved in this redevelopment of the internet as we know it. We are very pleased that the United States is now becoming involved. Despite international travel restrictions due to COVID-19, we have made great strides in recent weeks. Certain members of CRC are lodged at its facility, and we have various travel means in place for international travelers. Those who do not travel to the United States are also able to participate via video conference and live connection to the computers where all is being created. The basic structure is already developed and is now being tested and tweaked. The cleansing and protection aspects are in the beginning stages. There is still much to do, but we hope to be fully operative within six months."

Another Congressman asked questions about whether cleansing was just a patch, and whether it really did anything new.

Tad smiled. "You are exactly right. It really is like a patch, which is what we consistently say is what we have to get away from. But Interstellar doesn't completely exist yet, and we had to find a way to get rid of as much bad stuff as possible before bringing data into the new system. Since the existing internet is still the only connection, the cleansing process had to work with it, but it will deliver the cleansed data into the new system. And, yes, the procedure is unique and has not been utilized previously."

Kim introduced the new members of CRC from United States internet-based businesses and agencies.

A company representative began speaking. "We are so fortunate and pleased that we were invited to be a part of this coalition. Being involved from the outset allows us to continue our good works and offer protections that we hope are not needed in the future but could be. We are able to offer our knowledge in order to help us all in the development and future protection of the internet. The mutual respect and admiration of the various parties to the Coalition is truly astounding. While different businesses may have been competitors in the past, we are on the same page, and we believe that we can still offer protection and benefits to our users while distinguishing each of our businesses from others that offer similar services. And, Giga-BATS and its subsidiaries, had created operations that looked like many of ours while actually continuing its bad acts. So, we must be able to prove that Interstellar and companies that offer services but have been vetted are legit. We will be presenting a list of valid providers, and a list of known invalid providers."

After others delivered similar statements, Kim and Michele moved back in front of the podium and delivered a short summary. As the hearing closed and Members packed up, some Congressional Committee Members stopped by and thanked them for their excellent presentation.

******

On the flight home, the thrill of success spread through the cabin. It seemed nobody could be tired after this electric day.

Michele, Tad and Kim gazed out the window at Miami Beach, the Intracoastal Waterway, and downtown Miami as the plane continued southerly. When it veered to the right, Michele found herself reliving the harrowing moments of her escape from the Giga Blue.

"That's right where I dove off," she said softly, pointing out the window.

Tad squeezed her hand. "I'd be scared to death to be swimming in that water. You are extremely brave, Michele."

Suddenly, the pilot's voice crackled over the intercom: "Attention. We have been directed by the U.S. Air Force to circle out over the ocean due to a suspicious aircraft. Keep your seatbelts fastened and stand by."

The plane banked sharply to the left, circling back out to sea. Michele scanned the darkening sky for signs of danger. A military jet streaked past in hot pursuit of another aircraft. Time seemed to slow as a missile was launched from the military plane, leaving the trail of bright light through the night sky.

GIGA TROUBLE

The explosion lit up the horizon, debris raining down into the sea below. A collective gasp rippled through the cabin, followed by a heavy silence.

The plane finally touched down safely, and then the helicopter delivered them to their headquarters.

April 21, 2020

Chapter 27

The morning after returning from Washington, D.C., Michele stood at the head of the table, her fingers drumming an anxious rhythm on the polished wood as she and the other members of CRC waited for the news broadcasts to begin.

The first report flashed across the screen, a cacophony of sound bites and flashing graphics. Her hope deflated as she watched their carefully crafted presentations reduced to sensationalist snippets, their words twisted and taken out of context.

The reporter dripped with sarcasm as he said, "The brash representatives of a private company intend to scrap the long-existing and very safe internet and to replace it with a new one that would take away our privacy. Just like the pro-vaccine and pro-required-masks gang, these people intend to force us to take ridiculous measures for no valid reason. Congressman Foxworthy even called the computer tech fanatic, Tad Harris, the Fauci of the internet and the rest of them a bunch of nuts." The reporter laughed aloud.

Michele said, "Well, we expected this from some news outlets. Click to another channel."

The next news spot wasn't much better, focusing on the renewed battles between President Trump and Dr. Fauci, a reporter speculated, "I would imagine that the President will be bashing SASCCI and its newly created Cyber Renaissance Coalition on similar grounds."

"Whatever," Michele said, waving her hand dismissively. "Change the channel."

As they flipped through more reports, a pattern emerged: roughly eighty percent positive, twenty percent negative. But even the positive coverage felt hollow, failing to capture the true magnitude of what they were trying to achieve.

Michele turned to face her team. "We knew this wouldn't be easy," she said softly. "But we can't let public opinion sway us from our mission. The stakes are too high."

Tad nodded, his eyes meeting Michele's. "You're right," he said. "But we need to be prepared for continued opposition. This is just the beginning of an intense battle."

******

Soon thereafter, CRC members gathered for the weekly meeting to review the progress, setbacks and concerns about the creation of Interstellar.

Tim cleared his throat, his normally cheerful demeanor replaced by a look of concern. "I want to talk about some holes in the protection," he began. "I've seen some entries ... some searches of the system. And I think they are planted by internal moles. I don't see evidence of any attacks from the outside."

Tad shook his head, his expression darkening. "That's bad," he said, his voice low. "But coincidentally, Michele asked to speak to us today, and what she wants to discuss is right on point." He turned to Michele, gesturing for her to take the floor.

She said, "Good morning to you all. I understand that tremendous momentum has been made. Yet, the evildoers have attempted to attack us physically ever since the very beginning. Considering that this is a battle about cyber intrusion, it was a given that they would attempt to attack our computer systems in an attempt to stop Interstellar. Tad and others on the team have discussed the need to take a proactive approach. Tad, will you please present?"

Tad stood. "We have created safety backups of data and spread them out physically into different locations. Since CRC has at least eight companies that offer protection from cyberattacks, we are thinking that those companies could combine or separately protect our systems and data, which would create multiple levels of protection. And it would be more helpful to have each stage of creation and each combination among departments on a separate server. So even if invaders get one department's work product, they can't get it all."

As he stood, waiting for comments, ideas flew back and forth, each member adding to potential solutions.

A representative of one of the larger cyber protection companies said, "I had thought the same thing ... that here we are ... a group that offers such protection, but we are not doing so for our own data. And I think yes, we could combine forces as you suggest and still separately protect the data. Even the backups could have different protection from different companies. Right now, we have two secure backup facilities. We could create a couple more."

Tim leaned forward. "We really are working separately now anyway. We have different firewalls. We combine data from different departments when they need to be combined. So, for example, my department does its work, and others do theirs, and when we want to test them together, we could combine the data on totally different servers. Every time we combine anything we can move the combined data to a different server with different backups and different protection."

Tad nodded his head vigorously. "Let's try it."

As the discussion continued, Michele felt hopeful. They were adapting, evolving, staying one step ahead of their unseen enemies.

Summer, 2020

Chapter 28

Tad picked up his cell early one morning in June and saw Michele's face. "My lord, Michele. It's only been fifteen minutes since we separated and came to work. Do you want a rendezvous already?"

Michele smiled. "I wish that's what I was calling you for. You know those three agency men that dress like FBI guys and really seem to do nothing but spy on us?"

Tad nodded.

Michele continued. "Please remind me why we let their agencies be on the CRC planning board."

Tad frowned. "I know it was a mistake to let them join us. They are useless."

"Well, they have just basically ordered us to meet them in the small conference room to discuss something. See you there in two minutes."

When Michele and Tad entered the room, they encountered the three men seated at the table, all dressed up as usual, with masks on. Michele and Tad pulled out their masks and put them on.

The stern-looking, gray-haired guy who always took the lead motioned for them to sit on the opposite side of the table from the three men. "Thank you for seeing us," he began, his words muffled behind his mask. "Other U.S. government agencies have asked us to communicate concerns about the probability that Russia, China, Iran, and other countries repeat the internet-based disinformation campaigns of our 2016 federal elections."

Michele exchanged a quick glance with Tad, noting concern on his face.

The man looked at his two cohorts and then continued. "First, our agencies want to know which countries that have committed criminal acts against our country via the internet are involved in CRC work."

Michele took a breath before responding. "We did not pick and choose countries that were involved in the investigations in Cuba. All countries that were involved first dealt with Cuba, and later SASCCI." She attempted to keep her voice level. "Only a handful of countries that were involved in the investigations are now involved in the current work on improving the internet. But we do not follow accusations against other countries by our government. All I can say is that of the countries you mentioned, Iran was not involved in the investigation. China was involved in that but is not now involved. Russia was involved from the beginning and still is."

The leader nodded. "The U.S. government agencies demand that the Russian member be removed from CRC."

Michele shook her head. "We are not removing any party who has been involved and is cooperating and providing good information for the improvement of the internet."

The youngest of the three representatives, a man with closely cropped brownish hair, shifted in his seat and glared at Michele and Tad. "You are making a mistake. An agency of our government will take action."

The leader said, "It's not only about his being a part. As I stated earlier, we are concerned about Russia's intrusion via your new model of the internet."

Michele sat back, letting the silence stretch for a moment as she gathered her thoughts. Finally, she stared into the leader's vitriolic eyes. "We are building a technical process. We are not involved in how any party uses the current internet or the revised internet. You certainly know that CRC's work, of which you are a part, is in the planning stages. Expecting the internet to be revised overnight is kind of like saying medical experts should immediately create vaccines against COVID-19 without testing and knowledge."

Tad cleared his throat. "The new internet does not involve an attempt to control any kind of web presence, including social media. We intend to prevent malware, viruses and other means of stealing data, but we are not a police agency to restrict use. The main source of intrusion into our election process previously was via social media channels."

The leader's face reddened. "You are taking this too lightly. It is well-known what the Russians and Iran did to interfere with our 2016 elections. We must prevent it from happening again. And it is well-known that they are spreading false claims and disinformation about our government's and health organizations' stances on COVID-19."

Michele adjusted her position, trying to look strong. "We just told you that we will not control how any party uses the internet. We are building in safeguards to know who is posting and to prevent illegal activities, but we will not take any action about how a particular user operates. Interstellar will be usable by all social media companies just like any other application. As Tad already stated, while the revised internet is intended to prevent malware, viruses and other means of stealing data, we are not a police agency to restrict use. And also, remember this is an international endeavor."

The third man, who hadn't spoken previously, crossed his arms and sat back. "Our agency is probably going to terminate our involvement in your new creation."

Tad and Michele simultaneously shrugged their shoulders.

The youngest agency man spoke up. "On another note, the cybercrime activities have not diminished one iota since you located the criminals and other locations. A number of public utilities, transportation providers and governments throughout our country and around the world have been the victims of ransomware. We do hope that you are making significant progress toward the resolution."

Michele shrugged, as she glared from one man to another. "Again, you and your agencies are part of our teams. Maybe you should back out because you're not contributing and have no idea what's going on here."

Tad glanced at the agency representatives. "Maybe we do have one thing to offer in slowing down the attacks even before Interstellar is ready. We are on the verge of completing the cleansing software that would assure existing data does not bring ransomware and other malware into the new internet. Perhaps we could test it out by installing it in some of the networks that are still being attacked and help slow the continuing crime while monitoring whether our cleanser works to eliminate it. That would help us test and possibly reduce the crime even before Interstellar is ready."

As the agency representatives stood to leave, the leader said, "I guess that's something, but you'd better think again about the Russia issue."

******

GIGA TROUBLE

Days after the meeting with the representatives, military men wielding automatic weapons burst into the SASCCI offices, frightening Kim and Michele. Michele stepped in front of Kim with her hand up.

"Where is the Russian citizen?" one of the agents shouted.

Michele tried to determine how to handle this thunderous forced entry. The Russian would be working diligently on the Interstellar tech floor. Trying to defuse the situation, her voice calm despite her intense fear, Michele said, "Can we take you to him peacefully and quietly? We do not need drama in our facility."

The lead officer, his uniform adorned with more stripes than the others, glared at her. "No. We enter with guns drawn. This is a matter of national security."

"Bullshit," said Kim.

Michele tried to stand her ground as the officer growled, "Take us to the illegal or we will raid the place with weapons drawn."

Michele stood in front of the forceful man, jaw jutting. "No. You are not disrupting the work here with your belligerent attitude."

The man grinned malevolently, shouting, "You're the chick that tried to get over on the officers in Havana, aren't you?"

She remained silent, her jaw set in defiance, choosing not to inform the intruders that they were on the wrong floor.

As the agents moved loudly along the floor, glancing around pillars and into workstations, Michele discreetly called Tad.

"What's up, Michele?"

"A military group, guns drawn, is here to arrest the Russian."

The force headed back her way and banged through the door into the emergency stairwell. "Tad," Michele said, "They've entered the stairwell."

After a pause, Tad said, "Shit, here they come."

Through the open phone line, Michele heard the troop roar into Tad's area. "Sirs. Please," he begged. "There is no need to brandish weapons."

Michele heard banging as gruff voices yelled, "Where is the Russian? Produce him right now."

"Put the weapons down," Tad yelled, just as loud.

The Russian calmly said, "I'm right here. What do you want?"

Michele buzzed her dad on the office phone. "Dad. Emergency. Military personnel have intruded with guns to arrest the Russian."

Still through the open phone line, Michele heard the Russian being roughly tackled, while yelling, "Stop brutalizing me. I am not resisting."

Tad yelled, "Goddamn it. Stop. You're going to injure him."

"We'll take you down too if you don't shut up."

Michele ran down the stairwell and onto the tech floor. Two of the intruders pushed Tad roughly from behind, causing him to hit his head on a desk as he fell to the ground.

"You sons of bitches," Michele said, dialing Agent Banks' cell phone.

As he picked up, she said, "Agent Banks, U.S. military is in here raising hell and injuring people."

An intruder knocked the phone from her hand and tossed her to the ground too.

"You are both under arrest for impeding a military operation."

She struggled to keep from crying. "Tad, are you hurt?"

"I'm Okay. How about you?"

"I'd like to beat the shit out of these assholes," Michele said.

The Russian groaned as they tugged his handcuffed arms from behind.

Michele said, "Would you please stop?"

Franklin and Miguel rushed in. Michele said, "Dad, Miguel, these guys are out of control."

The men then yanked her and Tad up, also causing them considerable pain. "Let's go."

Franklin and Miguel rushed past employees who stood silently aghast. Franklin yelled, "This is a private business in a private building. Do you have a warrant or any government-issued document authorizing this attack?"

The soldiers ignored him and marched the three prisoners toward the stairwell. Franklin and Miguel tried to block them, but the soldiers elbowed them and marched through the area where workers stood dumbfounded.

An alert sounded over the loudspeaker. "The building is under attack. Move to the westerly side of the building away from windows. Run."

Michele tried to break free, but the officers refused to budge. She yelled to her workers, "Go. Run. Hurry!"

The window imploded as a massive drone crashed halfway through it, sending shattering glass through the room and bodies of workers and military men sprawling across the floor. The drone remained embedded in the dangling mesh of a plastic material and broken glass.

Through the haze of dust and confusion, Michele gasped at the sight of her father lying on the ground, a large shard of glass protruding from his arm. Blood streamed down and along his hand, pooling on the floor beneath him. She struggled again to get free to help her father.

Miguel rushed to his father's side trying to find something to staunch the blood flow. Finally, he tore off his tie and white business shirt and tied first the tie and then the sleeves of his shirt just under Franklin's underarm.

Workers from Michele's team rushed back to check on her, but retreated when an officer yelled, "Get away from the prisoners."

A worker hollered, "I hope there's no other explosive on the drone."

Security forces and medics who'd been stationed on the rooftop flooded in, pulled people away from the windows and treated the wounded. Soldiers in bomb squad outfits and carrying equipment to disengage bombs approached the drone.

One of the security men yelled at the troops who'd come for the Russian, "You idiots. Who told you to come in like this? The FBI called us to come here and stop you. Remove the cuffs from these three."

The officer in charge of the arrest of the Russian said, "No. We are enforcing a legal operation, and you have no authority."

The building security officers pulled guns and aimed at the intruding force.

Seeing two branches of her own government's military aiming guns at each other, Michele said, "You all are endangering everybody in our company. Put all the fucking guns down. Now."

But the two groups stood fast.

As the tension reached its breaking point, a new group arrived, their crisp white shirts and ties a stark contrast to the sea of military uniforms.

"FBI," shouted the apparent leader. "What in the hell do you people think you are doing?" They positioned themselves in between the groups with rifles.

The officers of the two groups looked at their respective leaders.

The head of the FBI group shook his head and said, "Children. Play fair. Stand down. Lower your weapons. Let these people go."

Again, the men of the two groups looked at their respective leaders and eventually received the look that told them they could stand down. They lowered their rifles and stood silently.

"Remove the handcuffs from these people," the FBI man said. Men moved forward and removed the handcuffs from Michele and Tad, both of whom had blood dripping down their faces.

"And him," the FBI man said, pointing to the Russian.

"No," the officer in charge of the first group answered. "We were sent to arrest him and expel him from the country."

The man dressed in a suit replied, "He did not resist. You attacked him without provocation. Un-handcuff him."

The men did so.

Michele and Tad sat down by Franklin as medics finished cleaning up and rewrapping his arm. Michele gazed around at others being treated wondering and worrying how long such abominations would continue.

****

In early August, Kim arranged a presentation at the SASCCI offices in front of a live audience, zoom attendees and reporters with their video and still camera people. The fervor of the chanting protesters several blocks away seeped through the walls like an insistent drumbeat.

Over fifty people filled the room, their faces a mix of curiosity, skepticism, and barely concealed hostility. The red lights of multiple television cameras blinked ominously, reminding her that every word and every gesture would be scrutinized by millions.

As Kim began her introduction, Michele tried to concentrate, thinking that the arguments of supporters and detractors of Interstellar seemed similar to the conflicting approaches about how to handle COVID-19, which seemed more divisive each day. She took a deep breath, centering herself for the challenge ahead.

She jolted back to the present as Kim turned the podium over to her.

As she began, her voice seemed steady despite the butterflies in her stomach. "Thank you all for coming today," she began, her eyes scanning the room. "We're here to provide an update on Interstellar and introduce some key members of our team who will share more detailed information."

As she introduced Tad and other CRC members, she could feel the tension in the room ratcheting up. Tad explained that Interstellar was still in preliminary stages and that over two thousand businesses and government agencies around the world were already testing the cleansing procedure. But when Tad announced launch dates in September, a ripple of murmurs swept through the audience.

Suddenly, somebody yelled, "This belief that the internet must be replaced is the same irrational fear that you people instilled before the turn of the century, the alleged Y2K issue!"

Michele struggled to keep her face impassive. "Who is 'you people'?" she asked calmly. "We were teenagers in high school when the Y2K fear existed."

"I mean you democrats," the media representative yelled.

GIGA TROUBLE

The room erupted into chaos, voices overlapping in a cacophony of accusations and rebuttals. Michele gripped the podium, her knuckles white. "If you wish to speak, whether here in person or on Zoom, please raise your hand and speak when called upon."

As the pointed questions continued, Michele felt like she was walking a tightrope. One misstep, one wrong word, and everything they had worked for could come crashing down.

The final blow came from a congressman, his words full of disdain. "I plan to file a bill to have all funding of SASSCI's and CRC's actions and proposals terminated."

Michele's eyes met Tad's across the room, and they both smiled and shrugged.

Michele looked directly at the man and said, "As you well know, the United States is not paying anything other than what the other countries that wish to participate are paying. If the United States stops paying its share, it will be out."

The man yelled, "You cannot remove the United States from its involvement in this matter."

Michele answered, "Oh yes we can, and we will."

******

Michele stood to the side as Tad took the podium before division leaders of CRC. Tad gazed around the room silently and then spoke. "We believe great progress has been made in having the cyber protection companies use their software to stop intrusions. Merging data on separate servers was a good move. Unfortunately, we're still seeing attempts at intrusion. Yet, they are not caused by a user accidentally accepting a link. An insider is installing the malware right inside our facility."

Michele felt the ripple of unease among the audience.

Tim stood from his seat. "I apologize for raising this in front of the numerous techs that are working from other locations, but is the intruder possibly someplace else? Are we sure that only legitimate members of CRC have that access?"

Michele felt everyone's gaze upon her as she struggled to decide how to respond. "We keep very good tabs as to who has access and their locations. We have a very robust procedure for regularly changing passwords and we are already using the additional proof, such as fingerprints, facial recognition, and similar means, which Interstellar will also be using. I cannot imagine how imposters could be entering our systems."

Yet, considering every potential weak link in their security, she wasn't so sure about the veracity of what she had just said.

Tim's next question jolted her. "Michele, I know that Pedro Rosales is family to you. But why is he in our department and what exactly is he doing? And what is his security level?"

Michele's voice sounded distant to her own ears as she explained Pedrito's role. But as Tim and the team shared their concerns, she knew that she'd relied on a false hope.

Then Tad spoke. "Michele, I was going to talk to you about this later. But now is appropriate." He paused, his eyes filled with a mix of concern and regret. "I've been going through memory chips from the yacht daily. I've found multiple communications between Pedrito and Doolittle, including a conversation in which they spoke about stealing the jewelry and funds of your deceased client."

As Tad laid out the evidence of Pedrito's betrayal, Michele felt as if the floor had dropped out from beneath her.

"I understand," she almost whispered. She had to acknowledge that Kim had been right from the beginning, and she'd ignored the signs.

Tad placed a hand on her shoulder. "Michele, he tricked us all. You couldn't have known."

As Tad left the room, Michele remained rooted to the spot, her mind reeling … the deepest betrayal, and the greatest threat to their mission had been right under her nose all along. She felt sick to her stomach.

September, 2020

Chapter 29

On September 15, just two weeks before the big day, the executives met to discuss various issues with getting Interstellar up and running. As Michele was absent while recovering from her first bout with COVID-19, Tad led the meeting. "Twelve countries do not intend to utilize Interstellar at all or not exclusively," he began. "And some countries that are suspected of internet intrusions intend to use it along with the old internet."

The audience was silent. Tad continued with a list of those that said they would not use it at all, ticking off the names on his fingers. "China, Iran, North Korea, Cuba, Venezuela. We'll see whether they're able to do business with the rest of the world."

A team member spoke up. "Attacks keep showing up on our systems. The tentacles of Giga-BATS still are doing their best to stop us."

As the meeting progressed, each department representative presented their successes and challenges.

Finally, Tad made the final statement as he closed the meeting. "The attacks won't diminish. We just need to keep protecting our systems and plug on. All systems still seem to be Go for September 30."

******

After the meeting, Tad tried calling Michele, concerned because she'd said she'd be attending meetings about the final preparations for opening day, but she hadn't. When she didn't answer her phone after several attempts, he rushed to her room. He banged and banged on the door but received no response.

In panic mode, he dialed Miguel's number. "Miguel, do you know anything about Michele? I don't know where she is and she's not answering."

Miguel sounded confused. "What? Where should she be? When did you last talk to her?"

"Early this morning. She said she was fine and coming to work. Can you ask your dad if he's heard anything?"

"I'll try to reach him," Miguel replied. "He hasn't shown up yet this morning."

Tad shuddered with fear, convinced that something was terribly wrong.

*****

The helicopter's blades sliced through the air as Michele peered down at her parents' home.

She burst through the back door and scrambled through the eerily silent house, while imagining the worst. Her voice grew hoarse as she called out for her parents while bounding up the stairs two at a time. She flung open the door to her parents' bedroom, gasped and froze as she saw her parents sitting on the edge of their bed, bound and gagged, their eyes wide with terror. Before Michele could react, the door slammed shut behind her. She whirled around, coming face to face with two men she recognized from Giga-BATS, their pistols trained on her.

As they bound and gagged her, pushing her onto the bed beside her parents, Michele tried and tried to figure out how to escape. She gasped in horror as she witnessed a young woman tapping away on a laptop, and then heard her own voice telling Tad that he needed to come help her because an accident had occurred in the home.

******

Tad's voice was sharp with urgency as he called Miguel on the phone and yelled for Tim to come into his office.

As they rushed in, he said, "Michele and her parents are in trouble. I think they've been kidnapped. And now I'm being asked to go to her parents' house. I think they're trying to sequester the leaders."

His fingers clicked wildly on his cell as he dialed Agent Banks, and then urgently begged for FBI assistance.

"I'm going there now, but wanted you to know," Tad declared.

Agent Banks said, "I'm not sure that's wise. We can get a rescue team there in a short time."

But Tad was already in motion, his mind made up. "That's fine, but I'm going too, in just a minute. Tim, can you put Pegasus or something like it back on my phone real quick, set up tracking and audio pickup, so you can be live with me as I enter?"

As Tim worked on the phone, Tad warned the others. "Do not fall for any phone calls or messages about this. I will not call. You will have my phone live. Do not stop operations. Tell our cyber protective agency members to safeguard all computers and servers."

With a final nod to his team, Tad bolted from the room, leaving behind a wake of stunned silence.

✶✶✶✶✶✶

In front of flickering screens filled with cascading data, CRC members frantically clicked keyboards while skimming for attacks.

Tim shouted. "I just got a call telling me to go to the nearest building where we have off-site backups. They must know where they are."

Another tech person, "I did too, but mine gave a specific backup location ... the one on Northeast 1st Avenue and Flagler."

Kim steadily relayed the information to Agent Banks. "Can raids be made on the backup locations?"

As the last senior executive of SASCCI still in the office, Kim urgently continued coordinating with law enforcement, fighting an enemy that seemed to be everywhere at once.

✶✶✶✶✶✶

Tad found himself cuffed and gagged alongside Michele and Mr. and Mrs. Morales shortly after arriving at the house. He locked eyes with Michele giving a slight nod in an effort to convey reassurance.

The woman at the laptop was dialing phones. But nobody picked up. One of her cohorts said, "What's going on? Why won't they pick up?"

"Who'd you tell that you were coming here," demanded one of the two men as he grabbed the front of Tad's shirt.

Tad silently glared back, as Michele gave him a worried look.

The other captor asked the woman who was operating the laptop, "How are the intrusions going?"

The woman shook her head. "Not well. They've got super firewalls ... multiple barriers."

"Shit," said the man. "Write to the boss and request new procedure."

The woman said, "The boss says to instruct our people at the back-up facilities to prepare to load ransomware directly in the systems, and if they fail, to blow up the servers. I'm writing them now."

Michele cringed and struggle to take hold of Tad's hand although she couldn't quite grasp it.

******

The quiet of the Morales neighborhood was shattered by the arrival of heavy-duty police and military vehicles. SWAT teams swarmed the yard and then crashed into the Morales home, their movements precise and coordinated.

The two intruders in the bedroom ran to the hallway but were immediately tackled by officers and handcuffed.

As Michele, Tad, Franklin, and Diana were freed, several officers, along with Agent Banks, dragged Pedrito into the room. Agent Banks said, "Your family member says he has permission to be here, but we found him working on his laptop in a closet downstairs."

Michele said, "So it was you. You lying thief."

Pedrito looked panicked.

Tad yelled to the officers, "Please allow me access to the laptops. They've instructed people in other locations to destroy computers. We need to stop them."

Officers holding laptops looked to Agent Banks, who nodded and said, "Let him try. I'm checking status of entry into those buildings."

As Tad operated both laptops at the same time, Michele texted Kim. 'Kim, it's really me. All four of us are freed and the bad guys on site are in custody.'

GIGA TROUBLE

Kim wrote, 'Michele, your brother is with me. Please type the family password for emergency.'

Michele typed, 'M&M.'

Kim answered, 'Thank God. Are you all okay?'

Michele wrote, 'Yes, nobody has been harmed. The FBI is about to enter all the server backup facilities, but Tad is also trying to enter the servers to change whatever they have done in the computers.'

Michele waited impatiently for some good news.

******

By five in the afternoon, all criminals had been arrested and CRC personnel freed. No server was harmed.

The team regrouped, tense and silent like soldiers who'd lived through a deadly battle. Each department reported on the attempted exploits, describing coordinated, multi-pronged attacks.

Tad spoke with cautious optimism. "It seems like having separated the data among multiple servers has worked."

Michele's felt relieved but still concerned. "All right. We must be prepared for more and more intrusions as September 30 approaches."

Monday, September 28 to Wednesday, September 30, 2020

Chapter 30

On Monday, September 28, the executives and their teams sat in the Zoom Room scanning multiple online newspapers and live news stories. Their faces, the building, snippets of videos, and reporters talking and talking about what was planned as Interstellar neared takeoff appeared on multiple screens all around the room.

As they could only hear one audio at a time, one would say, "Sound on Screen 25," and after a minute or two another would call for sound on another screen. The myriad of concerns, questions, beliefs and hopes was expressed by all media, some addressing certain topics more than others.

A reporter's face filled the screen. "Is Interstellar really necessary? Or is this just another Y2K-style panic ... for nothing?"

Before Michele could process the implications of that question, another voice hollered. "Switch to Screen 13!" The image changed, revealing a stern-faced anchor. "Is this Big Brother in disguise? What's to stop this new internet from becoming a tool for mass surveillance?"

Michele felt a headache building.

She finally spoke up. "This is like watching the elections, which by the way aren't too far away," she said, a wry smile playing at the corners of her mouth. "Since we can't hear everything at the same time, I'm going to go on what I see in their faces and what's posted, and say I think what we are doing is favored by at least a majority of the people, businesses, media and the world."

Kim said, "Many politicians are still screaming, saying that the timing is going to endanger their campaigns. Both Democrats and Republicans nation-wide are saying we are doing it to hurt that party's ability to present their case, and of course there's still also the Russian interference fear."

Michele clicked off the news reports. "We don't have time to worry about the reports. Luz, can you please give us an update on the procedure?"

Luz outlined the process for new users to access Interstellar. "Many intended users already have or will soon have their online access. Tomorrow, all media outlets will be provided copies of the detailed instructions, which will inform new users on how to identify themselves and gain access to Interstellar. Those who have already applied and been approved will be able to do so on September 30 while more fledgling persons can learn slowly.

Those who have computers without video cameras or smartphones can upload government issued IDs. Those who have anything with a video camera can use the one they like. This will be done through the party's web-browser with a login, or email account if not connected to a web-browser account. We intend that every person will have several methods to prove who they are. If a party seems suspicious, the system will ask for more data about the party's identification. In both situations, the internet provider must be vetted by Interstellar, which all major providers are. The entity users used already has a history on the user although not verified. The provider will change the suffix of the party's existing login or email to the applicable new suffix."

Each department again explained the status of that department's work and how it now meshed with the combined units. All seemed on track. But Tad felt the need to warn that there was more to consider. "We need to be able to allow initial entry into Interstellar in spite of more attacks on the existing internet."

Various members began presenting proposed solutions to this probable problem. "Is there a way we can send a connection?" Tad asked. "E-mail or message or something? How about if we use a VPN with its own browser and give them everything that way? Or we ask the internet protection companies whether they can give their existing customers a safe way to enter. We identify the customers, provide a log-in via the special connection, and they are in without going through the old internet."

The various internet protection companies confirmed that they could use the data they already had on their customers to give them access directly. The planning group seemed to collectively sigh with relief.

******

On Wednesday, September 30th, the room buzzed with anticipation, excitement and apprehension as workers entered and appeared on the Zoom screens. Michele, still wearing a mask as a precaution, was awed by the sea of faces before her—about half wearing masks. She scanned the room for Tad.

Suddenly, the doors burst open, and Tad rushed in with a small group of CRC members, their faces showing great concern. Tad motioned for the executives and department leaders to follow him away from the microphones.

He whispered, "We need to postpone for a few minutes. The main server we were planning to use has been hit by a DDOS to thwart the access to Interstellar. It's not able to function."

GIGA TROUBLE

Michele searched her memory for what a DDOS meant—Distributed Denial of Service Attack—a cyber-attack in which data is sent from multiple compromised devices at once in order to overwhelm a target server with traffic, so that the server cannot be contacted.

Ideas on how to solve the attack were thrown back and forth, but none seemed useful until Tad's eyes suddenly lit up with inspiration.

"Wait," he said. "The backup servers in the other buildings use different names and they are NOT connected at all to the main server, right?"

Heads started nodding earnestly. Somebody said, "Right. All the needed aspects of the full program are contained in all the new servers."

Tad said, "We've got different VPNs with built-in browsers on each server to submit the links without showing the origin. We'll contact you, Michele, by phone so you can inform media. For now, tell them to please hold. The instructions will change, but it will just be where the log-in procedures originate. Let's go to the one across the street and try to set up the log-in from there." Tad and the others raced back out of the room.

Michele stepped up to the podium and informed the waiting media of the delay and change of procedure, buying time for Tad and the team to implement their backup plan.

The minutes ticked by like hours as they waited for word. Michele and Kim huddled together, whispering about possibilities while trying to ignore the din of impatient speculation by media and the rumble of protesters outside.

The screens in the Zoom Room showed international news media, CRC members and many others. Reports of apparent dangers from the rooftop came in every few minutes but did not result in the need to flee.

Finally, Tad's call came through and in moments he was back in the room and thrust to the podium to speak on live television. "We are ready to launch. I'm going to give an overall summary first, so that those who already have their new logins and are tech savvy will not be slowed down by our explanation of details. Your favorite browser is not disappearing. You will have a choice among most of the existing browsers. It will look different and will show you that you are in Interstellar. Your prior apps, data and everything you have done in your prior system will not be lost. But everything will go through a cleansing process before it's available in Interstellar. In fact, if a company you've worked with in the past for email, password protection and the like has provided you a means of joining Interstellar, you may safely use that procedure. However, if you haven't been previously warned, all internet and similar companies operated by Giga-BATS are not permitted. You should immediately find a different company to use if you have not already. I am posting here a list of approved service providers as well as a list of the criminal enterprises we are aware of. No unidentified company or entity, and no criminal company can provide you access, but they might pretend that they have authority. Look for this code on all communications. Do not click into a hyperlink offered by any entity. We are not transmitting hyperlinks or QR codes." He showed a depiction of what hyperlinks and QR Codes looked like, saying "Do NOT use these. They are not legitimate."

The live meter showing new Interstellar users began to climb, slowly at first, then with increasing speed. Eight hundred thousand–one million–ten million. As the numbers soared past a hundred million, Michele felt elation. Tad smiled each time the meter hit another milestone on the numerous television channels. Michele's smile was hidden behind her mask but shining brightly in her eyes. Even reporters seemed awed by the rapid increase.

Michele's parents, Tad's dad and stepmother and Kim's parents, along with workers from the Roasted Oak chain, entered the room with appetizers and a rolling table with champagne glasses and iced bottles. The executives of SASCCI and their parents, some of the leaders of CRC and the two top administrative aids, Honesti and Luz, stood around Michele at the front of the table.

As bottles popped open and glasses were filled, Michele held her glass in the air, and announced, "Success is the result of the hard work of everybody in this room and afar who have worked tirelessly on this project. Thank you to all of you for your diligent work." She raised her glass higher, clinked with others, and said, "Cheers!"

"I also want to remind you that this is the beginning, not the end. We continue to have a huge job to do. We must maintain the goals that were the foundation of this enterprise. We must be wary of our opponents doing everything they can to destroy the protection for which Interstellar was created. We must combat attempts to clone it and trick its users. We, the countries who helped make it, and all the companies that have been involved, must continue to work together. We hope that all our employees will remain with us to keep the world free from cybercrime in the future."

She and the crowd lifted their glasses and sipped again. Then, Tad was at her side, pulling her into a tight embrace. Their lips met in a passionate kiss, eliciting cheers and whistles from the crowd.

As they broke apart, Michele grinned, raising their joined hands in triumph. "Yes, it's true," she announced. "Something else marvelous has occurred in our lives...."

The room erupted in applause once more. As Michele looked out at the sea of smiling faces, she felt a sense of pride and achievement she had never known before.

But then, Tad felt a vibration and picked up his phone. He tried to keep a straight, calm face as he read, 'MR. TAD HARRIS. YOU THINK YOU'VE SUCCEEDED, BUT YOU HAVE NOT.'

THE END

Made in United States
Cleveland, OH
16 March 2026

Fiction
Both 2026